DARK HUNTRESS

HARLEY JAMES

For Amy Bohanan

For your beautiful mind
& the secrets that bind.

CHAPTER 1

qua nightclub, Waikiki Beach, Hawaii

Death, darkness, demons. It was getting so damn old.

Katherine Evangelista breathed deep and stalked toward the Possessed. This one was a wild-eyed brunette who hadn't stopped talking since an evil spirit had shoved itself into her human body four hours ago.

Katherine stopped several feet away from the possessed woman, going over the best method to subdue her.

Step one: Force her into the massive Devil's Trap in the center of the dance floor.

Step two: Exorcise the evil within.

Step three: Wipe her mind and send her on her way.

Step four: Erase the episode from the non-possessed, human witnesses' memories and get everyone the hell out of the club.

Same shit, different day.

The chatty brunette lunged. Katherine's body flushed with heat as she thrust her arms out to block the attack. The brunette snapped her teeth, spittle flecking from her lips as she spilled question after question, her voice two octaves lower than it should have been.

"How much money do you make? Do you put out on the first date? How many people have you killed?"

The Possessed's teeth ground together, narrowly missing Katherine's throat.

Their scuffle backed them into a table, knocking it over along with several drinks and a hurricane candle.

"Ignesco," the brunette roared, and the table burst into flames.

"Stark!" Katherine shot to her feet and yelled over her shoulder for her lead security specialist. The Possessed charged forward, clawing at Katherine's face.

Konani, the club's most popular human mixologist, sprinted into the room. "Stark's out on the pool terrace rounding up the other crazies. Hold on." She grabbed an empty spray bottle and rapidly refilled it with holy water at her bar station, her gaze darting between the table fire and the possessed woman.

"Hurry the fuck up." Katherine slammed a rosary against the brunette's cheek, stunning her and giving Katherine time to direct her water element at the nightclub's emergency sprinklers.

Crystal chandeliers and champagne buckets rattled with the sudden power surge. Bone-chilling water doused Kat's face, her biomagnetism failing to shield her like it usually did when she used her water powers. *I am one hundred and eighty percent done with today, and at least forty percent done with tomorrow.*

The fire was out, and the brunette was temporarily docile,

but this final call for energy had consumed the last bit of Katherine's power. She was too tired to even turn off the emergency sprinklers. She'd never have enough energy to mind wipe the non-possessed humans cowering in the club's dark corners witnessing all this crap.

She'd probably need to call another Guardian for help, goddammit.

A dark corner of her mind sprang open, flash-burning her with heady images of a tall, golden Guardian.

Ari.

The only man who'd ever made her hunger, crave, beg. The only one she'd ever truly—

No.

She pounced on the memories, locking them away, deeper than before. One of these days, she'd find a way to eliminate them once and for all.

Aut viam inveniam aut faciam. Find a way or make one. Her favorite motto.

If people labeled her a bitch because she was assertive and goal-oriented, that was their prerogative. She had more important things to worry about. Like dealing with the rest of the fiends running amok in the club, courtesy of one of Satan's daughters.

Katherine shoved the brunette into a chair inside the Devil's Trap until she could be exorcised. The Possessed roared, staring down at the mystical sigils arranged between the five points of the pentagram.

Pursing her lips, Katherine studied the fingernail gouges on her wrists and the blood-stained cuffs of her soaked, white suit jacket. She wiped water out of her eyes, and her hand came away smudged with gray eyeshadow. She held it up to the possessed woman. "You see this? You've made today a colossal waste of makeup. Congratulations."

The brunette shook her long, wet hair, then turned and sank her teeth into the other Possessed inside the Devil's Trap. Just everyone's luck the male happened to be a fingernails-down-the-chalkboard shrieker.

Ugh. A person's reaction to demonic body invasion was as varied as the range of human personalities. Katherine turned to another member of Aqua's security team. "Maddox, get the iron chains soaked in holy water for this one. She's a biter."

The haunted look in the black man's eyes vanished with his assignment. Katherine had found Maddox homeless and delirious on Detroit's mean streets last year. He was human, but a powerful telepath who could hear the thoughts of others. Uncontrolled for years, the ability had nearly driven him insane.

Every week, she pushed him to delve deeper into his psychic nature. To gain mastery over it instead of turning to high dose anti-anxiety meds. Inhumane? Maybe, but she was a hard-edged bitch who didn't like the easy way out of anything.

And some day, she'd celebrate—privately—when those tormented shadows no longer darkened his eyes.

Maddox's tall, athletic form vanish into the storage locker, and Katherine wished she was anywhere but here right now. Guardian leader Alexios would flip his shit over how damaged these humans were before she got them exorcised, but right now she didn't give a damn.

She turned from the Devil's Trap to identify her next target in the nightclub's blue and white interior. But instead of finding another human ravaged by evil spirits, her gaze landed on the wet, white tank top plastered to her distant-relative-turned-best-friend's chest.

Jade Matson's honey-brown arms made the sign of the cross in front of every possessed soul. She swaggered toward

Katherine as though the emergency sprinkler system going full blast was the norm.

"I leave you alone for a couple hours to get some shut-eye, and the whole place goes to pot. This has gotta be a new record."

Katherine rubbed her temples. "Wow, aren't you disgustingly jolly?"

Jade pulled a rosary out of her pocket and flashed it at a foaming-at-the-mouth man running full throttle toward her. He dropped dramatically, then convulsed. "We're saving lives, Kat. It's a great way to start a Saturday."

"Morning people are so annoying," Katherine muttered. She grabbed the seizing man's arms, while Jade pocketed the rosary and scooped up his legs. Katherine blinked water out of her eyes, yelling over her shoulder, "The first person to shut off these sprinklers gets a five-hundred-dollar bonus."

As they lugged the writhing man into the Devil's Trap, Katherine felt Jade's gaze on her back. Too bad she wasn't in the mood to talk. They left the possessed dude in the trap and backed out.

"*Kat.*"

It was *that tone*. She'd never enjoyed a single conversation when Jade used it.

"Shh, no one cares right now, Jade."

"Lady K!"

Katherine shook soggy hair from her eyes and looked toward the second-floor balcony, receiving a series of hand signals from Stark. She nodded at him, then glanced back at Jade. "The crew rounded up the last of the Possessed from the upper balconies and pool terraces. Stark says there's five, maybe six more to go on this level."

"Okay, we can handle that, but first, I gotta tell you something..." Jade trailed off, and the expression on her face made Katherine's skin prickle.

"What did you do?"

"Don't freak out."

Katherine's pulse jolted, but she kept her features composed. "You know hysterics aren't my thing."

Jade hesitated. "I called Ari. He's on his way."

CHAPTER 2

Weightlessness rushed through Katherine. She sank toward the plush white leather of the nearest bench. Jade reached out to help her, but Katherine smacked her hands away.

"You did *what?*" Ari Grimmson was her Achilles' heel.

No, her Achilles' *Hell.*

Jade crossed her arms in front of her chest. "I called him. But, look, don't be mad because I'm looking out for your best interests."

"My best interests? Oh girl, I may like shopping, but I'm not buying that bullshit. *You*, Jade. You of all people know our backstory."

"I know. I know." Jade put up her palms. "But he was already planning to come after his assignment with the Dalai Lama."

Katherine pressed a hand to her stomach. "Seriously. That's your excuse? After everything I've told you?"

"Kat, you guys love each other. Hell, you *belong* together regardless of how pigheaded you've both been for the last three years. Ari's your soul mate, so he was bound to feel your growing weakness. You *had* to know he'd show up here one of these days."

Katherine shook her head repeatedly. "No. No, no, *no*. He's only a *potential* soul mate. I have a choice in this. Besides, he's the one who left." Even when she'd begged him —*pleaded* with him—to stay. As a free agent, Ari wasn't part of the Unholy Inc network of Guardian nightclubs. He could easily go—or stay—wherever he wanted.

He'd chosen to leave her.

She'd never known such soul-stripping humiliation.

Katherine's whole body trembled. She needed to hide. In a cave maybe, fetal position and all that.

Fetal. Oh God.

She swallowed hard. Her mouth felt coated with sawdust. *Speak slowly, don't stutter.* "You're fired if you don't call him back and tell him to stay away from me. From this whole island."

A stream of water from the overhead sprinkler slid down Jade's face, her blonde buzz cut as perfect as ever. "Fire me then. I don't care, but you need his help. You can't do these exorcisms alone anymore."

You can't. YoucantYoucantYoucant. Heat fired through Katherine's chest. *You can't save this baby* was what they'd told her as she lay in the ER, bleeding and crying for the life dying in her womb.

Helpless to stop it and the joy ebbing from Ari's eyes.

She pushed up from the bench, anger making her legs steady again. Konani moved past her, wrangling another possessed man into the Devil's Trap with a sterling silver crucifix and frequent streams of holy water from a spray bottle. "Can somebody please turn the sprinklers off? They're diluting the holy water."

Katherine was now juiced enough from Jade's 'you can't' comment to shut them off with a mere thought. Konani hollered a quick thanks, maneuvered her target into the Devil's Trap, then raced to the pool cabanas for her next mark.

Katherine scanned the club, the DJ lights rolling red, purple, and blue across the copper dance poles and white leather furniture. Stark, Maddox, and Konani's brother Makoa were tag-teaming the last of the possessions. But even with everything going on, Katherine couldn't prevent thoughts of Ari, that loathsome Viking—tall, muscular, and bronze all over—from escaping that locked vault in her mind.

Just the mention of him made her dizzy.

He would eat that up, arrogant, booming-laugh swashbuckler that he was. And she would go to hell before *ever* admitting she had a swooning bone in her body.

An unnatural wind swept through the club, shifting the diaphanous bolts of gauze that separated the dance floor from the outside pool terrace. The ground rumbled and shook, clinking the crystal chandeliers and raining chunks of wet plaster from the ceiling. Goose bumps broke out across Katherine's arms as she dropped into a crouch.

This was no earthquake. A manifestation of these elements meant the Archangel Michael was here. *Great.* Deep power filled the space behind her so that it seemed all the molecules in the room had compressed into a volatile state.

Katherine tried to swallow back her fear. *"I apologize for the Hell comment, Michael, but you should know by now that sarcasm is my native tongue,"* she said to him, telepathically.

"And you should know by now that sarcasm is indicative of passive aggression, which illuminates a flawed moral compass," he replied aloud, rather than with his mind.

She stood and turned slowly, noting with alarm that he'd frozen everyone in the club but her.

Oh, Lord, how could she forget how overwhelming the leader of Heaven's army was? Midnight hair, fathomless dark-blue eyes, dressed in black from broad shoulders to boot-clad feet... Michael had created the Guardians from piss-poor examples of humanity more than two millennia ago. And, beginning with Ari Grimmson in 847 AD, the archangel had structured the Healer class of Guardians to exorcise possessed humans.

"Yeah, well, if you didn't want your Guardians to be morally flawed, maybe the Big Boss should have chosen humans who'd lived exemplary lives instead of picking those of us who were bitches and assholes." Katherine crossed her fingers that the archangel wouldn't smite her with the power vibrating in the room.

Then again, being laid low by a celestial being might be better than having to face Ari in her current gutless condition.

Michael's dark eyes flashed with something that could have been humor. Which had to be a trick of light because the archangel had been nothing but somber in the hundred and forty-plus years since he'd given her this second chance at redemption.

Or rather, this Purgatory.

If I only knew then what I know now...

Michael raised an eyebrow.

"Oh quit it, you know I'm joking. Well, not about the bitches and assholes part, but that bit about Purgatory..." She paused, wondering how tolerant he was feeling today. "Kind of."

"Most humans who have endeavored to live a good and peaceful life do not have the necessary disposition to battle demons. That job is best reserved for those who are a hair's breadth away from the pits of Hell themselves. Those who know how to fight dirty when the situation demands it."

Nice.

It was fabulous to know she would've become one of the

black-eyed fiends if not for the final decision she'd made as a twenty-five year old human being. A single act of selflessness —an exclamation point at the end of her cold, egocentric existence. Katherine still didn't understand why she'd done what she'd done in those last few minutes of her life.

"You chose well at the time it mattered most. There is honor in that," Michael said.

"Jury's still out on me. My actions were probably a bout of temporary insanity. I doubt I'd make the same choice again."

She wanted to get a rise out of him, but Michael's expression remained inscrutable. "You hide your broken emotions behind bravado, Guardian. You will fail in your duties if you do not find a way to surmount your grief, despair, and loneliness. Failure is unacceptable, for the battle will soon arrive at your door."

Grief, despair, loneliness.

Her heart pounded, but she forced her mind to go blank so the archangel wouldn't see how close to home his words had hit. "Such apocalyptic commentary, but you don't scare me, Michael. If the End Times were near, you'd be polishing your weapons and strategizing with Gabriel, Raphael, and the rest of the God-squad instead of popping in at my lowly club. So spare me the lofty prose. This is obviously about Ari, and I'll have you know, I still don't—" She was going to say "want him," but Michael would pounce on that lie faster than a babysitter's boyfriend running out the back door when the parents' car pulled up. "I still haven't changed my mind. I refuse to bond with him."

Michael's eyebrows pulled down fractionally, and she felt a flare of triumph at getting his expression to change, even if it was infinitesimal.

She put a hand on her hip. "So you might as well undo this kumbaya thing between him and me. Or at least move me on to my next soul mate. Everyone assumes we have more than one because the Big G seems to place a lot of weight on free will. I mean, if we only had *one* person we could be happy with for the rest of our lives, well, that sucks."

Michael remained frustratingly silent. She took a step forward, intending to snap her fingers in his face, but thought better of it.

Unfortunately, staying alive trumped self-expression. "Well? Angels have to be honest, right? Tell me. *Please*."

Michael considered her for a moment like he was peeling back her deepest layers.

She tried not to squirm.

Finally: "You assumed correctly. There is no one person who is your only hope, as there is no limit on human happiness or human love."

"I knew it. This soul mate thing is just some shitty Guardian propaganda."

"*Enough*." Michael's form glimmered and the floor rumbled beneath her feet. "You disappoint me, Guardian. I shall be sorry should I have to relieve you of your duties."

She threw up her hands. "I'm bound to fail since I'm not rejuvenating after the exorcisms. I'm doing everything I always have for the last one hundred forty years— meditation, rest, and a good diet—but it's not working anymore."

"You have not tried everything because you have never truly opened your heart to possibility with the Viking." The archangel vanished as quickly as he'd come, unfreezing everyone in his wake.

"Oh really? What do you call making a baby with him?" she yelled at the ceiling as the renewed screams of the Possessed corralled in the Devil's Trap coincided with the pounding in her frontal lobe.

"An open heart is not a prerequisite for a biological event," came Michael's reply.

Katherine cursed. "Always have to have the last word, don't you?"

"*No.*"

She rolled her eyes and pressed her palms against her temples. And then Jade was in her face, her big brown eyes concerned. Katherine held up a hand before she could start her Southern, 'hey-girl-let's-hug-this-out' spiel. "It's a beautiful day to leave me alone, Jade. By calling Ari against my wishes, you've inspired my inner serial killer. Truly."

"Stop being so dramatic," Jade said. "You need to simmer down and wait to start de-deviling these people until Ari gets here. In the meantime, can you shut them up? Damn, they're a noisy bunch."

Katherine would've tried silencing the screamers, but since it annoyed Jade, she let them wail on. It would expend too much energy to quiet them anyway. Energy she'd need to mind-wipe the three freaked-out humans who still cowered beneath a table on the raised level beyond the dance floor.

She marshaled her resources then closed her eyes. Her molecules broke apart and refastened a split second later under the table with the humans. She placed her hand on each of their foreheads in turn, erasing their memories of the last several hours. Then she streamed to the bar, weak and nauseous, and watched the three dazed, but now-smiling humans crawl out from beneath the table and look around.

"*Aloha awakea!* That was some party last night, huh?" Konani hollered over to them. "Next time, no sleeping on the premises. Go home, eat a good breakfast, and drink plenty of fluids, ya hear?"

Maddox ushered the smiling humans to the door. Katherine glanced at Konani, wishing she had the time and energy to take their yearly trip to the Polynesian tattoo artist in Hilo. It had been their November tradition since Katherine took down the sex-trafficking ring that had enslaved fifteen-year-old Konani and her eleven-year-old brother Makoa.

Hard to believe that was ten years ago.

Harder still to believe that her Guardianship hadn't been revoked when she'd hunted down their pimp and fed him to the *pua'a* boars in the forest near Mauna Loa.

That *had* to have been against Guardian rules.

Maybe Michael didn't know.

Yeah right. The archangel was probably waiting to drop some massive judgment on her when she least expected it. Probably another 'biological event' that would rip her heart out. But if and when he did, it would be worth the satisfaction she'd felt exacting justice for Konani and Makoa.

Katherine rubbed her forehead, trying to ignore the rolling of her belly. "Nani, would you mind making me one of your chia energy drinks?"

Her gaze lingered on Konani's first tattoo—a scrolling wrist cuff that covered up the barcode her pimp had crudely inked to mark her as his property. The cover-up tattoo was a work of art, and for Konani, a symbol of mastery over the trauma of her past.

"Of course, Kat." The mixologist's long, dark hair slid across her shoulders with a nod and frown. "Don't do as many exorcisms as last time, all right? These devils aren't going anywhere, you know."

"She shouldn't be attempting any exorcisms right now," Jade said, grabbing a cold compress from the bar fridge and turning back to feel Katherine's forehead. "I'm not kidding, Kat. You think you're invincible, but you look like death warmed over after those mind wipes. It takes a lot, but Guardians can die, too, you know."

"I'm well aware of that, thank you." Too aware, in fact. If Leviathan made a play for the holy relic Katherine protected —the Chains of St. Peter, which had been strangely glowing for the last two weeks—Katherine wasn't sure she'd be able to stave off the archdemon.

So far, Leviathan hadn't performed any of the aggressive tricks that Nate Temple's invading archdemon had pulled at his Minneapolis club, but that wasn't necessarily fortunate.

The two low-key weeks since Leviathan had showed up in Hawaii were likely the calm before the storm.

"And thank you for your stunning lack of confidence in me, Jade. That always helps." She shook off Jade's attempt to apply the cold compress, turning toward the Devil's Trap. "Look at these cretins. Maddox, get that knave's mouth off the woman in blue."

To see their humanity vanish like this never ceased to unsettle her.

Katherine took the energy concoction from Konani, but was only able to drink a few swallows. She set the glass on the nearest table, her stomach churning as she wiped the perspiration from her hands on her ruined pant legs. Was she actually dying, or was it nerves because that damn Viking was on his way?

She'd sent him away multiple times in the three years since her miscarriage. The last time, he'd been furious. He wasn't angry by nature, but he obviously hadn't moved past those negative feelings because he hadn't returned since.

The staff members' eyes bored holes in her. "Everyone had better carry on with their day before I go on a pink-slip binge. Having to replace all of you at the same time would seriously displease me."

"You're always displeased," Stark muttered from across the dance floor, but with her Guardian hearing, his words registered loud and clear.

"That's no aloha spirit, boss," Makoa added.

Sweet Makoa with his unapologetic optimism, poetic eyes, and flawless Hawaiian good looks. How had he remained so hopeful and compassionate despite the horrors he and his sister had survived?

He was the only one she had a hard time bitching at. How irritating.

"The aloha spirit withers when in range of my shrewish shadow, Makoa. Now, out—all of you. I don't need any of you here for this part."

Especially if she passed out afterward.

Or worse, if she failed mid-exorcism and the rootless demon attempted to choose one of her team members as its new host. Of course, it wasn't likely to work because a host needed to be vulnerable for an evil spirit to take hold, but she wasn't about to risk her people in case they were having an off day.

"Why don't you at least change clothes first?" Jade suggested. "I'm sure you feel awful in that wet number."

Indeed. But her private quarters were twenty stairs away, and even the thought of getting there was exhausting. "Last I checked, I'm the boss. Everyone go get some coffee. When you come back, refill your holy water. Keep your rosaries, crucifixes, and salt close at hand at all times. And watch each other's back."

"Text me if you need anything." Konani's caring eyes felt like sledgehammers to Katherine's floundering facade of strength.

"I don't need anything. Now get out of here." Hopefully they'd stay away long enough to ensure their safety.

Konani grabbed her purse from behind the golden bar with its glowing nude silhouettes, then ran to catch up with Stark, Maddox, and Makoa as they walked into the bright sunshine on the club's main terrace.

Katherine's shoulders sank as she stared at the writhing mass of possessions in the Devil's Trap—now a half dozen of them—unable to suppress her desperation any longer. She felt more than heard Jade take a step toward her.

"*Don't*. Please, Jade. I hate that you think my directives don't apply to you." She dared not look back at the only living blood relative she had. Though six generations had lived and died between them, with Katherine's Guardian agelessness, they looked like contemporaries.

Three years ago when she lost the baby, she and Ari didn't know how to be a couple anymore. He left, promising to find one of Katherine's relatives even though she'd asked him not to. He thought it would help her heal.

It hadn't because even though the same blood ran in their veins, at the time, they were strangers.

Jade sighed. "Well, I hate that you carry this healing burden alone. I hate that you hide how much you care. And I hate that you don't love me enough to let me in," she finished quietly.

Katherine's lips parted momentarily in silent pain, but she summoned a breezy smirk before she turned around. "Now who's being dramatic? Go take a break, okay? I'll be fine."

"Listen. I met a psychologist who specializes in Electra complex."

Katherine gritted her teeth and willed her breath to slow. "I'll pretend you didn't say that." She turned to walk toward the Devil's Trap, finally ready to deal with these evil shits.

Jade's heels clicked rapidly toward her. "Daddy issues are nothing to be ashamed of. It's not your fault."

Katherine swung around to face her. "You want to go there after our last smackdown about this?"

"I won't abandon you, Kat. Not everyone is like that. I'll prove it to you if it takes my whole life." Jade's warm brown eyes were so earnest. So... loving.

A dark corner of Katherine's soul shivered and pulled the inky blanket tighter around her. How she hated when people ripped off the scabs. You'd think, having lived with Jade in her face for the past few years, she'd have developed scar tissue by now, but the free-spirited, good-hearted woman could shine light into the tiniest of cracks.

One of these times, Katherine was bound to implode.

One of these days, Jade would finally realize that her four-times-removed great-aunt was so grievously flawed she was past redemption.

And then, like Katherine's parents, her sister...even Ari...

Jade would leave, too.

CHAPTER 3

An hour later, on wobbly hands and knees, Katherine shook her head and groaned as quietly as possible. Her team had probably returned to the club by now and were hovering in the reception area beyond the second row of tables.

Her stomach pitched wildly again, bringing tears to her eyes.

One more exorcism and the humans they'd quarantined in the Devil's Trap would be free of invading malevolence.

Just one more.

It sounded so simple. And for the last century, it *had* been. She spoke the right incantations, drew the malevolent spirit into her body, blasted it with her bad bitch mojo, and *voila!*

Exorcisms "R" Us.

Not anymore.

The inside of her body felt coated in sludge. Black, oily, and unclean—with slithering worms piling up in her arms, legs, and chest. She'd tried meditation to rise above it, to initiate the natural rejuvenation that all Healer Guardians received, but she'd only fallen asleep. The twenty minutes nap hadn't helped. Nor had the rest of Nani's special energy drink.

I'm failing.

The worst F word of all. A word that had haunted her even before that horrific day on the beach.

Curled up and shivering on the hardwood floor, two feet away from the last possessed female, Katherine stared at a wooden table leg without seeing it. Instead she saw seagulls, heard the sounds of the ocean and children laughing. She was eleven, her sister Mary, only nine. She'd loved her new bathing suit, especially how the pretty blue color had deepened as she'd waded into the waves.

"Stop," Katherine whispered, closing her eyes. "Please."

The next wave washed away the fever dream, resettling Katherine in her childhood home. Father's low, angry voice lectured her mother behind closed doors two days before the accident. *Just wait, Annabelle, Katherine's headstrong ways will cause us more grief than Mary's tireless whining.*

How right he'd been.

Katherine rolled onto her back on the nightclub floor, covering her head with her arms, but it didn't stop how much it hurt that her mother had never defended her.

Tears leaked down the sides of Katherine's feverish face. This existence was hard. But she wasn't ready to give up. Wasn't ready for what came after failing her duty.

For better or worse, this Purgatory was her choice, and she'd make it again and again, though her motives made her a coward. She chose to help humanity not because she wanted to, but because she was honest-to-God, knees-knocking petrified of suffering in Hell for eternity.

"Michael, why won't you help me?"

"You're perfectly capable of helping yourself, Guardian, yet you choose not to," came the echoing reply. *"If archangels offer their aid, that is the beginning of the End Times. You know this."*

Yeah, well, screw him and his by-the-book anal-retentiveness.

A blast of air ripped through the room, so cold it made her damp pantsuit freeze to her skin. Her teeth clacked together. She managed to roll to her knees, panting to suppress the dry heaves. *Don't give him the satisfaction.*

"I find no joy in your misery, Guardian."

"Could have fooled me. Just..." Leave me alone. Even her voice inside her head didn't sound like her anymore.

The Possessed stopped crying and pulling her hair and started laughing and jeering at Katherine. After the worst of the nausea passed, Katherine wiped her mouth and staggered to her feet, looking at the bloodshot eyes of the still-taunting, possessed woman. "Keep that up and you're going to find your lip gloss replaced with a glue stick, demon."

Katherine turned toward the reception area as the evil spirit inside the woman erupted in rage. The screaming set Katherine's teeth on edge, but she forced herself not to cover her ears.

As expected, she found Jade, Stark, Makoa, Maddox, and Konani loitering near the host's station. They scrambled to make themselves look busy. Katherine plucked an upside-down menu from Konani's fingers, replacing it right side up before opening the club's front door.

"I'll be back in a few hours." De-demonizing the last one would have to wait. "If you burn the place down, make sure it looks like an accident for insurance purposes."

"Pretty hard to do that when the place is a fuckin' wet spa already," Stark muttered.

Katherine smiled inwardly, pleased with how much his confidence had grown in the two years since she'd exorcised a particularly robust demon from him, then forced him through heroin addiction treatment.

After that, she'd paid for him to finish his seminary

schooling online. None of it had been pretty, but they'd both managed to survive.

"I think you bitch more than I do, Stark. Impressive."

Pleasure flashed in his eyes before he turned away to grab a chair for her. "Sit your ass down before you embarrass yourself," he grumbled.

She knocked the chair over on her way to the door.

"Wait, where are you headed?" Jade called.

Katherine paused with one hand on the door, staring at all five of their serious faces, deciding if she wanted them to know. Telling them would be an admission of her exhaustion. Unfortunately, the need to be accessible to them won out over her damned pride.

"Home."

In thirty minutes, she was there. Normally, she'd stream home, but that was out of the question in her gutless state. The property was in Kailua, on the windward, lush side of Oʻahu. Her fortress. Five thousand square feet of privacy with both a sugar-sand beach and rocky outcroppings mere steps away from her tricked-out lanai.

She turned off the car and shucked her six hundred-dollar shoes, leaving them on the bench in the front entry. A soak in the hot tub would feel glorious, but she'd probably pass out and drown. She stripped out of her abused pantsuit, dumped it into the trash, and took a cool shower to clear her mind.

It only made her edgier.

Ari was coming.

She refused to look at her reflection in the mirror as she dried off, and then walked circles in her dressing room. She slipped into a breezy cotton shift and tried to make herself sit still.

Ari's coming.

She could feel his unique energy in the subtle pressure shifts of the salty sea air that was his Guardian element.

Ari.

Fatigue sat like two boulders yoked across her shoulders, but her pulse wouldn't let her mind relax and seek the rejuvenation that was critical to her existence. She arranged her still-damp hair into the low chignon that Ari had always called her 'proper librarian bun.'

Damn him for the memories.

She paced in front of the windows. *Breathe.*

Her hands balled into fists as she ran down the stairs and rushed out into the mid-afternoon sunshine. Her bare feet sank into the warm sand as she made her way toward the surf. Sweat pooled between her breasts. Panic—fresh, hot, breathless—flared to life, and she froze, as she always did, ten feet from the water's edge. The waves retreated, barrel-rolling tiny shells and strands of seaweed across the sand. She exhaled with a shudder.

The water element was her gift, yet her fear of the ocean —feeling the water rise up her ankles to drag her down and swallow her whole—nearly crippled her.

Such a paradox.

She stepped back five more steps and collected seashells, their smooth surfaces normally so soothing against her fingertips.

Now, each one gathered meant she was that much closer to facing Ari.

She sang an old Hawaiian song under her breath as the wind picked up and stirred loosened hairs from her bun as though pulled by Ari's fingers. He'd always taken her hair down, pin by pin. He said he loved to undo her.

Oh, how he'd succeeded.

Her shadow lengthened on the sand. She looked out over the ocean as dark, moody clouds overtook the sun. *Ari?* Her heart skidded to a halt, then jackknifed in her chest, restarting at an impossible pace. An unnatural wind drove the waves higher, crashing violently against the sand, forcing her to retreat until she stumbled onto the tiles of her lanai. This abrupt weather change had to be him.

She pushed back up to her feet and swung around to look out over the ocean.

I hate him for always making me feel. *I hate...*

Him.

Right there, standing before her on the wet sand. Still so rawly masculine. Always aware of his ridiculous appeal. Always smirking, though this time there was an edge of cruelty to the curve of his lips. White shirt, bare feet, and tan trousers rolled up and wet around the ankles, as though he hadn't just come from protecting the Dalai Lama in the frozen Himalayas.

He never felt the cold. Or self-loathing.

Must be nice to be born a Viking.

"*Katherine.*"

Her name fell deep and liquid from his lips, disorienting her. He stepped forward, crushing her in his arms, swinging her around. She grew dizzy from the motion and his sensual laughter. Memories poured through her. She let them come. Lost herself in the wonder, joy, and eventual heartbreak of them, knowing she was a fool for doing so.

Energy cleared the pathways in her mind, balanced her tummy, and heavens, she felt better than she had in *ages*.

Too bad they were so wretchedly unsuited.

She pushed out of his arms, conjuring a geyser of cold water to blast him in the back of the head for taking such liberties. He shook the water out of his eyes and from his sun-streaked blond hair—longer than she'd ever seen it—as he laughed in that captivating way.

Pure Ari.

His laughter was as intoxicating as his kiss.

She turned abruptly and forced herself not to dash into the house. He grabbed her hand, swinging her back around, the blue of his eyes clouding abruptly. "No more walls, Kat."

CHAPTER 4

Ari's euphoria bled away as he watched the storm break across Kat's face. Her dark curling lashes framed washed-out irises, a feeble reminder of the fierce blue-green she'd been born with, the snapping intelligence in them a shadow of their former glory.

And her waterworks —which normally landed him on his ass—were now a squirt to the back of his head.

He swallowed back his shock. She was truly ill. He rubbed his thumb across the underside of her wrist where her pulse jumped. His initial elation at seeing her warred with his anger at her past rejection, as well as a new, unwelcome uneasiness about her well-being. "Kat—"

"No!" She jerked her arm away. "No more walls, you say? That's rich coming from someone who was so emotionally unavailable you couldn't even stand to be on the same island with me after I f-failed you."

He blinked, taking a moment to process what she'd said.

Even she looked startled by her outburst.

"Whoa. The only failure we're both guilty of is a breakdown in communication," he said.

She held up a hand. "Let's not reanalyze why we don't belong together, okay? Jade obviously grossly overstated whatever trouble she called you to tattle about. I'm fine. Just like I've been for the last three years."

Without you.

The unspoken words hung between them, as daunting as any enemy fortifications he'd ever faced.

"You've never been a decent liar. Your eyes show your struggle, and I feel it in your body. It's time we mended our discord." He stepped toward her, maintaining eye contact. He pushed through the ether that stretched between them to seek out her heart's rhythm with his Guardian senses. When he matched his heart's cadence to hers, the thrill of their intimate connection surged through his blood. The white grains of sand at his feet grew luminous.

Marvelous.

Hues, feelings... *her*. It was all entwined, coming back in a rush that made him want to throw back his head and howl to the Valkyries like the crazed Viking berserkers from his ancient raiding party. He'd forgotten how a Guardian's senses stormed to life when in sync with his soul mate.

He slowed his breathing. She remained rooted to the spot while he threaded his fingers through her chilled ones to increase their skin-to-skin contact. The need to comfort her, to soothe her racing heart, and bolster her dangerously low energy levels quenched his anger. Softened his bruised pride.

His other hand cupped her cheek, once so soft and full. Now it was sunken, the skin pale and dry. Touching her, impressions cascaded through him—pain, darkness, hopelessness. He frowned, clasping her hand tighter, but she shook her head and forcefully broke their connection, wiping her cheeks.

"Stay out of my head. You have no right."

"Kat, my God..." Fragments of his own grief drifted

through him like murky shadows in fjord caverns. He'd been patient these past three years, giving her time to realize that his actions—finding Jade—was his way of helping her deal with the loss of their baby and her soul-deep scars from losing her family at such a young age.

She'd had far more loss in her life than anyone should have to bear.

But she'd been so wrathful when he'd returned with Jade.

"I won't allow you to suffer another day."

She flushed briefly before resuming that aloofness that was her hallmark. "You will gladly offer your body in service to my weakness because it's your duty, right?" Her lips curled coldly. "I'd rather purchase new batteries for my hand-held, so you can go stuff your damn soul mate obligation. And my name is Katherine."

He stepped closer, watching with satisfaction as more color rose in her cheeks. He'd missed every reserved, bitchy edge of her because he knew better than anyone what was down beneath it all. Still waters ran deep. And those passionate undercurrents belonged to him whether it pissed her off or not. "No vibrator in this lifetime or the next will satisfy you the way I can."

"Get over yourself, Viking. And for Heaven's sake, stop crowding me. I don't have the energy to pretend I like you."

"I'm not sure I like you either, so we're even. However, if you expire, you'll no longer be able to boss people around. I know you'd hate that."

"Stop acting so sanctimonious, Ari. You're only here because if I get too sick, you'll start feeling it in your bones, too."

"I'm still pissed, yes. How much rejection do you expect a man to take? Nothing I said would change your mind so I buried myself in my duties. But if you think I'm only here for myself right now, you never really knew me."

He was ashamed at how much he wanted to hear her deny his words. How much he hungered for her to say she *did* know him. That she was sorry for all the times she pushed him away.

Without answering, she walked away from her house, toward the rocky shoreline. Another rejection. He should go and stay gone this time. But the ache to touch her, to feel her body rise and fall over his, to laugh together the way they often had after making love...that ache never went away, regardless of how many oceans he put between them.

In the good times in her arms, he'd felt as free as he ever had on the high seas.

Suddenly, a wave of dark energy detonated through the air, turning flowers, shrubs, and trees black. Birds fell from the sky and their treetop perches.

A chill darted down Ari's spine. He turned to look out over the ocean. In the distance, a woman garbed in inky blue hovered over the suddenly still water. The ocean—unmoving —was the most unnatural thing he'd ever seen.

After Jade's urgent call this morning, he'd reached out telepathically to Alexios, wanting to find out if there was anything he should know before showing up in Hawaii. The Guardian leader immediately mentioned Leviathan—one of the archdemons freed at Nate Temple's Minneapolis club during last month's rending of an Earth-Hell Seam.

Alexios, an honorable Spartan warrior from 521 BC and sole exception to the you-have-to-be-an-asshole-to-qualify Guardian selection process, had spoken of Leviathan bringing waters of chaos.

Ari squeezed his fists at his sides, a bygone, yet familiar aggression rising as he watched Satan's daughter hover over the water. He opened his palms toward the sea, calling to the air masses that had freakishly deserted the vicinity around the archdemon.

The archdemon's halo of chestnut hair seemed to have a life of its own. She shook her head and yelled something in an otherworldly language that made the hairs rise on the back of his neck. Had to be Enochian—the language of angels.

But she wasn't an angel, so how could she speak it? Had her father, the original fallen angel, taught her?

Ari squinted, his acute Guardian eyesight bringing her —*heartbroken?*—expression into focus.

Definitely not the look he expected. "Go in the house and refortify your wards with all possible haste," he told Katherine, keeping his eyes on Leviathan who extended a hand, then let it drop.

In the next instant, the demon princess was gone.

What the hell? When the tide resumed, some of the fallen birds staggered to their feet. Ari glanced behind him, but Katherine was nowhere in sight. Once more, he sent his senses among the competing air pressures in all directions around the property—this time searching for Katherine's essence.

She was in the house, but he couldn't detect any lingering traces of her wards. He frowned. Guardians had always called upon her when powerful protection spells were needed. Usually those talents extended to her own fortress.

Her now unprotected home spoke volumes about her physical decline.

How long had she been so sick? For the last three days, aches and pains and nausea had washed over him at unexpected times. It wasn't until Jade called that he realized his symptoms were coming from his connection to Kat.

He reached into the ether, opening the Guardian pathway to contact Alexios about Leviathan. Moments later, Alexios appeared on the sand. His haunted amber eyes hinted at a tormented soul, capable of extreme violence.

And the type of love that goes down in history books.

"You didn't have to come all this way. I know you haven't been able to find Sophia in this lifetime—"

Ari was ass-down in the sand before he could even blink.

"We're not discussing my business." Alexios's low voice rumbled in the air. "Katherine has suffered for too long, Grimm. Does your arrival mean you will no longer neglect your duties to your soul mate?"

Ari rolled to his feet. "I'm not going anywhere." He brushed his hands on his pants. "I will care for her." It would leave more scars, but after she was well, he'd try to forget her on the open seas...or maybe he'd return to the Himalayas. Mount Everest was not nearly as cold as Kat's heart.

Alexios assessed him. "You and Katherine need to lay aside your wounded vanities. Disharmony between soul mates creates weakness within our ranks. With four archdemons loose, there could be no worse time for vulnerability."

Ari made no comment.

If only it were that easy to heal two battered hearts.

"Let me know if you need help with the water demon," Alexios said. "I haven't faced her before, but there've been reports that she's a loner in Hell."

Ari nodded. Loners could be the most dangerous opponents because they were good at keeping secrets.

No one knew how Alexios obtained his information, but besides being Archangel Michael's favorite, he was one of the few Guardians who could manipulate the ether—the metaphysical energy of the atmosphere and inherent in all living things.

Every Guardian had one physical element they could control, but Alexios could harness the power of all of them. He could stir the sea, propel the wind, detonate volcanoes, and grow mammoth sequoias from aught but a seed.

He could also destroy a man's mind with a whisper.

Ari looked out to sea. "Leviathan was right there, watching Kat's house, and she was very much alone."

"Did she attempt contact?"

"No. She drew further into herself when she felt my energy. She looked upset. Almost lost. It was odd. Maybe she was feeling the ill effects of being in daylight for too long? I don't know. If she's here to take possession of Kat's relic, why hasn't she made a move for it in the two weeks she's been here?" Another thing he hadn't known before Jade's call, otherwise he would've come sooner.

Alexios shrugged. "I gave up demon psychology a thousand years ago, but what we started seeing last month at Nate's club is that these archdemons are able to tolerate sunlight a lot better than when we've faced them in the past."

"One more Guardian advantage we can no longer count on."

Alexios nodded. "Be ready for anything. And don't trust a damn thing any of them say."

"I won't." Ari glanced at Kat's house, anxious to set his own wards there. "I have a good tracker in the Himalayas if you haven't looked there for Sophia yet."

Alexios vanished in an explosion of beach. It took Ari the better part of a minute to extract himself from the sand-pocolypse.

Touchy.

Then again, he would be too if his soul mate was hunted by demons in each of her reincarnations.

Lately, all the Guardians were uptight.

Ari shook the remaining sand out of his hair and refilled the ten-foot hole in the beach using massive pulses of wind. Then he opened his palm and moved his arm through the air to send highly charged molecules into all layers of the atmosphere to serve as tripwires, alerting him to encroaching evil energy.

Because Leviathan *would* be back.

But he—and Kat—would be ready.

CHAPTER 5

Katherine slipped out of her cotton shift and into a sleeveless designer dress and python knee-high boots. Her gaze kept wandering out her second-story bedroom window that overlooked the beach. Ari stood there like a Norse warrior venerated in stone. How such a vibrant, restless man could stand so still like that had always fascinated her. He was either a cyclone or a statue.

A man of contradictions.

But of course, not many of them were visible until you really got to know him. *Trust him.*

That was probably true of everyone, but she'd never bared her soul to anyone like she had to Ari.

Katherine went to her dresser mirror to repin her bun, fingers shaking slightly. His presence had rejuvenated her more than all the sleep, meditation, and nutritious food she'd had in the last several months. It would be irrational to deny herself such healing.

The problem was how to convince her heart to turn off its *boom-badda-boom-boom* every time he curved his sexy lips at her. Because they didn't work as a couple.

Katherine glanced at Ari on the beach once more before hurrying down to the garage. By the time she slid into her convertible, Ari was opening the passenger door. She squelched a flush of pleasure. He'd always been able to gauge her location, having some sort of thermal-sensing air GPS where she was concerned.

She frowned, put the top up on the convertible, and started the ignition. "I'm going to work. There's bound to be lots of chaos when the club gets into full swing. When I left, there was a Possessed on the premises. There's probably more by now."

"Perfect. You know I thrive in mayhem. And I look forward to a complete tour of Aqua. I only got through the upper terrace before you threw me out the last time."

She held back a snort at the thought of anyone besides Alexios, Raj, or an archangel physically removing Ari from anywhere. If he'd really wanted to stay, there would have been nothing she could've done to make him leave.

She pulled out of the garage and sped toward Highway 61 to Waikiki Beach. "You only stay when it's convenient for you," she said finally, wishing she hadn't opened her damn mouth when she heard him sigh.

"You're wrong, Kat. I've tried to be respectful of your space these last few years, even though you misunderstood my intentions when I left to find Jade. But you clearly need me to stay this time."

"You are so full of yourself. You think you were being heroic for finding my long-lost family member and giving me time to get over losing the baby, but what about *you*, Ari?" She glanced over at his steely jaw. "Have you ever thought that maybe you left because you couldn't deal with your own feelings?"

He'd robbed them of the chance to mourn their baby together.

His gaze swung from the view out the windshield to her. "Are you kidding me? We've never been a touchy-feely couple. Talking about my emotions and how gutted I felt when our baby died wasn't going to help anything." The miles sped by as the silence deepened in the car. Ari looked out the passenger window. "Besides you, I wanted our baby more than I ever wanted anything in the thousand-plus years I've been alive. You were drowning in your grief. I wasn't going to heap my pain on yours."

Katherine's head leaned back against the headrest. "But that's what people do—they share. It reminds us we're not..." *Alone.*

What if all along he'd only been pursuing her out of a sense of duty as her soul mate?

"Guardians have always assumed we have more than one possible soul mate, but Michael confirmed it this morning." Her words hung in the stifling car air. His gaze on her face felt like scorching sand under her bare feet, but she kept her eyes on the road.

"I've always known that, Kat. I choose you anyway."

She wriggled her nose when her eyes started to prickle. She flicked the radio on, and Chopin's "Raindrop Prelude in D-Flat" filled the car with its haunting piano. Ari promptly switched the station to heavy metal. She didn't dare glance at him before looking down to switch it back to classical.

"*Woman.*" Ari grabbed the steering wheel and swerved the car back to their side of the road. The passing vehicle's shrill horn made Katherine's hair stand on end. The slight tilt to Ari's beautiful lips meant trouble.

"I know my rakish good looks and masculine charm are distracting, but really, Kat, you need to pay more attention to the road."

"Oh, shut up," she muttered, grateful for the levity. *No more heavy shit—no matter how much he baits you.* He hadn't come up with any kind of response to her sharing comment, which only confirmed her belief that he didn't have it in him to be that kind of partner.

He'd always be a Viking wanderer at heart, happier exploring and fighting than living a quiet life with a family. It shouldn't surprise her.

Or hurt so bad all over again.

She scowled so other emotions would stay buried. "And, just so we're clear, when Leviathan showed up, I did *not* go inside because you told me to. I was already on my way to get my crucifix and holy water. So don't go thinking you have any influence on me."

He shrugged his broad shoulders as he flipped to a jazz station. "Wouldn't dream of it."

Okay then. His easy acceptance was way more annoying than it should be. She promptly turned the radio off to irritate him.

Then realized they were back to silence.

Ari had always been a chatty one. He'd told her how he used to prattle on with his enemies before running them through with his sword. Must've been all those hours on a ship with only the faces of his blood-thirsty comrades. Barbarians, all of them.

Just her shitty cosmic luck to be a reserved, homebody suffragist tied to a loquacious, nomadic savage.

He swiveled in the seat to angle toward her. No easy task when his knees were already pressed against the glove compartment.

Her fingers squeezed the steering wheel until her knuckles paled. "Stop. *Staring.*" *You loquacious, nomadic savage.* Yes, she was going to use that description to remind herself not to go to bed with him. He'd make her feel amazing up until the moment he departed.

God.

His gaze now felt like a warm waterfall with her standing naked beneath it.

"How do you plan to handle Leviathan if you're not going to let me touch you?" he asked softly.

She shivered even though it had to be pushing ninety degrees outside. He seemed so unrattled by Leviathan's strange arrival. Then again, Alexios had probably already told him that the archdemon had set up camp around Honolulu.

Alexios, Ari, and Raj—another free-agent Guardian like Ari—had fought more archdemon uprisings than any other Guardians. "You can go back to globe-trotting if all you're going to do is suggest intercourse."

"I'm open to discussing all kinds of topics with you, but if you're unwell, you're worthless against the dark ones. And as my soul mate, that's my problem, too. However, if you want to focus on intercourse right now, I'm more than happy—"

She held up a hand in front of his face. "And this is why I've ignored you all these years. We can't go two minutes without wanting to kill each other."

"You're exaggerating. It's been at least eight minutes, and I definitely don't want to kill you. I want to—"

"Let's just forget it." She snuck a glance at him. Those damned blue eyes were crinkling at the corners. How many times had she woken up to those eyes looking down into hers as his body slowly, exquisitely, merged with her own?

She wanted that breathless loving again. Wanted it with a desperation that shamed her.

How could she be so aware of wrong choices, but still desire to make them? It was illogical. "I really think you should go back to the Tibetan monks."

"I'm gratified you've been keeping tabs on me after all." He ignored her *pfft*, to rudely continue, "It's only natural that you would. Females can get very possessive of their mates, you know."

Don't even look at him or dignify that with a response.

"Some females have even been known to get sick if they go too long without—" His eyebrows raised like he'd had a revelation. "Ahhh, so that's what's wrong with you."

His laughter made her gut feel like it was blooming birds of paradise. *Stupid.* She stopped her car under the canopy of a banyan tree on a quiet street a few blocks from Aqua. "You know what? This is an exercise in futility. Just go and save us both the trouble." *And heartache.*

His palm cupped her wrist where it had dropped to rest on the gear shifter. "You're always so serious, woman. Maybe stress is another reason you're sick. I wish you would've called for me. No matter how much you piss me off, I'd do anything to help you."

She did know—maybe that's why she didn't call.

She could keep him out of her heart if he wasn't in her face. Ari in full living color was impossible to resist. "Well, looks like I should have, 'cause little old me can't *possibly* handle all those big, scary possessions by myself."

"Stop being such a harpy. Why do you always think the worst of me?"

Acid flushed through her belly and warmth coated her cheeks. She pulled her hand out from beneath his and looked down as she clasped hers together on her lap. She should apologize, but that would only encourage him.

He twirled the prism that hung from the rearview mirror. "I knew Jade wouldn't replace the baby we lost..." He cleared his throat. "But I thought she would give you a sense of family."

The shadow in his voice caught her off guard. She looked over at his profile, a chink fissuring in her wall. Her breath caught, and she quickly looked out the windshield at all the people passing on the street. "Thank you for that, Ari. Honestly. But I can't be with someone who won't stand beside me when I'm at my lowest."

Her palms were starting to sweat again. This sharing bullshit was not for the faint-hearted. *Need air.* She opened the car door and stood, unable to breathe or stay in her seat one moment longer.

She heard the other car door open and shut, but she still jumped when Ari's breath fanned the back of her neck.

"I wish I could go back and do it differently. But all I can do is be here now when you need my help."

She closed her eyes, fighting the little voice that told her this time might be different. *Everyone thinks it's going to be different the next time.*

It never was.

She took a deep breath and turned around to face him. "Even if I believed everything you're telling me, we're still too different, Ari. Think about what sets your soul free— adventure. You were born a Viking. Eleven hundred years hasn't changed your drive for exploration. The exhilaration of the unknowns beyond the horizon. It's not fair to expect you to change. I probably wouldn't even like you then anyway."

"Not everything can be perfect, Kat," he said, brushing the back of his fingers against her cheek.

She ached to lean into his hand, to forget their obstacles and pretend like it would all work itself out. "I know, but this is big picture stuff, can-I-be-happy-with-you-forever stuff. I'm a homebody. I appreciate order and planning and consistency. So we're stuck, attracted by some absurd, misaligned soul mate matching"—*that feels so right*—"that's completely wrong."

Her stomach was twisting, her throat was swelling, and if she cried right now, she would be *so* pissed.

"It's a cosmic mistake if you...ask...me." Her breath caught on the last word. She blinked rapidly to clear her eyes, appalled at the wavering quality of her voice.

She could see the truth reflected in Ari's for-once serious gaze. And that look was like the death knoll to their love...or whatever honest connection they'd shared.

Perhaps she'd been keeping him away all these years so she could keep the dream alive that maybe it would actually work. That maybe no differences were too great to make their love irrelevant.

Now that everything was in the open however...

Oh, Ari.

She wrapped her arms around her torso as he ran a hand through his hair. As painful as it was, she couldn't stop looking at him. The tanned, sinewy forearms, powerful biceps, and broad shoulders that had so often anchored her in the quiet hours before dawn. He would rise above her, silhouetted by gauzy street lights streaming through her open shutters. She would whisper to him, and he would answer with everything he had...

She bit her lip, turning back to her car, ready to barter with the Devil not to let the prickling in her eyes well into a blur of tears.

His hands came around her waist, his voice next to her ear. "We can figure this out, Kat," he whispered.

She swiped at her eyes, but didn't turn around. "You can't unsheathe your sword and fix everything with pure brawn. If it was that easy, I would have had you do it ages ago. But something like this doesn't work that way."

Lord, this hurt. Made her chest ache and her whole body lethargic.

But it was better to be sad now on a smaller scale, than know the devastation that would eventually come when his restlessness became too much to ignore.

He'd leave.

He would come back, yes, but then he'd leave again. Over and over. She couldn't bear it. How did Alexios stand it?

Even worse, he had to watch Sophia *die* in every lifetime. *No way*.

She slipped into the convertible. Ari stood by her door, looking down at her. "I don't know what to say."

If only you could deny everything I just said.

But Ari was always honest, and too impulsive to be devious. Too self-assured to lie.

Even when it cut to the quick.

She started the car and rolled the window down. "I'll talk to Alexios. Maybe he can convince Michael to sever our connection. There's got to be a way. I really think it's for the best."

"Not for me," he said.

His eyes were so bleak. Her heart hammered and her fingers itched to turn off the ignition, open the car door, and step into his arms. To erase that desolate look on his face.

"Just because two people love each other doesn't mean they should be together." Those were Susan B. Anthony's wise words to her over a cup of tea so long ago. Flinging them now at Ari, however, extracted far greater pain than when she'd delivered them to a nineteenth-century stockbroker who'd asked to marry her one full-moon night after a women's rights rally.

When she met Ari, she finally understood why she'd told that stockbroker no.

Very few people could set your soul on fire.

Katherine made herself stare into the fervent blue eyes of the one man who not only set her on fire, but burned her down and made her rise again. "You will find new adventures to lose yourself in. You'll be fine."

He shook his head angrily. "No. I've made mistakes. Lots of them. You accuse me of being afraid of your grief, but what about you, Kat? You've always been afraid, hiding behind condescension and fancy clothes. But you're still that sad, abandoned little girl who pushes people away before they get close enough to hurt you."

Burning coals dropped in her gut. She stomped on the gas pedal, but he raised a palm to apply counter wind pressure to the front of her car. Her tires burned rubber, raising acrid smoke that singed her nose and eyes. She let off the gas and pounded on the steering wheel. "Damn you! Why can't you leave it alone?"

"Because we've—" He straightened suddenly, pivoting away from her. Katherine leaned around him to see what had alarmed him.

The hairs tingled on her arms. A pale, beautiful woman stood in the middle of the street in a tailored, navy pantsuit. Everything about her communicated culture and elegance except her curly brown hair. It frizzed like a fuzzy halo around her head and all the way down her back. *That hair.* It made Katherine uneasy. And the fact that all the people in the vicinity were now frozen in shards of ice.

"Leviathan," Ari whispered in Katherine's mind. She startled at the intrusion. It had been so long since she'd let him in telepathically. She didn't even realize she'd allowed the pathway.

"I hate how daylight doesn't seem to affect them anymore."

"I couldn't agree more." Ari built pressure around them. She tried to unbuckle her seatbelt, but it was stuck.

"Let me go, Grimm, or I swear you'll regret it."

"Can't," he shot back.

"You mean 'won't,' you chauvinistic creep."

Leviathan clapped her hands, her laughter tinkling like mid-toned wind chimes. Katherine felt violence rise in Ari. Wind howled through the trees, bashing empty soda bottles, food wrappers, and other garbage against the stuccoed walls of the buildings around them.

"Can she hear us?" Katherine asked Ari, still telepathically.

"Not our words, but she knows we're communicating. And she can sense the discord. Ergo, she delights in our conflict. Fucking demons."

"Let me out of this car. Now."

Leviathan put an elegant hand on one hip. "How positively quaint! A pseudo-chivalrous man in the twenty-first century endeavoring to protect his lady love. So fascinating to meet you Mr. Grimmson. I've been looking forward to inspecting the one who reinforced Katherine's hatred of men."

Ari didn't respond, but formed a high-pressure air mass to warm the ice shards encasing the bystanders. As soon as they were free, Katherine sensed infrasound vibrations that indicated he was sending out pulses of mind control at frequencies below the normal threshold of human hearing. The humans scattered in various directions at a dead run.

Katherine had never seen him do that. Mind control was something he'd dabbled in while they were together, but he'd obviously mastered it in the years they'd been apart.

"Very impressive, Viking." Leviathan sauntered toward Katherine's car, her gaze never straying from Ari, her long legs and hips moving like she was taking a turn on a European catwalk. "Aren't you curious why I didn't stop you?"

"No. Nothing any demon does is ever interesting."

Leviathan stopped. Her shoulders dropped, and she suddenly looked like a lost little girl.

The hairs on the back of Katherine's neck rose. *"Ari, I feel like a sitting duck here, plus you're making me look weak."*

Her seatbelt unlatched and a pulse of wind made it retract. She quickly stepped out of the car to stand beside Ari.

"Leave this island, dark one. This is your only warning," he said.

"I see I've gone about this all wrong." Satan's daughter waved a pale, long-fingered hand in the air and that strange, lost look was replaced with a warm smile. "It makes sense that you're being overprotective. But I mean Katherine no harm. On the contrary." Leviathan's intense gaze locked on Katherine's, and Kat felt a sort of raw honesty down to the tips of her designer shoes. "I mean to offer you my protection," Leviathan finished.

Ari's booming laugh echoed down the street.

Katherine didn't feel like laughing. "From what? You?"

"Kat, deals with the Devil end in fire," Ari warned.

The archdemon froze, the pain in her eyes so...human. "I am *not* my father."

Katherine felt Leviathan's emphatic declaration deep inside. The emotion in Leviathan's voice carved a hollow in Katherine's gut and stayed there.

Leviathan clasped her hands in front of her. "You understand, don't you, Katherine? We have done wrong ourselves, but the sins of our fathers are not our own. How long are we supposed to pay for their mistakes? Your parents let you down when they should have held on to you."

...let you down when they should have held on... The words ping-ponged inside Katherine's mind. Leviathan took a step closer, then stopped when Ari raised his hand. Katherine pushed his arm down. Leviathan looked at her. No, looked *inside* her.

She felt stripped bare. Yet understood.

No one else could possibly perceive the complicated twist of guilt and anguish she lived with unless they, too, had lived through something so horrible. Unless they, too, had a mountain of baggage that went hand in hand with having a parent whom people whispered about and from whose daughter they kept their own children far away.

The daughter of Lucifer would probably understand that kind of pain better than anyone.

Ari attempted to usher Katherine back to the car, but she stepped away from him, moving closer to the archdemon.

Leviathan stretched out her hand briefly before letting it drop. "I know you, Katherine. I know what drives you to protect this island, and I know what dreams haunt your sleep. No one understands you like I do. We are two sides of the same coin. I am here to protect you, for you are too good to fight what's coming."

"This is bullshit," Ari growled telepathically.

Katherine's vision grayed as one of his sonic booms erupted around them, shielding them while a straight-line wind roared down the street, blasting Leviathan violently back before she had a chance to react.

Katherine ran to the vibrating shield Ari had created, heart in her throat, but Leviathan was nowhere to be found. She spun to Ari. "She didn't do anything to provoke such rancor!"

"She's an *archdemon*, Kat. What the hell?"

Of course he wouldn't understand. He'd led a privileged life as the son of a Viking jarl. "You would judge people based on their parents' actions?"

"Well, if their daddy is Satan, I'd have to say...yeah."

Ari's glib discrimination pissed her off. Or maybe it depressed her. She walked to the curb and sank down, suddenly too exhausted to even make it to her car.

If people were to be judged by the sins of their parents, she was fucked.

Her father had killed her mother in anguish over their middle child's death. Then he took his own life after telling Katherine it was all her fault.

My fault.

Mary's death was her fault as surely as if she'd held her little sister's head under the waves herself.

Katherine put her hands on her cheeks and tried to stop the tears. But her mortification was complete when she was lifted into strong arms, and the molecules of life broke apart.

CHAPTER 6

A ri held Kat tightly as he streamed them back to
Aqua, ready to deal with the fallout if any humans
witnessed their unconventional arrival. A tall, lean
man with a military haircut glared at him and handed an
energy drink to Kat when they materialized in the foyer. He
didn't look surprised to see them appear out of thin air, so he
was obviously in Kat's inner circle. "Where are Ms.
Evangelista's private quarters?"

The man met Ari's fierce stare, nothing but challenge in
his gray eyes. "You'd already know if you mattered."

Kat squirmed in Ari's arms. "Thank you, Maddox. There
is surely a raise in your future."

Ari lowered his fuming woman to her feet, then slapped
Maddox good-naturedly across the shoulders. "Good show,
young man. At least Kat has some decent help."

His laughter brought Konani and Makoa running into the
club's entryway. The brother and sister's wide, welcoming
smiles reminded Ari of happier times.

"Aloha, Grimm," Konani said, coming forward for a hug.

Katherine moved past Ari toward the Devil's Trap,

sinking to her knees beside a possessed woman weighed down by iron chains. Ari's nerves stood on end at the precise moment Katherine's eyes rolled back in their sockets and her body crumpled. He caught her before she hit the wood floor, her head lolling against his shoulder. His breath sawed in and out of his chest.

No Guardian should be so weak, especially when in the continued presence of her soul mate. "Someone better tell me *right now* where her chambers are," he growled.

Makoa pointed down the hallway. "Second level, last door on the left."

Ari streamed there, settling down with Kat in his arms on the semi-circular gray sofa with its sumptuous gold and silver pillows. He eased back, comforted by rise and fall of her chest and the pink hue blooming on her cheeks the longer she was in his arms.

When was the last time she'd had a decent night's rest?

He should've known she was too stubborn to ever tell him she was in trouble.

He'd layer wards at her home and here at Aqua. He'd make her stronger than she'd ever been and learn what he could about Leviathan. The archdemon had to have sensed Kat's flagging power. That meant she'd likely make a play for Kat's relic soon, or she'd try to draw Kat further into her web, hoping she'd fall for her lies.

He'd be ready for either tactic.

But after Leviathan was dealt with—what then? What of Kat's accusation that they were too different to make a relationship work? Everything she said about their personalities was true. He'd never taken the time to evaluate the hows and whys of things. He was more about the do's and let's go's of life.

His temples beaded with perspiration. He looked around the warm, oak-paneled office, pulling his shirt collar away from his neck. He drew in a slow, even breath to distract himself from her beautiful face and the fidgety feeling in his legs.

The room was a two-story circle with floor to ceiling bookshelves, polished wood railings ringing the second story. A giant black chandelier hung in the middle of it all. There was a permanence to the room with its graceful antique desk, gold and silver silk drapes, stately lamps, and hardcover books that huddled on the shelves like old women whispering secrets.

The elegant room suited the glitzy public persona of Katherine Evangelista perfectly. But where was the tribute to who she was under the controlled, condescending mask she put on for the world?

His eyes tracked along the shelves, top to bottom.

Ah, there. The ardent red Moroccan lantern they'd bought in a Marrakech market the first night they'd made love.

His lips curved slowly remembering the draped bed, saturated fabrics of purples and reds, textiles of all weaves and thicknesses, and Kat reclined upon them, her blue-green eyes dark with passion and provocation.

His breath fanned the blonde hair at her temples, his hand skimming over the curve of her hip. His restlessness fell away. She shifted on a sigh, and his hand paused under the swell of her breast, fingers curling into her, her tiny movement rubbing his groin.

Thor's beard. She felt incredible. How he'd missed her. The weight of her, the insolent set of her lips, the respectable bun that was part of her armor, the smart mouth and inexhaustible mind she used as defensive weapons.

Everything about her pleased him. Surely that would conquer their differences?

At least until their next fight when her well of hatred for him would resurrect all their pain.

He wrapped her tighter in his arms, wanting to set her aside, to avoid what was probably inevitable, but...

He loved her still.

It must be a sickness to love that which promised nothing but insecurity.

Katherine woke, wriggling out of his arms to stride toward her desk where she sat down, pushing stacks of paper around.

"What are you doing?" she asked without looking at him.

Her color was back to normal, thank Freya.

He stretched his arms overhead to calm the war in his brain. "Plotting world domination and helping you save face. You collapsed as soon as you laid hands on the Possessed in the Devil's Trap, in case you don't remember."

A deep blush stained her cheeks. "No, I mean what are you doing *here*?" She tapped the table with a manicured finger. "Aqua is my club, my business, and you need to leave. I didn't give you permission to stay."

Ari stood up. "I don't need your permission to do anything, least of all take care of my soul mate."

She made a rude noise. "So we're back to duty."

Maybe that's all it was ever going to be.

Maybe this long sojourn on Earth—loving Kat, yet never being good enough for her—was meant to be his punishment after all. "I guess we are. You don't remember the Hell Queen trying to mind-fuck you less than an hour ago?"

She waved a hand in the air. "I can handle Leviathan. She and her horde have been loitering for two weeks already. Things are under control." She sat down and fumbled with a pen and paper with shaky hands. She looked up and caught him watching. She sent him a glare, then started digging in her desk drawer.

"Has she approached you before the two times today?" he asked.

"No."

"Then she's used the last two weeks to lull you into complacency. It's a classic move, Kat. Don't be naive."

"I'm a lot of things, but I'm not gullible, you boil brain."

He would've smiled at her old-school insult if he weren't so agitated by her laidback response to Leviathan, her deteriorating health, and the continued strife between them. "Lulled is exactly what you were an hour ago when that spawn of Satan was talking to you. You were damn near catatonic."

Her hands smoothed her loose hairs into her bun. "I'm fine, Ari. I'm always fine."

"You don't do nonchalant well, Kat. In fact, it's probably your worst tell. Or should that be, your best tell?"

"For the love of God, call me Katherine."

He raised his eyebrows. "If you'd say 'for the love of Odin,' I might."

She pursed her lips. "Odin is God, and Buddha's God, and Allah and Jehovah and Brahman and Jesus...they're all God. For the love of all of them, please call me Katherine."

"Your parents hated when people called you Kat. I hate your parents. Fuckers. Ergo, I prefer calling you Kat."

She stood up, scooting back her desk chair. "You never knew them so you are not at liberty to judge."

"So snobby... Don't you remember that turns me on?"

"Thinking with your other brain again, I see. If you pretend to be intelligent, I'll pretend to care."

He laughed out loud. "You know I'll end up pissing you off by doing it anyway, so you might as well give me your blessing...*Kat.*"

"No."

"No?" he repeated.

"Did I stutter?"

You little shit. He advanced on her, enjoying the minute

widening of her eyes. "You're being needlessly mulish." Unfortunately for him, it looked good on her.

"Thank you," she replied tartly, brushing by him to the door. "Now if you'll excuse me, my club opens in three hours."

He shoved a hand on the door to prevent her from opening it. Standing behind her, he could see the pins holding all that thick, silky hair in place. How many would he have to extract before that mass came tumbling down? He wasn't usually a patient man, but he knew he would wait with bated breath for as long as it took to take them all down.

Because when her hair came down, her walls tumbled.

He leaned forward to brush his lips against the velvet skin at the side of her neck, knowing full well that his actions were a slippery slope, but helpless to stop himself when she was this close.

She stiffened and her breath arrested, so at odds with the wild gallop of her heartbeat which was as loud to his supersensory hearing as his own.

"I haven't missed your high-handedness, Ari," she whispered.

His nails raised goose bumps along her bare arms. He leaned down to sniff her neck again. "You are a terrible liar," he whispered back. "You feel energized by my nearness. I can see it. *Feel* it. Your color is better, your pulse is stronger, your eyes have revitalized to that jeweled sea-blue that wakes me in a cold sweat."

She turned to face him, her sudden indrawn breath his cue to place his other hand on the door to bracket her in. The heavy pulse in his groin another slip down that dangerous slope, but he'd worry about the emotional fallout later. He leaned down, but before his lips could take hers, the fingers of her right hand came up to press against his mouth.

"As mentioned earlier, I will talk to Alexios about undoing

our match. Surely the powers that be will see their mistake. We are total opposites, and therefore incompatible."

It came out in such a rush he wondered who she was really trying to convince. He watched her in the silence. Her eyebrows—a darker blonde than her hair—were perfection. He smoothed his thumb across one sweeping arch. "*No.*"

Her eyebrow tensed under his thumb. "No?"

He smiled slowly. "Did I stutter?"

"Wow, aren't you original? Out of my way, peasant. I have a demon to exorcise."

Don't we all? He traced the side of his finger across her full lower lip which she promptly slapped away. "When did you become so afraid of your sexuality?" he asked.

"Oh, Christ. Whatever, Viking. Last year I actually read the Kama Sutra, not just looked at the pictures."

Well, hell. That was hot.

He was ready to grab her thighs and start replicating some classic Kama Sutra moves, but she pursed her lips and closed her eyes—her quintessential *I'm-about-to-go-left-brain* look.

Always entertaining.

He smiled and waited.

"This..." She opened her eyes and fluttered a hand next to his jaw, "sexual arousal between us is purely physiological. Biologically, we're both stuck in our twenties, so it's only natural that we have strong organic responses to sexual stimuli. And since you're a large, virile male—which translates anthropologically to being more capable of protecting offspring..."

She faded off, and his gut bottomed out the same time hers must have by the stricken look that passed over her features. He reached for both of her hands. They were as cold as the Vatnajökull glacier in Iceland. His heart slugged at his ribcage as he squeezed her hands. "I will always regret not being able to save our child."

She continued to look at his chest, unblinking. "There was nothing you could do. It was...my fault," she finished so quietly he wasn't even sure he heard her right.

He frowned, squeezing her fingers. "Nonsense." She pulled her hands gradually from his grasp, and something about the action made the blood chill in his veins. He tilted her chin up so she'd look him in the eye. "Miscarriages are devastating, but unfortunately for millions of us, very common. You can't possibly blame yourself. I never did."

Her eyes swam with tears that refused to fall. "The days I wished I *wasn't* pregnant outnumbered the days I did. I...I didn't know how much I wanted that child until I l-lost it." Her hands flew up to cover her face as her tears spilled over. "I'm sorry. I didn't deserve to be a mother. I would have continued a sad legacy."

Rage surged sudden and hot. It scuttled through his sinew and bones, rawer and more elemental than the heated aggression that followed him into battles on foreign shores. He curled his fingers into her arms. "Don't you dare compare yourself to your parents' failures. You are nothing like them. You hear me? *Nothing*."

She shook her head, her cries drowning his anger in the need to comfort her. He crouched down to bring himself eye level, tugging her hands from her face. "Katherine, open your eyes." He brought his palms up to frame her jawline. "See me, *elskan*. Please."

Her eyelids snapped opened. He'd never seen her eyes so green. "I *hate* this, damn you. Why did you have to come back?"

He brushed a kiss on her forehead. "Our love has seen many troubles, and is sure to see many more. But know this... I have always wanted you. And nothing can ever shake my confidence that you'd be an amazing mother."

She brushed at her eyes. "All the evidence says otherwise."

"What evidence? That you weren't sure you were ready to be a first-time mother? What newly pregnant woman doesn't have that worry at least once? What else? That you might walk in your parents' shameful footsteps? Well, let's look at the facts... you've been rescuing the oppressed and exploited for years. Look at Konani and Makoa. How many others have you pulled from despair to give a new life?"

She looked down between them. One of her hairpins was loose, sticking up on the right side of her bun. He reached to pull it out. When she looked up at him, he smiled. "You can't argue with the facts." He leaned over to look for another pin. That one followed the first to the floor. She shivered, and he inched closer. "Plus, you should know by now, I never lie."

Her hand came up to rest on his chest over his heart. He closed his eyes, marveling at how such a simple act could provide such succor.

He kissed her, tasted the salt of her tears, and it was like plunging into the deepest, darkest part of the ocean, fighting for breath, but never wanting to come up for air. He descended into her, fingers weaving into her hair, stripping every last pin, bringing her down into the darkness with him.

He groaned into her mouth, the fragrance of her hair intoxicating, the curves and hollows of her flesh like silk against his fingertips. She moaned low, her hands tracing the muscles of his back under his shirt. He leaned back to unzip the front of her dress, his gaze holding hers. "We should try again."

Her hands stilled on his heated skin. "What?"

He blew out a breath, not sure what he was even about to say. "Another baby, Kat. When you're well."

She eased her hands from his shirt, stepping away gingerly like he was a lunatic with a bomb strapped to his chest. "You can't be serious."

He ran his hands through his hair, then dropped them back at his sides. "But I am. I actually am."

She visibly swallowed. "Then you're more insane than I gave you credit for."

When she moved toward her desk, he resisted the urge to reach out and make her look him in the eye. "I have loved you since the day you rained hell on an incubus at the turn of the century in that swanky New Orleans brothel. My going away was not because that love had died. It was because I needed to act." He balled his fists, then stretched the fingers of both hands as far as they would go. "I was determined to find someone from your family. I thought it might ease your grief. I see now I did what *I* would have wanted done for me. And in doing so, I failed to understand your needs."

The air in the room thinned as he waited for a sign that she'd heard him. His senses wove through the atmosphere, trying to detect her heart rate and respiration for clues to what she was feeling, but she'd cloaked all her systems.

In all the years he'd been away, he'd maintained the belief that they would reconcile. She could cut him into tiny little pieces, throw his gory bits to a pack of demons, and he'd still love her. It was a sickness perhaps.

Maybe Hell was individually based instead of a massive, burning lake of fire like everyone believed. And maybe his Hell was knowing what he wanted desperately—Kat and a houseful of their children—but never being able to make any of it come true.

Kat chose that moment to turn around, her eyes brimming. "I have zero faith in my body to carry a child at this point."

In three steps he was by her side, hands on her shoulders. "I refuse to listen to such negativity. If we want a life together, we can make this work."

She lifted his hands from her shoulders and slipped past

him as he stood frozen by an uncharacteristic despair. "We're done here," she said, and he felt the finality of it like an open-air pyre cremating the remains of their love.

But these icy winds wouldn't carry his soul to Valhalla.

Kat yanked open the door, and Jade stood in the hallway, her arm raised to knock.

"What now?"

Jade's arm lowered slowly as her gaze flicked over Kat's shoulder to Ari. "We've got trouble."

CHAPTER 7

Thank God. Something else to focus on besides making babies with Ari.

Katherine wiped her eyes as she pushed past Jade toward the hallway that led from her private staircase to the main lounge. Jade's boots clicked down the hall behind her.

"Makoa was returning from lunch when two possessed females pounced on him outside of the club. He could have handled one with his crucifix, but the second one came at him from behind, saying she had a message from Leviathan."

"Lovely. I'm assuming Makoa's all right since you're not organizing armaments for World War III." When Katherine reached the main room's twenty-foot-long bar, Konani and a couple other bartenders were organizing the liquor displays.

Ari had already streamed there, his charm casting its usual spell on her people. He winked at her when she approached the black marble-topped bar, but the twinkle was gone from his gaze. She stared at him after he turned away. Something was missing in his body language.

"Stark was making a pass on the second-story terrace and

saw it all go down." Jade's gaze settled briefly on Katherine's head of security. "Between him and Makoa, they got both possessions contained in the Devil's Trap in the employee lounge."

Katherine looked back and forth between Jade and Stark. "What was Leviathan's message?"

"She said she looks forward to working with you. What the hell is that supposed to mean?"

It meant that Leviathan knew how well she'd gotten under her skin. Knew they shared a lot of the same pain. Daddy issues, Jade had called it. Katherine's stomach tumbled unpleasantly. "She's crazy, of course. She's finally letting loose the dogs of war—or in this case, the demons of war. Isolated terror attacks orchestrated to begin unraveling our nerves before the real battle begins."

According to Jinx Tanaka, another partner in the Unholy Inc network, it was a classic archdemon tactic she'd seen played out in her Tokyo nightclub more than once. Katherine pulled a stool out and sat down. "Are there any other irregularities at the moment?"

"When I was restocking the poolside bar, a demon was staring down at me from one of the hotel balconies next door," Konani volunteered.

Katherine's heart pounded. "You're certain?"

Konani nodded. "He had black eyes with no color in the irises."

Damn. Another person whose soul had lost the battle. Konani's announcement was bad news. Usually Guardians welcomed both the Possessed and full-fledged demons into their clubs, setting wards to trap them *inside* so the evil could be dealt with—either by exorcism or extermination.

Nightclubs were the perfect venues for luring the Possessed—humans whose souls hadn't lost the fight yet and still retained their eye color. The Possessed who wandered into Aqua, or were brought in by Katherine's small team of informed humans, were usually healed by her before last call.

But since Leviathan's arrival in Waikiki, Kat had reversed half of her usual wards, still allowing the Possessed to enter, but repelling full-fledged demons. So if a black-eyed demon had managed to push through her reverse-ward, it meant one of three things: the demon on the balcony next door was being powered up by a fallen angel; it was a fallen angel in disguise; or, her reverse-wards—and probably her regular wards—were failing.

Fallen angels meant Rephaim, Nephilim, Succubus, or Incubus. All scenarios indicated five-alarm trouble.

And then of course, there was Leviathan, Satan's offspring via a Succubus. An archdemon had powers second only to Satan himself...if he ever managed to escape the cage the Archangel Michael had put him in when time began.

Katherine wiped damp palms on her dress. *Don't panic and don't exaggerate a problem until it's warranted.* She could and would deal with Leviathan's tricks and aggressions. Maybe the demon next door who breached her reverse-ward was an astral projection.

Last month, Raj had tracked a demon in South Africa for two weeks before realizing it was a setup. Apparently some fallen angels used astral projection to trick him, so their true forms could pillage and destroy an entire city while Raj was occupied with the false image in another location.

Katherine was ill, yes, but surely she wasn't so feeble that her wards had failed to such an epic degree. She rubbed her temples, turning to where Ari leaned his hip against the bar. His eyes were calm, but alert and almost clinical. Fully focused on her, but bereft of their usual warmth. She'd never been on the receiving end of that look.

Like she was a stranger, and he was sizing her up.

She didn't like that look one damn bit.

She wasn't some stranger. She'd lived with him. Had battled for and healed souls beside him. He'd been in her mind and in her body—and she in his. Her heart beat on a slow throb as her gaze mapped a course she'd once loved traveling. Chiseled jaw, sinful lips, tight ass, powerful arms, and those *baby-I-got-you* shoulders that did her in every single time.

One side of his lips tilted up lazily as though he could read her mind.

"Stay out of my head, Grimm," she pushed at him.

"Settle down, kitten. You've got your walls up so high I can't hear the exact words unless you harpoon them at me like you just did. But I can sense the tone. And I'd be delighted if you kept that naughty train rolling."

"Put your adolescent hormones away. You're embarrassing yourself," she replied, but heat sang through her body at the outrageous images that she imagined.

Ari rapidly straightened and vaulted over the bar like an Olympic gymnast on steroids. "High five, I'm all-in for woman on top."

Katherine tried to calm her thundering pulse as she stared pointedly at his raised hand, then up into his burning blue eyes, feeling the gazes of her staff locked on her and her wicked Viking.

Ari's heat felt so much better than that Godawful chill that had emanated from him moments ago. "Some people need a high five in the face with a chair."

He laughed in that hedonistic, full-bodied way that made her knees weak. "You really need to start taking some things personally," she snapped.

"If you chose to share more of the explicit thoughts you had just now, I'd be more than happy to take it personally."

The male bartenders snickered, but pivoted to straighten

their expensive top-shelf bottles the second they met Katherine's *you're-on-borrowed-time* glare.

Ari smirked. "Is it sexy in here, or is it just me?"

The laughter in the room rankled. Even crabby Stark hid a chuckle in a cough she heard clear across the dance floor. Jade was the worst offender, though. Tears of mirth rolled down her cheeks by the time she got herself under control.

Katherine rubbed her temples. "I hate all of you. Now, someone had better start telling me about the human witnesses who observed the Possessed whaling on Makoa. Any mind-wiping needed?"

Jade dried her eyes, smudging her smoky black eyeliner. "It happened by the benches next to the trees out front. A few tourists had their cameras out, gigglin' and promising to come back tonight when we open. They thought it was a skit to drum up more business for the club."

Thank heavens. Katherine briefly closed her eyes and rolled her shoulders back. She despised going in search of humans who'd witnessed something they were never supposed to see. Mind-wiping had never been one of her strengths. If you weren't careful in singling out the nightmare episode, you could accidentally erase something important, a memory that could never be replaced.

Stark laid his towel on the bar. "You want me to contact Spencer to see if he can get his tech guys to watch out for any strange Waikiki Beach YouTube videos that show up?" Spencer Jameson was another Unholy Inc partner whose San Francisco club was a Guardian intelligence-gathering hub.

"Yes, that's a good idea. Thank you, Stark." He nodded at Katherine and headed to the office on the main level. When a loud cry ripped through the air, he broke into a run. Katherine and the others followed, but Ari beat them there.

Two possessed females in the employee breakroom had broken free of their bindings and had gone after the possessed woman in chains whom Katherine had left unexorcised earlier when she'd gone home.

Now there were blood and chunks of hair on the floor where all three rolled around, unable to resist the malevolent wills attempting to take over their human souls.

Ari stepped into the circle and pulled the wild brunette off to the side as Stark and Konani sprayed the other two with holy water to immobilize them. The brunette snarled and writhed in Ari's iron grip, but he held her fast against his large body, speaking ancient words of the exorcism rite in her ear. The evil inside the woman made her scream and convulse as though in unspeakable agony.

Katherine shuddered. It was so rare that she was on the outside, watching someone else perform an exorcism. When she was the one absorbing the evil, the one scrubbing a human soul, she didn't think about what was actually happening. She acted on the innate knowledge Healers had been given to complete the steps of the ritual.

She'd watched Ari do this hundreds of times, but his process was so different than hers. Whereas she placed her hands on the Possessed's forehead or chest, he held the person tight to his frame. It was a testament to their differences. He was such a physical man, always relating to the world with his whole body.

It fascinated her. What would it be like to be so literally, physically, in touch with life? She had trouble even letting someone shake her hand, much less give her a hug.

"Boss, a little help with these two!" Konani yelled. "I don't want to damage their skin too much with all this holy water!"

Jade blocked her. "No, Kat, you're still too weak." Jade turned to Konani, yelling over the screaming, but weakening, brunette in Ari's arms. "Hold them off—just a little more holy water—until Ari can fix them up, too."

Katherine shoved Jade's hand off her arm and hurried

across the threshold into the Devil's Trap toward the taller of the two possessed women, whose skin was steaming from the effects of the holy water.

"Kat, no! Please don't do this!"

She ignored Jade's censure, knowing her human staff wouldn't defy her standing orders to never enter a Devil's Trap. Trusting that Stark and Nani would keep the holy water flowing on the third possession to protect her while she did this.

She breathed deep, trying to find her bitch mojo. *Don't fail.* Not in front of her staff.

Definitely not in front of Ari.

She stared into the hazel eyes of the tall blonde and saw the woman's humanity hanging by a thread. The evil spirit was close to overcoming the good inside her. And once it was gone, it would take a tremendous ritual—if not a miracle, if one believed in those—to overcome the full-fledged demon she would become.

Katherine had only moments to save her. Only an instant before the disabling effects of the holy water would fade and the monster inside the woman would attack. Katherine closed her eyes, shut out all the sounds around her and built the light within. Hot, brilliant, it was a calm so perfect it made her doubt her faithlessness. She smiled inwardly at the irony, opened her eyes, and stretched her hand toward the woman's forehead.

"*Exorcizo te, omnis spiritus immunde, in nomine Dei Patris omnipotentis...*"

The sudden rush of hate that barreled into Katherine's mind and body sent her to her knees. Her contact with the woman's forehead was lost, and the evil inside the blonde roared with triumph, following Katherine's to the floor as though in slow motion.

The fluorescent lights of the room blinked out, but only a

moment, confusing her. Then...*a small child's body.* Following her down through the murky water.

Down, down.

Down.

DROWN.

Mary, no! Please somebody help my sister! Help her, she's drowning!

Her own screams, echoing, and she was suddenly so very cold.

Frozen.

She couldn't see anything through the churning, gray ocean. Teeth clacked. Hers and...another's.

Tearing. Searing pain in her chest, stealing her breath, her fingers suddenly wet and slippery with something warm and, as she brought them level with her gaze, scarlet. What was happening? *I've lost control.* The worst sin. Something bad would happen now.

Was happening.

Katherine fought to separate illusion from reality. From somewhere in the gloaming, Ari bellowed her name. Then all went silent. She struggled to open her eyes. Ari lunged for her, his beautiful face twisted in anguish, tendons in his neck standing out furiously, his lips moving, but she couldn't hear the words. Couldn't hear his deep voice that was like coming home. Could only hear her heartbeat.

Ba, bummm. Ba...bummm.

Heartbeat.

Slowing.

Ba...

bumm.

A sudden release of pressure on her midsection. A body flying. Ari lifting her.

Stay with me, Kat, goddammit!

Please, warm me, she tried to say. Wanted to run her finger across his lips like she often had after making love, his ardent gaze melting the iron forged about her heart like a blowtorch to a candle.

Don't leave me.

Ba...

bum—

CHAPTER 8

A ri's gut wrenched, breath stopped as he looked down at the woman in his arms. He couldn't hear his soul mate's heartbeat any more. He stood there, holding her, muscles frozen. His hands, arms, chest—all covered in Katherine's blood. "Kat-*Katherine*," he gasped. "Stay with me." Her body was so cold.

"You can't save her, big man! You big, tempting, violent man!" one of Possessed screeched, then laughed, her unearthly high tones like shattering glass.

He jolted when Jade's hands pounded against his back. "Take her, Ari! Heal her—hurry!"

Hurry. The word mobilized him.

He streamed to Kat's quarters on the second level. He burst into her bedroom, carrying her straight through the sunlit space to her bathroom where he entered the shower fully clothed. He shielded her from the water until it ran warm, then angled his body so the water sluiced down his shoulders to gently cascade over her, washing her blood in red rivers down the drain.

Heal her.

Skin to skin always worked best, but the possessed woman had fused pieces of Kat's dress into her flesh with a fiery brand of her demonic hand. Would thinking his soul mate's clothes away damage her more when her muscles were bonded to the dress?

He boosted her higher in his arms so he could kiss her cheeks, her closed eyes, her nose and eyebrows.

He hadn't protected her. "Fight, Katherine! You can't be finished tormenting me yet." His body shook, his breath fast and hard. What if he couldn't revive her?

Gingerly angling her toward him, he watched her chest begin to knit together. *Thank fuck, yes.* He could heal her with his body. With his touch. It was the natural order of things for Guardian soul mates.

He leaned back against the shower tiles, light-headed.

A small sound, barely audible, made his eyes open. "Katherine," he whispered, letting water—her beautiful element—stream down the sides of his face, thrilling in that simple sensation now that she was on her way back to life.

To him.

She wasn't awake, but he sensed her Guardian consciousness rise, could feel her heartbeat begin to throb against his chest where he cradled her.

His head bent down once more to taste her lips when her eyes opened. With the extent of her injuries and the state of exhaustion she'd been suffering for so long, she wouldn't be completely herself for a while. He held her gaze, his body surging to life when desire darkened her eyes.

Her hand lifted to the back of his neck. "I need."

"I am yours."

Their mouths met, and she came alive. She drove her fingernails into his scalp, her torso twisting, shifting upright. He resituated her, hiking up the remaining strips of her dress, pulling her legs apart to wrap around his hips. As her center met the heavy ridge of his wet denim, her gasp flowed into a moan. The water swirled around them with her rising passion. His fingers tunneled under the elastic of her underwear and curled into her soft buttocks, finding her seam and following its curve until he reached her slick heat. He ached to put his tongue there and taste her as he had in an outdoor shower in Bali before he'd carried her inside their hut, and they made love so fervently they created a life.

Miraculous what love could do.

Memories poured in on him in a rush. Her soft smiles by candlelight. Her flashing eyes and imperious posture as she challenged his every belief. Her hand in his, laughing that full-throated sound as he pulled her along toward new adventures.

His head on her belly, listening to the sounds of their baby.

Relief flooded him as her skin knit together becoming whole again. He turned to ease her against the smooth gray and white tiles. Wet locks of her hair stuck to the wall as his hips rocked her up and down. "Command me, *elskan*," he whispered. "I am yours."

Her sudden release came with a scream that echoed off the marble and filled him with joy, pride, arrogance. Love. He wrapped his arms around her and buried his face against her head, fearful of what she might see first if she peered too closely.

Then she went limp in his arms.

How had she carried on so long when she was so sick? He'd never seen another Guardian this depleted who managed to pull through.

He grabbed two plush towels off the counter as he carried her into the bedroom. He laid her down, thought her clothes away, toweled her off, and then lay down beside her, pulling her close. For two hours she slept, utterly still. Endless minutes while the sun crept across the late afternoon sky, and he had nothing but his thoughts.

It was odd to be so stationary while awake. He usually puzzled things out while in motion. Fighting, running, sailing, exploring. These quiet moments with Katherine lying in his arms were foreign.

Not altogether comfortable.

The setting sun cast peach rays against her upholstered headboard when her fingers curled on his belly. He froze, hardening instantly. He knew what was coming. As much as he thought he was prepared for it, how could a male Guardian ever fully calm himself enough to be merely an instrument for his mate's healing?

Her Guardian spirit was on autopilot—survival mode— sensing her soul mate, seeking his body as the quickest way to restore her power.

Her fingertips slid down the center line of his abdomen, pausing to dip in his belly button before continuing down, following the fine-haired trail down to his erection. Her fingers wrapped firmly around the base, the thumb of her other hand slicking across his damp slit. He groaned low, his heart thudding as she brought that thumb to her mouth, sucking his essence with a shiver of pleasure. His entire body pulsed with a fire to cover her, fill her, heal her.

Dying to touch. Bury myself so deep we are never parted again.

She smiled at him—soft, sweet, coy.

He inhaled and exhaled slowly, painfully, as he angled from his side to lie back down on the bed. Her eyes tracked across his body, darkening when they focused on his erection. He curled his hands into fists, the fingernails biting into his palms doing nothing to ease his need to move. To be in control. To orchestrate her release.

No. Let her lead. Use him as she wished. It was the only

hope he had that she wouldn't hate him when this was all over.

"*Nos et cedaums amori.*" *Let us too yield to love.* His whispered submission in the old language between soul mates unraveled the last of her hesitation.

The sheet fell from her body as she rose to her knees, her breasts beautiful in the twilight glow with their puckered, light pink tips, and the creamy undersides perfectly circular. She bent over him to run the ends of her silky blonde hair over his nipples, down, down, to tangle in his body's precum. She chuckled deep in her throat when his hips jerked. She was going to kill him.

But oh, what a way to go.

She pressed a kiss to his head, then licked the long, hard length of him like she was enjoying the most decadent popsicle.

Thor's blood.

When her warm mouth closed around him, he growled, his hand shooting into her hair for a moment before he came back to himself and let his hand drop beside his thigh. She frowned and shoved his legs apart, settled between them and looked up at him, his cock in her mouth, her eyes daring him to move, damn her.

He sat up, sweat rolling between his pecs, his muscles tense all over. A frown marred the smooth expanse of her forehead like she couldn't understand why he wouldn't touch her, and he was sorry for it.

"Use me, *elskan*." The words rasped from his throat. "Take everything you need."

She blinked and sat back on her ass, lifting her legs to drape them across the tops of his thighs, scooting forward, her sweet lips parting only inches from his cock. His hands slid roughly up her shins, knowing she might vilify him if she remembered he touched without permission.

She raised one leg, settling the back of her heel on his shoulder, one hand going to her pussy, rubbing slow circles that made his breath erratic and his cock pulse with yearning.

"Kat, *yes*, baby..." He grasped her hips, watching her play with herself, her escalating moans like the final seconds of a ticking bomb, ready to tear his body apart. He bent his knees, feet touching behind her ass to give her more space. Her legs shook, her eyes squeezed shut, but her orgasm wouldn't come. He wrapped his arms behind her back, supporting her as she struggled to find release. She opened her eyes, her gaze pleading with him.

Fuck this. She needed him.

He grasped her waist, lifted her, spreading her legs over his hips and sliding her along his length until her moans grew louder than the wet sounds their bodies' slick flesh made. Up, down, hot, slippery, perfect. "Look at me," he demanded. "Tell me what you want." He didn't know how much longer he'd be able to hold out. Felt *so* good.

She pulled her leg down from his shoulder, scooted up to her knees, and his breath stopped. She wrapped her arms tightly around his neck, pressed her lips to his pounding carotid, and lowered her body over his, taking him in, restarting his heart, body, and soul simultaneously. His arms squeezed her closer, closer, his ass contracting, reaching up into her as she lifted away and then returned all that heat and acceptance. The essence of her that he would never get enough of.

She loved him, slow at first, her movements limited because his arms wouldn't relax his hold on her. Little hip rocks, slight shifts, the pleasure built. It flowed out of their mouths—breath, pores, sighs, all of it an expression of their connection.

"*Ari.*" Her hands wedged between them to press against his chest. His arms unlocked around her, sliding down her backside, cupping underneath to feel their intimate joining. His breath shuddered out of his mouth, eyes slitting, hungrily watching her breasts bounce faster as she took her pleasure from him.

Her vocalizations rose and fell, building with each stroke. Ari looked into her eyes. *What can I do to make your walls come down and stay down? What can I do to trust you won't reject me over and over?*

He grasped her hips, grinding her against him every time she descended, until that beautiful contraction within her meant imminent release. Gratitude rippled through him as her cries filled his ears and her breasts crushed against him. She stilled in a moment of perfect implosion, and he absorbed her pleasure greedily.

"Give it to me," she demanded. Buried in her, he felt her energy, her light, her power rise several notches.

Finally okay to let go.

His orgasm wrenched violently through him, spurting into her as she curled around him, wrapping her arms and legs about him, whispering to him in the old language. Thanking him, spurring him on with warnings and promises. Wringing power and healing and energy from him. He thrilled in his loss because it meant she would rise from this bed strong and restored.

He was shaking when it was over.

She was asleep even before he eased her back down onto the mattress and cleaned her with the towel he'd dried her with earlier. He balled the towel and chucked it across the room, then tucked in beside her. As he pulled her into the shelter of his body, she whispered in her sleep, "*alis volat propriis.*"

She flies with her own wings.

Aye, she certainly did.

He closed his eyes, angling his head on the pillow by her

hair, desperate for sleep. He'd need it in the coming hours when she woke and sought his body again.

And again.

Needing him like this would likely seal her hatred of him for all time.

He sighed and reopened his eyes to stare out the windows at the growing darkness, wondering if he'd ever find peace.

CHAPTER 9

Oh, warm. This dream was incredible. Katherine burrowed further into the heat, squeezing her eyes shut more tightly against the brightness, wishing she'd remembered to draw the curtains before going to bed. And, heavens, something smelled divine. She wanted to laze here for hours and hours, shirking all responsibility to humanity.

The heat curled tighter around her left hip like it had a life of its own, turned her gently to her other side, then pulled her a short distance across the silky sheets till she felt a pulsing wall of warmth pressing solidly against her backside.

The heat slid up her bare belly as soft as angels' wings toward her breasts where it explored the tender undersides like they were a boundless mystery. A moan slipped from her lips, and she shifted restlessly on the bed.

A deep breeze, suffused with the most erotic sound she'd ever heard, feathered in her hair at the shell of her ear. She shuddered, undulating her body back against the furnace. Again. And then once more. Against the shaft that hit her in the most perfect spot. The warmth lifted her upper leg in a tender vise and set a carnal rhythm against her bare flesh that soon made her breath rush between her lips, her mind imagining laughing blue eyes and a pair of broad shoulders she would forever yearn for. Her body arched at the exquisite peak of her passion, head thrown back, her chin caught in a firm grip. Pressure, like that from a thumb, tugged across her lips before delving into her mouth.

Liquid fire roared in her veins.

Ari.

Another flutter of wind at her ear, a seizing behind her, then, *I am here, elskan.*

As you are meant to be... Her sated body drifted in a drowsy cloud, listening to the chirp of fairy terns. There was also a heartbeat.

Actually, two.

What?

Birds and heartbeats.

The heartbeats were in unison. She hadn't felt that sensation in—

Her eyelids flew open, the bright daylight making her blink in rapid succession until her full consciousness arose. She was in bed at her Aqua apartment. She glanced down, cringing to see a heavy forearm dusted with golden hairs draped over her arm, a tanned, sculptural hand nestled between her breasts.

Oh *damn*. And here she was, buckass naked, pressing her nether regions into his groin like an animal in heat.

"Blazing hell! No, no, no." She shot up and away from Ari, her knees and feet tangling in the sheets. She yelped, tumbling headlong toward the floor until strong hands grasped her upper thighs and hauled her back onto the rumpled bed linens.

"Did...did we...?" Her voice squeaked, knowing the answer, but asking anyway.

He laid on his side and propped his head on his arm when she kicked his hands away, his smile more beautiful than any Hawaiian sunrise.

"Repeatedly."

The satisfaction in his voice made something give way in her chest.

She felt amazing all over. Like she could run marathons, climb mountains. Maybe even wade into the loathsome ocean.

This was *terrible*.

She didn't *do* happy. The few times she'd tried, it didn't end well.

She rolled out of bed, grabbing a barely-there robe off the hook on the door. The urge to rail at him, to accuse him of forcing her to go to bed with him ran her hard, but it would be a lie. Some of her actions were fuzzy in her mind, but she knew in her weakened state her Guardian instinct had sought restoration in his body.

Had demanded it.

Heat poured through her face and down her neck. Yes, it would be a lie to say he'd had his way with her without her permission. The best thing to do was pretend it didn't mean anything and move on.

Don't look at him or you'll want to crawl right back into that bed and never leave.

"I appreciate your...services,"—he raised an eyebrow at that, but she soldiered on—"but you can go now. I've got a lot to do before the club opens in..." She picked up her phone to check the time and gasped. "How can it be Tuesday? Where did Sunday and Monday go?"

All traces of humor fled his face. "You almost died, Kat."

Memories of starting the exorcism, feeling the evil press into her, and then the rending of her flesh came pouring back. She plunked into the chair by the nightstand. "Well, that sucks."

Ari ran a hand though his hair and swung his powerful legs to floor. Sitting naked at the edge of the bed, all his golden skin was dangerously appealing. Her gaze tracked hungrily across the washboard expanse of his abs, up his rock-hard chest, to his eyes that burned with black and blue fire.

"Come here."

Her joints softened at his low tone. "I can't."

He lifted a hand toward her. She wanted so badly to take it. "Of course you can. Right leg first, then your left."

"Knock it off."

"As your soul mate, nothing brings me more pleasure than restoring your vigor."

Her heart squeezed. *So stupid.* "I despise the fact that this is your duty. Don't you?"

He stood and stalked toward her. "Not at all. I am one hundred percent focused on you because I want to be."

She held up a hand when he got close enough that she could feel his body heat. "Stay back, Ari. Please. I can't deal with our stuff right now. Not with Leviathan breathing down my neck."

"I'll help you handle her. Then we'll sort out 'our stuff.'"

"You make it sound so easy. You always do that. I hate that," she retorted. "It's like you expect to pick up where we left off."

His eyebrows pulled down, and he raked a hand through his hair. "I can't go back and change my actions, but I'm here now. I won't leave you again."

Oh yeah, he would, and it wouldn't even be his fault. His restless soul would make him. But his assurance broke her heart, especially because she knew——at this moment——he believed it.

CHAPTER 10

Ari laced his fingers behind his head and leaned back in the chair, his gaze following the path of Kat's fingers as she eased a black suede boot over her knee and up her delicious thigh. She repeated the process with the other boot, then stood in front of her gilded floor mirror and added an intricate black lace choker that picked up elements of the spindly, black flowers embroidered on her white, V-neck dress.

God, she was beautiful.

"Your style is as alluring as ever. It's a shame Leviathan doesn't expire with envy for your unrivaled fashion sense."

Her gaze found his in the mirror as she put the back on a glittering earring. "Life would be awesome if sweatpants were sexy, but alas...no." She sighed as she turned to face him. "We're lucky she didn't attack while I was out of commission. But now, I wish she'd just get it over with. This waiting for something to happen is worse."

"That's what she wants—nerves eating away at you. That way, when she does attack, you'll already be frazzled and emotionally drained." He eased forward to rest his forearms on his knees. "We could always go on the offense, you know."

She walked to her dressing table, uncapping a stick of dark red lipstick. "It's going to be a long night. Where's my coffee?"

One side of his mouth lifted, but a full-on smile wouldn't come. Not responding to his suggestion to go on the offense meant she wasn't feeling as well as she was letting on, she was scared, or both. "I'm happy to be at your service in bed, but you can get your own damn coffee, princess."

Her eyes narrowed. "Feeling puckish, are we? Poor Viking, being trapped in this room with such a heavy obligation must've cramped your style."

He leaned into her barbs, buttoning down a surge of anger that her emotional walls hadn't budged even a little in the past few days they'd spent wrapped around each other. Of course she'd been in healing mode, but still.

"You're just mad that you needed me. I respect your independence, but even great leaders can't do everything on their own. Don't fault me for doing what any Guardian would've done for their soul mate."

"I'm not saying it was your fault. I'm saying I blame you."

What? He stood up from the chair and grabbed her hand. "Blame me for what? For letting you use me for pleasure and healing? Excuse me if that's beyond the pale."

Her lips pursed for a moment before she sighed and tried to pull her hand from his. "Release me, unless you want to give my resuscitated water element a test run."

"Sarcasm usually masks fear," he said quietly, letting her go. "You're afraid of so many things. Why didn't I see it before?"

"Nooo," she drew the word out like he was some dimwit. "I'm allergic to stupidity so I break out in sarcasm."

"I think you'd actually like it if I spanked your ass, you little magpie."

"Whatever makes you feel better about your savage self." She ran a hand down her flowing sleeve, looked up at him, then quickly back down.

"She came to me in my dreams."

He stopped breathing for a moment. 'She' meaning Leviathan. He was surprised Kat had admitted it. "I figured. What did she say?"

She frowned. "You did?"

"Three times in the hours before dawn you pulled away from me and thrashed around, fighting harder when I tried to soothe you. You didn't settle down until I spoke the words of the binding ceremony." He'd wanted to tell her earlier, but from the current stiff set of her shoulders, she clearly didn't want to hear about it. Well, too bad. "I'm beginning to think neither of us will find peace until we accept our match."

"Does it really matter if we're together or not? We're damned if we do, and damned if we don't. Ours is not meant to be an easy path."

"Vikings never shy from a challenge." They stared at each other while the bass from high-end speakers struck the first chord in the club below. "What did Leviathan tell you in your dream-state?"

Kat picked up a glass perfume bottle, spritzing something exotic and spicy on the insides of her wrists. Then she set the bottle down like it was an explosive device. "Nothing new. She believes we're two of a kind, and that we can help each other."

"She's weaving a web."

"I know that, Ari. As crappy as I feel, my mental faculties are still in working order."

"You weren't as skeptical the last time you saw her. What changed?"

"I don't know. Honestly, I don't feel like myself."

He ran the back of his knuckles down her cheek, frowning. "You still feel sick?"

She held his gaze, her eyes glinting with challenge. "Would it wound your alpha pride if I was?"

"Don't be spiky, Kat. It just concerns me. When we don't feel good, sometimes our judgment gets clouded, and we don't—"

Kat spun away and marched into her bathroom, slamming the door.

"—make the best decisions," he finished with a growl. He swiped his jeans off the floor, as frustrated with himself as he was with her. He'd made her feel incompetent—one of the worst offenses in her book. But the words had rolled off his tongue before he could stop them.

He understood Kat's walls. Anyone who'd endured a childhood like hers needed protective measures. Using her smart mouth to mask insecurities, guilt, and abandonment issues was better than addiction or other self-destructive behaviors.

Still, her pain was carved so deep he wasn't sure how to reach her.

Did she still love him the way she once had? Her behavior the last few days hadn't given him any indication that she did.

He looked at Kat's bathroom door, rubbing his neck, then turned to stare out the second-story windows where the full moon glimmered on the ever-rolling Pacific. The ocean called to him. The feel of the wind in his hair, the salt on his tongue, his ship rolling under his feet, the crack of the sails...

For him, there was peace on the water. A rightness and a belonging.

He'd once had that with Kat.

He hungered for both, yet feared never the twain would meet.

He walked to stand in front of the bathroom door, his hand poised over the handle. He could sense nothing beyond the door. No noise, no heartbeat, no current of her essence. She'd masked it all from him.

His hand lowered to his side, and he quietly left the room.

CHAPTER 11

C lub festivities were in full swing when Ari made his way downstairs and headed for Konani's station. Kat had created one hell of a nightclub. Its seductive turquoise lighting glowed off luxurious white leather seating that ringed a gorgeous, trapezoidal dance floor made of native koa wood. Its grains were so fluid the entire floor seemed alive with movement.

Inlaid in the wood was an exceptionally large Devil's Trap in its usual configuration—a circle with five magical sigils inscribed between the legs of a star. Next to the dance floor, south of the bar, was the large stage where a young woman in a barely-there glittering leotard defied gravity with her aerial dance on a silk rope suspended from the ceiling.

Ari scanned the other side of the dance floor, where the sound tech and DJ booths took up most of the wall next to the wide doorway leading outside to the terrace, pools, and swim-up bar.

Liquor was flowing, and humans were flirting, laughing, and dancing.

Status quo. Ari's shoulders relaxed as he turned back to the bar.

"Hello, handsome, where have you been all my life?"

Ari caught Konani's eye roll before he looked down at a curvy brunette blocking his path. He smiled. "Chasing demons and learning how to meditate in India, Nepal, and Bhutan."

The brunette cocked her head. "Good-looking, well-traveled, *and* intelligent. Maybe you can tell me more about your adventures over a drink?"

"Much obliged, but I have to decline."

"You damn right, he does." Jade inserted herself between him and the brunette, her hands doing all manner of communicating to the shorter woman. "Now, *bye.*"

The brunette's gaze shot to Ari's over Jade's head. He shrugged with a grin. When the young woman melted into the crowd, Ari slung an arm across Jade's shoulders and continued on to the bar.

"You start smilin' at every pretty young thing who bebops into your path, and this whole place is gonna go down in a waterpocalypse if Kat finds out," Jade huffed.

"She'd actually have to like me to be jealous of another woman."

"Stop acting stupid. She never would've let you keep her in bed for three days if she didn't like you. And damn, by the sounds we heard coming from the apartment, the shit you two have been doing, neither of you oughta be walking upright."

Ari eased to the crowded bar in front of Konani, who promptly slid Jade a glass of chardonnay and then uncapped his favorite stout. His mouth watered looking at the label.

"You remembered." He toasted Konani and took a long swallow, while Jade bartered with an arguing couple for their stools. He smacked his lips. "Liquor perfection."

Konani nodded with a smile, pouring blue curaçao into a martini glass for a server. "Dried cherry and fig aroma. Kat always makes sure we're stocked."

Jade wiggled her eyebrows at Ari. "That should tell you something."

It did, but he wasn't sure what. That Katherine expected he'd come, and she wanted to make sure his favorite beer was on hand? Unlikely.

More probably, she'd tested it on her customers, and it had become a crowd favorite.

Christ, stop with all the speculation. He put his elbows on the bar. "So, Nani, did you ever finish your teaching degree?"

"Kat would've skinned me alive if I didn't." She loaded up a server's tray with four colorful daiquiris. "Now, I co-teach math to eighth graders. I love it. And when I'm not here or at school, I keep books for GAN, the charity Makoa and I started for homeless and sexually exploited youth. We named it the Guardian Angel Network because Kat was our *ānela kia'i*—the guardian angel who saved us. She gave us the seed money to open our doors. Don't tell her I told you though. She'd be mad."

Ari leaned back in his stool. Most people loved announcing their good deeds, raising themselves in the esteem of others. Not Kat. She didn't want people to know she had a heart of gold. She'd rather they assumed she was cold and indifferent so they kept their distance.

Less chance to be hurt that way.

Kat felt more comfortable in the shadows rescuing the forgotten, the sick, the broken.

Elskan. My love. Ari reached out telepathically, finding her essence in the hallway that led to the bathrooms, club office, and sanctorum. She startled before quickly blocking him, but her walls had been down for a brief time. *A small victory.* He celebrated by downing the rest of his stout. As much as he wanted to go to her, it was better to let her come to him when she was ready.

He swiveled on his stool, surveying the scene. All ages filled the dance floor, where laughter and leers and too many beers usually spelled demon trouble before the night was through. Club security generally spotted the Possessed and demons right away. If not, and the demons realized it was a Guardian nightclub, one of Kat's complex wards would prevent them from leaving until they were dealt with.

Most nights, the security team was able to publicly subdue the evil because the majority of humans assumed the offenders—who were being carted off for exorcisms or extermination—were juiced up on drugs.

Security also looked for humans who saw beyond the veil and recognized what was actually happening. People who suddenly realized demons walked among them. Katherine dealt with those panicked individuals, usually by mind-wiping.

At the bar Jade was talking to Maddox and Stark about their strategy for the night. As the men dispersed into the crowds to consult with the bouncers, Kat appeared on the second story overlooking the dance floor. Her long fingers curled over the ornate balustrade, her eyes finding his through the colored haze cast by the flashing lights.

"You've built a solid, loyal team," he pushed at her. *"Everything is going to be okay."*

There was silence in the space between them, then, *"We can't know what Leviathan is capable of. All I ask is that you guard my staff to the best of your ability. They are...my family."*

His gaze traced the tense line of her shoulders, the whiteness of her knuckles. How could she ever think she wouldn't be a good mother? All she did was protect and elevate those she loved.

He nodded, watching her shoulders ease slightly. He

would do whatever she asked of him, but no one's safety would come before hers.

Three hours passed unremarkably. Feeling restless, Ari made another round of the club, spotting Kat amusing a bachelorette party table. He walked by, his fingertips skimming her ass.

"Holy fuck, it's Adonis in the flesh! Come here, sexy. I'm ready to put my yoga practice to work!" The girls at the table burst into raunchy laughter.

He smiled and kept walking.

"Good news, ladies." Kat's voice was more animated than it had been all week. "That fine piece of man-flesh will be going up for bachelor auction if he's still in the area next weekend."

You little vixen. He glanced over his shoulder and winked at the women who broke into hoots and applause.

Downstairs near the entrance to the kitchen, Maddox was in a heated conversation with Jade. Ari moved closer, catching snatches of troubling dialogue on the high-pressure currents he pulsed around the room.

"Everything okay?" he asked.

Maddox swung around, his eyes angry, entire body stance ready for battle.

Ari spread his hands wide near his hips. "Hey, take it easy, brother. I'm not the enemy here."

"You are not my family," Maddox gritted out, "and it remains to be seen if we'll be enemies."

Jade patted Maddox's shoulder, looking at Ari. "We're a little edgy tonight."

"Jade—"

She turned back to Maddox. "We can trust him. I promise."

Maddox stared at Jade a long time before he nodded.

She leaned closer to Ari. "Maddox is psychic. Most of his

life it's been a traumatic experience, but Kat and a specialist have been working with him for the past year to control his abilities. A few minutes ago, his senses jumped into high alert."

Interesting. Kat probably planned to mentor Maddox in casting out demons. Human psychics could be powerful exorcists once they'd mastered their gifts. "What are you sensing?"

Maddox rubbed the scruff on his cheeks. Ari drew closer, focusing on the intense young man, trying to latch onto a thread of his thoughts, but he only encountered a disconcerting silence.

Maddox turned to Ari with vehement silver eyes. "Something's coming...and it's *bad*."

CHAPTER 12

Ari scanned the stage, dance floor, and, upper balcony. Nothing seemed amiss, but things could go to hell quickly. The DJ announced a popular new song, and the dancers erupted in cheers and spilled beer.

"Tell Ari what you explained to me," Jade urged Maddox, yelling over the heavy bass of the music.

Maddox's eyes took on a faraway look. "I hear wailing behind the walls. People suffering, pounding, trying to get in. In here, I see flames on people's bodies as they dance. And when they turn my way, blood runs from their eyes. Then I blink, and all the impressions are gone."

"Have you told Katherine?"

Maddox nodded. "The whole security team knows, too."

"We have a cache of demon weaponry stashed at multiple checkpoints around the club. We're ready for anything," Jade said.

Ari wasn't so sure about that, but he wasn't going to undermine her confidence. "Did the chrism oil finally get here?" When Jade confirmed, he relaxed a little.

Wards, Latin incantations used with ash, and salt across

doorways and windows kept demons either in or out, but if Leviathan was the one triggering Maddox's psychic sensitivities, they'd need all the firepower they could muster.

Chrism oil, made from olive oil, scented with balsam, and consecrated by a bishop on Holy Thursday, was more powerful than holy water, which was fine for use on run-of-the-mill demons.

A Molotov cocktail of holy water and communion wine was almost as powerful as chrism oil. When lobbed with an incantation, it incapacitated all demons within a block radius so they could be dealt with.

Ari, Kat, and the rest of the team would need all of that and more.

Even then, it might not be enough to fight Leviathan.

"Stay open to your impressions. They could be our only advance warning. Nice work." He lifted his hand to Maddox, who hesitated a moment before shaking it. "I know your exposure to all that darkness is a sacrifice."

Ari turned away to find Kat when a harsh scent overlaid the club's piped-in essential oil blend. This new odor was pungent and...acrid. Ari frowned, expanding his senses beyond the dance floor and surrounding tables—where he encountered a suspension of carbon particles. *Smoke.*

People began to yell and scream.

"Fire at the DJ booth," he pushed at Kat as he streamed there.

Kat was right behind him. Members of security herded people toward the exits as the emergency sprinklers went off, and Stark used a wooden cross to back a broad-shouldered, black-haired man into the Devil's Trap. A woman shrieked from her position on top of the bar, pointing at the pair.

The sprinklers weren't putting out the fire so Ari gathered a blast of hot air from the flames to form a ring around the resisting, possessed man.

"Ari, be careful! That's Makoa!" Kat yelled and circled around behind the tall Hawaiian. "What happened?"

Stark switched the cross to his left hand, brushed the wet hair out of his eyes, and reached for the vessel of holy water that another security team member brought him. "He didn't look well about twenty minutes ago. I told him to go outside to get some air. He came back in like this."

"Get out of my way." Kat raised a shaky hand toward the sprinkler above her to direct water at the DJ booth to put out the fire. Ari dropped the fire ring around Makoa to contain him. Then he built the pressure in the air to give Kat's water a push and to keep Makoa from leaving the room.

Every time the brawny, young Hawaiian attempted to run away, he bumped into Ari's invisible air force. The demon inside him howled, looking for a way out or a body to hurt.

"Makoa, stop this madness. You are goodness and light. *Fight* this." Kat's voice was faint.

Ari glanced sharply at her. *What the fuck?* Her cheeks were draining of color, her eyes becoming a washed-out blue. *Impossible.* She shouldn't be so exhausted after such a minor encounter. Certainly not after three days in his care.

The sound of sirens grew steadily louder.

"Can you make the emergency responders turn around?" Kat weakly pushed at Ari.

"I thought you didn't like my use of mind control."

"Only when you use it on me."

"I wouldn't ever make you do anything you don't want to." Unless it was for her own good. He was almost ready to call on Alexios to force Kat into an ether sleep until he figured out why she was so compromised.

"Just do it now!" she snapped.

He compressed his lips, sending a massive pulse of 'all's well' to the emergency responders. Then he created a vacuum around what remained of the DJ booth blaze, depriving it of oxygen, and the fire went out instantly. In the next breath, he lifted his hand, creating an air pressure lasso around a snarling Makoa, pulling him closer to the Devil's Trap.

Jade and the security team got the last of the drenched partygoers outside where Ari did a quick group mind wipe, while Kat, Maddox, and Stark moved to defensive positions in case Makoa found a way to escape. When Ari came back inside, Makoa looked unhinged, groaning and holding his head with both hands as he lurched forward, finally pitching into the Devil's Trap.

"Makoa, stay with us. You are strong, *kaikaina. Aloha au ia 'oe.*" Konani's golden skin was pale, the shadows under her eyes pronounced as she moved to the edge of the Trap and pulled out a rosary. Makoa wailed when he saw what was in his sister's hands. Konani shook her head, glancing at Ari. "I don't understand. Out of all of us, my brother should have been the least vulnerable to invasion."

That had been Ari's initial impression as well, but over the centuries, he'd learned that people hid all manner of disturbing secrets behind serene exteriors.

Suddenly the front door of the building caved in and half a dozen Possessed scattered inside like ants fleeing a razed colony.

"Heads up!" Jade yelled, chasing in on their heels with a crucifix in one hand and a St. Michael medallion in the other. "A posse of demons were waiting for hosts out there, and guess what, those bastards found 'em after you finished the mind wipes, Ari."

Ari grabbed one by the back of the neck as another pair of newcomers tore into each other, nails rending skin, teeth biting, falling half-in and half-out of the Devil's Trap. One of them pulled a small knife and gouged a painted chunk out of the wood floor, destroying the protective circle of the Devil's Trap.

Ah, shit, no—

Ari didn't make it in time before Makoa trampled over the fallen bodies and escaped the Devil's Trap. Ari shoved the man he was holding into a chair in the Trap, then used air pressure to push the fallen Possessed the rest of the way inside the circle. After he resituated the wood chunk in the painted circle, he reinstated its binding power with an incantation.

By the time he turned around, Makoa had found the one place that didn't have counter pressure holding him inside the building—the dead air zone by the DJ booth where Ari had suffocated the blaze.

Makoa spun around beside the cabana, closest to the swim-up bar, his possessed senses immediately alerted to the Guardian at his back. His whole body twitched with the strength of the war being waged inside. "You're *nooo* good for her."

Ari knew it didn't pay to engage in verbal skirmishes with demons, especially when they were in that near-feral state, trying to stake their claim on a host.

He also wasn't a hold-back kinda guy. "You presume to know what's good for Kat?"

Makoa walked stiff-legged toward the edge of the pool, his body jerking every couple steps like he didn't want to move, but didn't have a choice. The demon was probably whispering to him that if he didn't give over, he'd drown his body, then find another host. "Sheeee doesn't like to be c-c-called Kat."

Once upon a time she did. Could she have changed so much?

Stop. This is exactly what demons did. Mess with your mind until you didn't know which end was up, and you fucked yourself without any extra help from the demon.

Ari sent his senses inside the club to gauge other threats as well as the progress the team was making to manage the

Possessed. Kat's group was getting the last of them into the Trap, but there was something dark gathering around the building. *"You feel that?"* he asked her. *"Outside in the front."*

"I do. Stay with Makoa. Don't let anything happen to him."

I might, he thought, but didn't let Kat hear it. The young Hawaiian would have to prove his worthiness. Ari looked up, gathering the wispy nighttime clouds high above them, swirling them violently as a distraction for Makoa's demon. It would be best if the young man could overwhelm the demon himself so they didn't have to exorcise him. It'd give him confidence in his abilities to aid and protect Kat. "It's time for you to go back to Hell, demon. My soul mate won't be happy if I let you take over her pet employee, so you can either leave peacefully, or I'll make you howl on your way out."

Makoa's eyes flashed dead black to green, and then back to black again, over and over. "Let...me go," he gasped, toppling into the deep end of the pool. His body undulated underwater, his massive legs kicking him toward the bottom, his mouth opening like he was screaming.

Ari streamed to the edge of the pool, a cold sensation flooding through him. He squatted down to peer into the blue-lit water, not entirely sure if it was the man or the demon who was attempting to drown the body. Something about the way he fought. When humans were gaining the upper hand in a physical possession, it was a jerky business—like learning how to drive a stick shift. But when demons were winning, the movements were smoother.

Everyone said Makoa was the purest soul on staff, but then how come he was the one invaded? Was his '*let me go*' plea meant for him—as in, don't bother saving me?—or was it a final entreaty to the demon trying to wrest his soul from him?

Ari pushed air bubbles down around Makoa, shoving

oxygen into his lungs, maintaining a steady stream of air in and out his nose and mouth to prevent him from drowning. If he couldn't defeat the demon, Ari wouldn't let him anywhere near Kat.

Ari was about to enter the water to start the exorcism when Makoa surfaced, sputtering. His eyes were now green, his body still shaking, but not in that jerky, I'm-waging-a-battle-for-my-soul kind of way.

Ari hadn't seen the demon's mist form leave Makoa's body in search of its next victim, but it easily could have in that bubble bath he'd created trying to keep the big man alive underwater. Plus, the pool was huge. The demon's shade could've shot away underwater and exited behind the swim-up bar.

"You good now?" Ari grabbed him by the back of his shirt and hoisted him out of the water, not because he was feeling particularly friendly, but because he wanted to touch the man to see if he could register any evil still circulating in his body.

Strangely, he didn't feel much of anything—human or demon.

He frowned, pulling Makoa along, the large man as weak as a child, protesting and stumbling as he tried to keep up with Ari's long strides. Ari passed the Devil's Trap and the charred, sodden embers of the DJ booth, rejoining Kat and the others at the bar.

Everyone was wet and cranky. Stark was...

Sanctifying a vat of water in a terra-cotta pot.

"Well, holy shit. Look at that." Ari's lips curled up in spite of the situation. He deposited Makoa on one of the low-backed leather couches nearest the bar, then turned to Kat. "You finally got a priest on staff. About time one of you Unholy Inc partners got smart about that. Why haven't you used him in the exorcism rites?"

Stark looked up with a glare as his lips spoke life-affirmations at the water. Kat's gaze stayed on Makoa. "Stark finished his seminary program only a few months ago. He needs experience and time to mature before I ask him to do such a hellish rite."

Stark closed his Bible and tucked it under the bar. "I can do it. I survived the hell of heroin withdrawal. I can damn well square off with a demon."

Ari nodded. "Good. Go get your vestments, or whatever you need for the ritual. You can start tangling with your first one shortly."

Kat swung around. "*No.*"

Ari raised an eyebrow at Kat, but pointed at Stark. "You're babying him, and I'm sure he doesn't appreciate it. The man spent *years* of his life to become a priest, so let him do the work he's called to do."

"I'm not babying him, I'm protecting him. Jesus, Ari, you know how vicious exorcisms are," she shot back.

"Which is exactly why you need the help. You're sick, woman. You should've been able to deal with that stage fire with one hand tied behind your back, but using your water element sucked nearly everything you had. I doubt you can even do an exorcism right now."

"Nice to know you have such faith in me." She stalked up to him, her lips in a tight line. "Well, just watch me."

She marched away, obviously intending to go to the possessions in the Devil's Trap, but Ari grabbed her hand. "Stop your ridiculous tantrums," he whispered harshly. "Don't mistake love and concern for faithlessness. Everything I'm doing here is in support of you."

They stared at one another for a long while—or rather, he stared and she glared.

Ari kept the air pressure in the room high so he'd be able to detect the slightest movements of anyone coming or going.

There was something not quite right about Makoa even though Ari couldn't detect evil in him anymore.

The young man remained slumped on the sofa, his wet clothes plastered to his body, his face relaxed, his eyes glassy, but their normal color.

Konani wiped her eyes as she fumbled with the stopper on a holy water flask, then went to sit down next to her brother. "Is he okay?"

"I'm not sure," Kat replied slowly, turning to look at Ari. "What happened outside in the pool?"

"He almost drowned." He pushed the thought at Kat so Konani wouldn't be upset, quickly following up aloud with, "He fought the demon well, but I'm not sure where it went, or if it went at all." He could tell by the tightening of Kat's lips that she wondered the same. He looked at each member of the Aqua team in turn. "Has he been depressed or mentioned any personal issues lately?" He paused. Then when no one said anything, "How about suicidal comments?"

Konani's indrawn breath broke the silence. "Why do you ask such a thing?"

Ari grabbed a bottle of holy water from the stash behind the bar, uncorked it, and splashed a stream onto Makoa before anyone could blink. The young man's body bowed on a great bellow. Skin steaming, he panted and snarled, gnashing his teeth at Konani who jumped way from him. "His demon is still here? Why couldn't your Guardian senses tell?"

"Maybe it's a fallen angel," Jade said. "Get him in the Trap!"

Kat paced while the others steered Makoa into the Devil's Trap with sprays of holy water and blessed objects. "Not so much water, Jade, you'll hurt him. His skin's already starting to smoke," she snapped.

"Well, excuse me, but he's gotta have some low-down

dirty secrets if the demon was able to take him over so easily," Jade said.

Kat stopped pacing to plant her hands on her hips. "I'm getting really sick of your judgmental ways, Jade."

"We don't need your high and mighty ways either, but you don't see me bitchin', do you?"

"From where I stand it sure looks a whole lot like bitching, but far be it from me to know everything like you do. For future reference, though, what do *you* call it?"

"I call it motivational speaking, baby. Now let's all just simmer down." Jade's pointer finger jabbed at the air, punctuating her syllables.

Bad move, lady, Ari thought. Kat hated people pointing in her face.

A muscle jumped in Kat's cheek. "Screw you, Jade."

Ari stepped between the women. "Hey, let's focus—"

"Kat, dammit! I hate this. Can we just start over?" Jade tried to push Ari out of her way, but when she couldn't, she resorted to jumping up and down to see Kat's reaction.

Ari suddenly felt a wave of lightheadedness. A quick glance at Kat's pale face made him realize the sensation came from his connection to her. Using his element, he brought more oxygen-rich molecules into his respiratory system, doing the same for Kat as he grabbed her and hoisted her in a cradle hold.

"What are you d-d-doing?" Her teeth chattered like she'd been dumped naked in a snow bank. He streamed to her bedroom, setting her down on the edge of the mattress and wrapping her in a blanket rumpled by their loving. "Fighting with Jade isn't going to make you feel better."

"They sh-shouldn't have been able to g-get in. None of them. I s-set reverse-wards." Kat's teeth clacked together and her lips were turning blue. She blamed herself. She always did. He started taking her hair down from its severe bun so it could lay warm against her neck.

"D-don't do that," she scolded.

"Stop talking, you're going to bite off your own tongue with your shivering. This is not your fault." He condensed the water vapor around her, releasing heat against her skin.

She sighed in pleasure. He seized the opportunity to place his hands on her thighs.

"You make me look bad in front of my staff when you manhandle me. Don't ever do that again. But...thank you for stopping...*you know*."

He *did* know—stopping World War Z between her and her best friend. His hands tightened on her thighs before she brushed them off. She was weakening, and it was more than physically. She seemed a shadow of her old self, much like she had when he'd first arrived. She still had those abrasive edges that made her seen invincible, and she worked to keep people at a distance. But the closer he probed, she seemed...

Fragmented.

He wasn't the worrying type, but this was deeply troubling. She should be getting stronger, better, happier the longer they were together.

Before he could figure out what to say, they both heard a scream followed by shattered glass.

Ari was about to demolecularize, when she grabbed his shoulder. "Take me along. I'm too tired to stream."

"If you're too tired to stream, you're in no shape to fight."

"Then you'll have to pick up the slack. Besides, that breaking glass sounded like my nude silhouette behind the bar. I have serious ass to chew if that's the case."

Instead of arguing, he latched onto her essence, streaming them both downstairs where the silhouette had indeed been broken and three new humans ran around the room with various weapons raised in outstretched hands like they were part of a low-budget horror flick. It was almost comical until he saw their black eyes. They had become full-fledged demon, and the only way they would stop hurting others was a miracle...or death by Guardian.

A dozen more black-eyed demons followed in their wake. "Where are they coming from?" Konani yelled, stepping over a chunk of glass.

"My wards have utterly failed. I'm either dying, or this is the beginning of the End Times."

Kat's telepathic words reverberated in Ari's mind. *Maybe she's right.* Kat's wards were second in potency only to Alexios's. *"You are not dying. You still have eons to torment me."*

Where to attack first? He materialized his ax and hacked his way to Kat, killing two demons on his way to the temporary Devil's Trap Jade had scribbled in black marker in the second-row seating area, next to one of the stripper poles.

"Jade, how many do you have?" Ari asked.

"At least five, and they're getting bloody. Bastards!" Jade looked over Ari's shoulder. "Kat, look out!"

Ari spun wide to shield his soul mate from whatever Jade had seen. Struck from behind, pain slashed from his right shoulder diagonally to his left hip. He staggered, looking up to find Siolazar standing behind him, the notorious Rephaim's red eyes and leathery gray face smiling with satisfaction.

No wonder Kat's wards had been breached.

Ari threw a gust of pressure to disorient the Rephaim, then rolled away in a new rush of wind that unbolted tables and sent chairs and champagne ice buckets flying. From the corner of his eye he saw Kat rushing toward him. "Stay back!"

Siolazar used his long, skeletal fingers to tear into Ari's windpipe, then he slammed him in a choke hold up against the wall. Ari's neck tissues shredded for several seconds before they began repairing themselves. Too slow. *Something's wrong.* His vision started going dark.

"Use your element, Ari! Oxygen!" Kat yelled in his mind.

Oxygen. *Yes.* He marshalled the air. In a rush of energy, the darkness faded, his muscles responded, and he pulled at the hands of the demon trying to strangle him. A jet stream of Kat's holy water singed the back of Siolazar's bald, gray skull, making the walls shake with his bellow and his skin begin to slough off his body.

Still the demon's fingers were crushing Ari's neck as fast as it was repairing itself.

"Now would be a good time for that nasty Viking sword of yours!" There was panic in her voice.

Ari blinked the holy water out of his eyes and materialized his ancient *Ulfberht.* At these close quarters, he couldn't deliver a killing blow, but he swung the sword as hard as he could at Siolazar's body. The demon roared again, dropping to his knees. Kat's holy water stream was keeping the Rephaim rooted to the spot, his skin melting down his body like a thick, sludgy oil spill, but it wouldn't hold him for long.

"We're going to need something stronger than holy water for this bastard," Ari said.

"Finish this, Ari. I need to protect the Chains."

The Chains of St. Peter.

Of course, the fallen angel wanted Kat's relic. If Siolazar managed to steal it, he'd take it to his brother, Lucifer. Everyone assumed Lucifer's cage would only break open with the power of multiple relics. But what if it only took *one* holy relic—one key—to free Lucifer? If that was the case, no one could know which relic was the key that would unlock the cage.

Either way, the loss of any relic threatened Armageddon.

Siolazar hissed amid the steaming slide of his gray skin. Ari shouted orders for Kat's staff to guard her as he swung his sword in wide arcs. The Rephaim were taller, faster, and stronger than most Guardians, but they could usually be outsmarted. Ari stabbed and swung, breathing heavily, lulling Siolazar into believing he was weakening and getting backed into a corner.

Five more feet and the demon would be in perfect position under a Devil's Trap inscribed on the ceiling.

A new scream splinted the air, pulling Ari's attention to the main entrance. Through the filtered dust and debris in the besieged club, a horde of black-eyed demons poured into the building to flank their leader Siolazar. Ari risked a glance up and swore. The Devil's Trap wasn't large enough to encompass all of them, and worse yet, while he was distracted, Siolazar ripped a stripper pole from its base and smashed it against the ceiling to break the circle. The Rephaim opened his arms as though offering a macabre embrace. "How does it feel to be the loser, Viking?"

"Vikings don't lose, you warmongering son of a bitch." Ari tried to dematerialize and stream to a better location, but Siolazar compressed the air molecules to such a degree that Ari's form wouldn't fit through. *Fuck*. The Rephaim held his raw belly and threw his head back to laugh, the sound like a wire brush scraping across a chalkboard.

Ari glanced at the bar where Kat's security team was holding their own, but their supplies were dwindling. *"Kat, you'd better be in the sanctorum by now."*

He threw his sword upward at the light fixture over the demons, bringing the light down on top of three of them in a cloud of dust and glass. He dropped and rolled under the nearest table, then stood explosively to launch the table at Siolazar and the demons who were still standing, barreling them off their feet and smashing them against the nearest wall.

Ari took advantage of the precious seconds he'd bought to charge down the hall toward the sanctorum. The door was wide open. Inside, Kat stood by the reliquary door, which led to the inner chamber where she kept the relic. She'd formed a protection arc around the doorway with chrism oil, so demons shouldn't be able to break through it. But it was clearly draining her.

Anger and confusion rushed through his blood again. Why hadn't her rejuvenation lasted? And why the hell hadn't he forced her to complete the bonding ritual when they waited for their child to be born? A mistake he'd always regret.

Standing in the sanctorum doorway facing the hall, he materialized his sword once more, ready to fight off whatever came their way. "When this is all over, you're in my bed for a month," he barked over his shoulder.

She ignored him, her lips chanting ancient wards. He could feel her desperation—like the breathless listening at a fallen comrade's chest—as he lunged into the hall and raised his sword against the first demon sprinting his way. The host body crumpled, the demon's black mist evacuating through the human male's nose, mouth, and ears, shooting back down the hall in search of a new host before time ran out and it was sucked back to Hell.

Their damn black eyes. They were so unnatural with no white, no emotion.

No soul.

As the centuries wore on, it seemed more and more humans were losing the battle for their souls. Which meant more exorcisms were necessary, yet the powers that be didn't seem to be creating enough Healer Guardians to pick up the slack.

Another black-eyed demon stalked down the hall in front of a renewed Siolazar, who now wore a blood-red bodysuit over his gray skin. Ari manifested a protective shield around himself and Kat, then built the air pressure to skull-crushing levels in the hallway. The demon crumpled with a hideous peal, but Siolazar continued forward, unaffected. The Rephaim leader raised his right hand and the walls of the hallway began to liquefy, the gold paint running like shiny tears down the gypsum plaster of the sagging and warping drywall.

As the heat continued to spike, a roaring from below shook the now-naked wall studs. Ari dropped his sword and summoned his ax as he lunged toward the fallen angel. He attempted to cross out of the safe circle, but found himself bound inside. He hissed in frustration and spun on Kat. He could override her power binding, but it would hurt her. *"You don't need to protect me,"* he said. *"You're only draining what little reserves you have left. Release me before he awakens an entire legion."*

"He's feeding dark energy into the walls to scramble our thoughts. I can feel the darkness calling me. Almost like it's inside me. Eventually we won't be able to communicate."

Ari's gut bottomed out. "What the fuck do you mean 'like it's inside' you?"

Kat shook her head as though chastising him for speaking out loud. *"No time for discussion. You can't fight him alone, Ari,"* she responded in her thoughts.

"Kat!"

He would have grabbed her to make her answer. To make her reassure him that she was exaggerating. But she blasted him back with a surge of energy she shouldn't be expending, goddammit. Then she turned on the emergency sprinklers, spraying holy water throughout the hallway to counteract the melting of the walls.

Siolazar's demon companion sizzled, rolling and screaming on the floor until the Rephaim shut off the sprinklers with a snap of his fingers, oblivious to his own peeling—and, this time, rapidly regenerating—skin.

Ari kept his eyes on the fallen angel, shifting back and

forth, looking for the demon's weakness. Kat was right about one thing. It was growing more difficult to push his thoughts at her. He took a deep breath to bank his anxiety. *"Whatever you think is going on inside you, you can fight this. I'll help you, Kat."*

"Stop thinking about me, Viking. You have a job to do. If he kills you, I'll be so pissed. I might even drag you back to life to destroy you myself."

"How sweet...a lover's spat." Siolazar's serpentine blood vessels and wiry muscles pulsed and rolled under his red bodysuit. Ari's mind spun. He needed to get out of this safe circle before Siolazar got any closer to Kat or the relic.

No time to reason with her. He widened his stance, gripping his ax tighter. "Kat promised to warm my bed for the next month if I get her out of here alive. And I fully intend to collect on that promise."

"You're talking about sex when this son of a bitch is ruining my club?"

Bingo. Ari broke from the circle when Kat's telepathic censure weakened her hold on him.

Siolazar launched, fangs bared, eyes afire. Ari raised his ax, lunging toward the Rephaim, but before they engaged, Siolazar froze mid-air, unblinking red eyes fading to a sick yellow, his gray leathery face shriveling. He crumpled to the hardwood floor, twitching, his features twisting in agony while his mouth belched great clouds of steel-colored smoke.

What the fuck? Ari's gut clenched, his gaze moving beyond the Rephaim down what remained of the gutted hallway. Both bathrooms and the kitchen were now fully visible without their walls.

Leviathan walked calmly into view, a pale, clenched fist at the end of her outstretched arm. Her face and lips were as sallow as her fist, except for a pinkish-orange coloring around her striking blue eyes. A silk, sand-colored blouse floated on her tall, willowy frame, a wide pearl choker nestled below her chin, and a sleek, chestnut braid coiled from the right side of her forehead, under her chin, to her left ear, tucking into a shiny bun that defied gravity.

Ari couldn't understand his sudden fascination. He slowly stood and took a step toward her.

"Ari, stop!" Kat snarled.

Ari shook his head to clear the buzz that had started at the base of his skull.

Leviathan's ashen lips curved seductively, her eyes warming. "Like what you see, Viking?"

"Hell, *no*."

Leviathan's lips turned down, and she twisted her wrist, making Siolazar scream. Jade and Stark emerged at the mouth of the hall, stopping abruptly when they saw the archdemon. Jade wrenched her crucifix out of her pocket, while Stark uncapped a flask of chrism oil.

Kat gasped. "No. Go back and protect the others! I mean it, go now!"

Ari gave Jade, Stark, and the rest of Aqua's core team a mental push toward the storage room off the kitchen. Any remaining staff who'd managed to stay alive, he compelled home.

This was a terrible spot to make a stand against a Rephaim, much less an archdemon. He needed a more open area to manipulate air pressure to their advantage. Fortunately, the DJ booth was open on both sides to the pool terrace. Ari built a gust from outside, forcing fresh, oxygenated air inside.

"We need to build a storm."

Kat coughed, then nodded. With Kat's water and his air elements, they could create a greater calamity than he could make on his own. As Leviathan began speaking in the old Enochian language, Siolazar quaked, his movements pulling down more Sheetrock and tearing down two-by-four framing posts. Sweat rolled between Ari's pecs. He'd been in confrontation with an archdemon only twice in his eleven hundred years, but both times he'd had Alexios at his side.

He sent out a call to their Guardian leader, then raised his ax and zeroed in on his target. "Leave now or in pieces, Dark One."

CHAPTER 13

Katherine moved away from the reliquary door toward the demolished hall to watch Leviathan with morbid interest. What could she do to help Ari? She could feel him stoking his considerable power. It was both arousing and terrifying. But looking at the archdemon, she also felt frozen by a strange sort of detached horror mixed with admiration and...affinity?

"I'm sick."

"Aye, very sick, elskan."

Kat closed her eyes and forced Ari from her mind. She felt the drain of their disconnection almost immediately.

"Don't waste your resources so foolishly," Ari chided, angling his body between her and Leviathan.

She didn't have the strength to respond.

Leviathan tilted her head back and laughed euphorically, then opened her fist. Siolazar stopped smoking from his mouth and staggered to his feet. He demolecularized instantly into a stream of twinkling red vapor. The vapor twirled into a mini cyclone, ripping down a crystal chandelier as it shot toward the reception area, then blew out the main entrance door. The melted plaster and Sheetrock from the walls bubbled one last time, then hardened to a milky white on the floor.

Leviathan's friendly smile sent chills up and down Katherine's arms even as it made her want to sit down in a warm room and divulge all her secrets. "Temper tantrums, violence, and insanity... Siolazar has never managed his emotions well," the archdemon said softly. "Hence he's Rephaim instead of Nephilim."

Katherine felt Ari trying to communicate with her, but if she let him influence her, how would she ever know Leviathan's true intentions? She'd been on the wrong side of people's judgments far too often herself. She'd be damned before she'd be like them.

If she could look beyond the Devil's daughter's shell, beyond the evil story, maybe others would give her the same benefit of the doubt.

Kat's legs wobbled. She reached out to support herself against what was left of the wall, her stomach churning. *I'm not myself.*

Leviathan's blue eyes seemed to see into her soul.

Ari's knuckles whitened as he gripped his ax, stepping closer to the archdemon. How stupid to think she could keep him contained. Kat had known he wouldn't force down her puny binding because it would hurt her, but she hadn't counted on him baiting her, distracting her so he could slip out of her bindings without harming her.

How could she protect him?

This was all her fault. She couldn't stand it—would just want to *die*—if something happened to him because of her. She moved forward and grabbed his arm, feeling his warmth, his need to charge in full-on Viking mode, but recognizing he needed more mojo.

Mojo he should have been able to count on her for.

He shook off her grasp and made his body bigger as though to shield her. More aggression, but that wasn't the answer. Was it? She was so tired of fighting. Fighting to keep people the right distance from her brokenness. Fighting the evil around her.

And the darkness within.

It was growing, that darkness—whatever it was. She could feel it spread through her cells, a slow-moving but relentless taint, sapping her Guardian life force.

Her legs quivered, then gave out. Ari was there before she hit the floor, his back and legs pressing her into one of the few remaining walls so she didn't slump to the ground.

"Let me heal you, Katherine," Leviathan called fervently. "You can't carry on this way." Her smooth voice wrapped around Katherine's limbs like the Bible's serpent.

"The day you touch her is the day this world ends."

Kat blinked at Ari's back as his words rumbled out. How could he sound so calm? Leviathan would kill them all, take the relic, and disappear into Hell where she'd horde the Chains until they secured enough relics to free Satan and start Armageddon. *And I can't even hold myself up.*

Leviathan clucked her tongue. "Such bravado, Mr. Grimmson, but so far, I've seen nothing to back it up." She moved into Katherine's line of sight. "Beautiful Guardian, regardless of what my brothers and sisters have come for, I'm not here to fight you or destroy this beautiful island. I wish to get to know you and help you. Most of all, I want to know what it feels like to have a friend."

Ari laughed, though his body remained rigid. "That's the biggest crock of bullshit I've ever heard. Nice try, demon, but *you're* what's making her sick."

"Katherine, surely you can do better than this overgrown cave dweller who kept women as slaves. As a protégé of Susan B. Anthony and Elizabeth Cady Stanton, that's got to rankle."

Katherine closed her eyes, imagining what Elizabeth would have thought if she knew her apprentice was in league with a Viking. Sure, she'd been a women's rights suffragist in those days, but hers had been self-interested activism. When she'd run away at fifteen, she received boarding from a friend of Elizabeth Cady Stanton. She'd been spoon-fed women's right ideology by the very leaders who'd made history.

She'd only wanted a place to feel safe. So she listened to their speeches and attended their meetings. But she never felt their passion. Their unrelenting drive for equality.

Life wasn't fair and never would be.

Agitation pumped blood back into her limbs, and she squirmed against Ari.

He shifted, letting her stand on her own, though he didn't turn away from Leviathan. "Thralls were paid workers. They could even buy their freedom from their masters."

Leviathan rolled her eyes. "Thralls, huh? Polite vocabulary never ennobles slavery. The fact is, you Vikings were brutal plunderers—of women, land, and culture. Quite frankly—"

"Quite frankly, you can turn the TV off and go back to school. We were farmers and explorers. When we raided, most men didn't take the time to rape anyone."

Leviathan laughed. "So inconvenience was the deterrent to rape, not morals?"

"You're twisting my words, demon. Vikings love and respect women. Rape was severely punished." Ari glanced back at Kat. "Viking women could freely divorce their husbands. A society that gives women that kind of power isn't barbaric."

"Yet you captured innocents in violent circumstances and brought them back to serve you as spoils of war. In any age, that's called human trafficking, Ari," Katherine said quietly, feeling the loss of her vigor once more.

Ari's cold stare made her stomach feel warm and twisty.

"I'd never condone that anymore. Come on, Kat, you know it was a different world back then."

"Indeed. How about...diabolical?" Leviathan supplied, and Kat knew her mentor Elizabeth would've agreed.

Ari threw down his ax and summoned his sword. "This is rubbish. I'm sick of your meddling. Go find some other planet to terrorize, you treacherous bitch."

Leviathan's face revealed none of her feelings. "Real classy, Mr. Grimmson." She turned to Kat. "I'm deeply sorry that my presence has brought out the wickedness in him, but perhaps it's for the best. He will only cause you pain."

"Kat, don't listen to her." He placed a hand gently on her shoulders. "Look at me. *Look*." He crouched down slightly so she was forced to stare at him or look childish with her continued refusal. "You know this is exactly how demons operate. The more vulnerable someone is, the friendlier they come on. They suck you in, steal your soul, then leave you an empty shell. Don't let her do this to you."

Leviathan sighed loudly. "There he goes again, lumping all demons into the same tired stereotype. Are all humans the same? Are they all good, all bad? No. Are all Guardians the same level of fucked up? No. Neither are demons. Use your logic, Katherine, then let me know when you want to talk. Remember, I'm not here to make trouble, as I've demonstrated by my timely dispatching of the Rephaim."

Katherine's skin prickled as a loud whoosh of air flushed through the space. Compressed molecules quivered like Jell-O shots spilled on the bar, and she thought her body would implode. Ari lunged at Leviathan, throwing his sword, severing her braid as she spun away. She raised her hand to freeze him mid-leap and encased him in solid ice. Ari's frozen prison was so thick it nearly blocked the entire width of the demolished hallway and made the black of his T-shirt appear a murky gray.

Leviathan flung the entire ice block out of the hallway onto the dance floor.

Katherine's fingers wrapped around an exposed wall stud, trying to breathe. She could feel Ari yelling in the ice, trying to communicate. But looking at Leviathan, Katherine couldn't remember how to reopen their pathway.

"I didn't want to do that." Leviathan sighed again and brought her tired gaze to Katherine. "You won't have to worry about anything. I'll keep a tight rein on Siolazar and his horde. I'll also help you get this place fixed up in time for tomorrow's busy crowd. Let me help, okay?"

Trading one problem for a more deadly one? "Let him go."

Leviathan stared at Katherine like she was actually considering it. "Would that make you happy?"

Katherine nodded, her pulse a heavy knock in her carotid. The archdemon seemed so calm. Too calm? It was surreal having a conversation with one she expected to loathe on sight. Was Satan's daughter for real? Could she truly only want someone to understand her...

To *like* her?

Katherine had experienced the trauma of losing her family because of her own horrible decision, so how could she not give Leviathan a chance?

She understood the desolation of isolation. The need to feel like you belonged somewhere, anywhere. But everywhere you looked, people whispered and shunned.

It crushed the soul.

Especially when she felt so physically weak lately.

Leviathan fingered the severed ends of her hair, then looked down at her hands like they were a stranger's. Finally, she brought her gaze back to Katherine's. "I want to please you, Guardian, but I believe the Viking will be as cranky as a vampire without blackout curtains if he's rescued by a woman. For that reason, we may want to let him figure it out himself. However, I will defer to your judgment."

A trap? There was no way Leviathan would do as she asked...would she? And if she did, would that somehow come back to bite her?

"Ari?" Katherine tried their intimate pathway, but heard only static. She pressed her palms to her temples as the buzz grew louder. Leviathan took one step closer, a look of concern settling on her fine features. "Are you okay?"

God, no. Katherine dropped her hands to her sides and wriggled her fingers to try to get the feeling to return to them. "Fine. I'm completely fine."

Leviathan held her gaze for a moment longer. Katherine brushed sweat from her temples as she shivered. "If you really want to help, convince your siblings to stop attacking Guardian night clubs and stop this awful search for a way to free Satan. As long as you don't try to take the relic, I can repel the Rephaim on my own."

Leviathan's shoulders sank. "Sadly, I don't think so, Katherine."

"Don't think what? That I can repel the Rephaim—"

"Well, that too, but even *I* cannot stop the other archdemons. The beauty of our creation is that we are implicitly self-directed. No one can influence us. Not our succubus mothers. Not even Lucifer, our father."

A low sound like the chanting of a dozen bass voices seemed to come from far away. Katherine shook her head to clear it. "I don't believe that."

"Your disbelief in our self-determination doesn't make it untrue."

"You don't want to stop the other archdemons."

"If it would make others believe in my goodness, I would stop my siblings any way I could."

Leviathan had never looked so earnest, or so young.

"I don't understand what you want then."

Leviathan's alabaster skin glowed with an otherworldly beauty. How could someone supposedly so evil be so lovely? "Exactly what I told you moments ago. Understanding, friendship, the chance to be seen as something other than the spawn of Satan."

"But that's exactly what you are. You're a fallen angel's daughter." The low chanting in Katherine's mind expanded, and the remaining chandeliers Siolazar hadn't brought down began to rattle.

Leviathan glanced around with wide eyes as though only now hearing the chants for the first time. She raised a hand toward Ari's ice prison.

Katherine jerked away from the wall stud. "Stop! If you do anything else to hurt him, I'll destroy the relic!" It was out before she could stop the words. Destroying the Chains would mean her own immediate dispatch to Hell, but she was gambling on the archdemon being unaware of that clause in the Guardian rule book.

But was it really a bluff? Looking at Ari in that ice coffin, she realized, *yes*, she'd do it if it meant saving his life. He was more powerful than her, and therefore more important in the fight against evil.

And, of course, she loved him.

"I don't want—or need—the relic, my dear," Leviathan said. "The sins of my father are no more my own than you're responsible for your father's mistakes. I'd think you, more than anyone, would understand that."

Yeah, she understood the whole *sins-of-my-father* trap, though it was so difficult to outrun the guilt. That kind of thing always managed to defy logic. The heart was never reasonable. It felt what it felt. Even when it knew a restless Viking would always have to leave her to feel whole.

She'd held Stark in her arms as he shook and spasmed

violently, his heroin detox neither quick nor kind. She'd shushed him and sang to him and promised him that blunting the trauma of his past with opiates wasn't the path to happiness.

Now, she wondered if she'd been lying to them both.

And she wondered if her fleeting memories of love—and her ever-present guilt—would ever go away and leave her in peace. Medicating them away was perhaps the path to contentment after all.

The room shattered in shards of ice that shot outward at velocities that could pierce concrete blocks. Shards the size of daggers stopped twelve inches from her face, then zoomed backward by the pull of Ari's hands. He shook ice from his hair and rematerialized his sword as he advanced on Leviathan, glancing at Katherine once more.

"Get your head in the game, Kat! Lucifer has been the father of lies since time began. Lying and manipulating is all archdemons know. You're smarter than this, come on!"

"So circumstances of birth and nurturing are one hundred percent unalterable?" she fired back.

"Of course not." He kept his eyes on the archdemon, who'd now rematerialized to a more defensive spot near the exit to the pool terrace, looking around her like she was going to be ambushed. Katherine could only see her because the hallway walls were obliterated.

So tired of all this. But she needed to see to her people. "You must think so, though, if you're so vehement about this. And if you believe that, what must you think of me?" After all, she'd had an alcoholic father who'd blamed her for her sister's death.

The kicker was, it was true.

Her father had killed her mother because she couldn't stop grieving for their lost child. Then he'd shot himself in remorse for murdering his wife.

All because she'd begged Mary to come into the water.

"She's twisting this all around. Human beings and demons aren't subject to the same rules. You're not your father, Kat. You never were, and you never will be."

"You don't know that. We became Guardians in the first place because we were rotten examples of humanity. Perhaps I'm one meltdown away from..."

Becoming my father.

Ari's lips were moving like he was yelling at her, but she couldn't hear him all of a sudden. Her vision grew hazy. She slid slowly down the sanctorum door to her haunches. She blinked, feeling another increase in air pressure and the sounds of chanting before an air mass enveloped her. Leviathan's face registered alarm as she spun in all directions looking for an invisible threat. Katherine's heart pounded, attempting to rise to her feet.

Ari was chanting something she should recognize. It *felt* familiar, but she couldn't place it. The air vibrated, and the walls that hadn't been leveled shook. Then she heard the voices of several Unholy Inc partners—Nate, Spencer, Jinx, even Alexios—join in on the incantation.

"Kat, add your voice to ours." Ari's push into her mind was so potent her vision blacked out for a moment.

Ut fiat templum Dei vivi, et Spiritus Sanctus habitat in eo...

Katherine tried to form the powerful words the telepathically linked Guardians were using to cast out the darkest evil, but the phrases wouldn't come. Her eyes locked with Leviathan's. The archdemon's gaze held sadness, the skin on her face like tissue over rock, the luminescence of her skin now a pasty gray. "I know it's hard for you to trust one such as me. I'll go now, but think about my words. We're not so different. Together we can protect this island from the Rephaim. From the other archdemons, even. I *swear* it."

Ari snarled the final words of the incantation, and the

room detonated in a light so bright it whitewashed the blue-painted ceiling.

Before Katherine's vision restored, she was hoisted into the strong arms she'd recognize anywhere. Leviathan's abrupt departure was a relief, but also a little like...

Loss.

She couldn't begin to understand why. What was the point of *any* of this struggle between good and evil? Why did she care? And why did she choose to come back to an eternity of this shit?

Talk about a lack of foresight.

Ari's arms tightened as his steps slowed. She dashed at the infernal watering of her eyes. "Put me down, I'm not going to break."

When he set her on her feet, her surroundings came back into focus. He'd brought her into the kitchen, facing the storage room door where he'd compelled Jade and Aqua's core staff in order to keep them safe. As soon as he unwarded the door and dissipated the air pressure against it, Kat's team stumbled into the kitchen, talking all at once.

"Shut up, all of you, I've had enough social interaction for one day," she said, trying to find her reserve of anger to overcome this awful sense of vulnerability and hopelessness. Her team deserved better than this...from her and from life. Anger had been her go-to emotion for decades. *Rage, don't fail me now.* "Where's Makoa? If you've lost him, you'll wish the Rephaim had gotten to you after all."

"You planning to kill everyone, or are you just gonna eat us and spit us out?" Jade grabbed Katherine into a fierce hug, whispering into her ear, "Thank God, you're okay. I thought you were done for."

Me, too, she thought.

"If she ate you, her stomach acid would kill you, so you're fucked either way," Stark said.

"If Kat assassinated everyone who annoyed her, it wouldn't be homicide, it'd be the Apocalypse," Ari drawled. Everyone snickered, but only she saw the worry in his eyes.

Drawing back from Jade, Katherine smothered the urge to lay down and never get up. "Strange how humor darkens in correlation to vile circumstances. I'm not always a bitch, you know. Sometimes I'm asleep. Now, is Makoa here or not?"

"Relax, boss, he lit out when that gray-skinned monster blew open the doors, but Leviathan brought him back and trussed him up on the stage, neat as a bow," Stark said, grimacing when Jade smacked the back of his head.

"You idiot, all you needed to say is 'he's here.'"

"Nani and Maddox designed a new Trap on the stage and weighed Makoa down with iron chains, so he's not going anywhere," Ari said behind her. She felt him move closer and lay his hand at the small of her back. She allowed herself a moment to absorb his warmth and solace because she wasn't sure what to do next. Siolazar was on the prowl, half of her club lay in ruins, and Leviathan was...what exactly?

A tormented, but neutral soul? An unexpected ally? Pure evil?

Not knowing if you could trust someone was quite possibly the most unsettling feeling of all.

But Ari was trying to keep everyone—including her—calm. Makoa was on the premises and the Holy Chains were still safeguarded, so she supposed she should be grateful.

Turning back to Ari, she saw dark shadows under his eyes and a drawn pallor to his face before he quickly put up another smile. That white-light exorcism bomb he'd orchestrated with the telepathic help of the other Guardians had obviously fatigued him.

She frowned, clasping her fists at the sudden tightness in her chest. *Not good.* Especially when she was in no shape to protect him. "We need to make fresh salt lines across all the windows and doors. After that, Maddox, see if you can get some contractors in here to clean up this disaster. Stark and Konani, make sure our weapons—especially the Molotov cocktails—are topped off and ready. Jade, call the other members of the team to make sure they made it home okay, and then put your feelers out there to see if we can locate Father Angus."

They were going to need him as desperately as she needed sleep.

Please let me regenerate this time.

Normally, if she brought Ari with her, it'd go a long way to healing them both. Even more so if they made love. But she couldn't expose him to the burden of her dread, thoughts of Siolazar and Leviathan chasing away any hope of rest. And what if whatever she had—this darkness inside—was somehow contagious? He'd already felt slivers of her experience.

No, she wouldn't expose him. So she'd try to lay down and quiet her mind...alone.

Yeah, right. She'd never be able to fall asleep, wondering when the demons would come again. Would it be hours? Days?

The only certainty was that they *would* come.

As her team dispersed to fulfill their duties, the hair on her arms and the back of her neck suddenly stood on end. She spun to face the wall of small, square windows above the kitchen prep counter. Her heart pounded inexplicably as she stared out into the dark Hawaiian night that shared no secrets.

Seconds later, the Waikiki Beach sirens began to wail.

CHAPTER 14

Ari stood on the stage where Makoa had curled into a mumbling ball in the middle of the Devil's Trap, weighed down by more than a hundred pounds of chains. At the bar to his left, Kat was talking to Stark, looking deceptively strong. But it was a facade. He'd bet his prized shield that Leviathan was the one behind this current citywide emergency, not the Rephaim, like Kat believed. There probably wasn't even an emergency. It was likely another stunt meant to further unravel Kat's nerves.

Why couldn't Kat see through Leviathan's lies? Her ploy seemed so obvious. Yet the archdemon had some kind of hold on her, fabricating a shared life experience based on Kat's grim childhood.

He jumped down from the stage and crossed the dance floor toward what was left of the hallway. He retrieved his sword from the rubble instead of materializing it in order to conserve strength. That nuclear-style Guardian light bomb he'd detonated with Kat's partners' help had emptied his tank more than he'd expected. He reached into the ether to thank the Unholy Inc team.

"No worries, mate. How's Kat?" Nate asked.

"You in over your head, Viking?" This from Jinx.

"Things are little rough at the moment, but it's nothing we can't handle," he pushed back, hoping they didn't pick up on the sirens still roaring in the background. They didn't need to know the details—they had their own problems to deal with. Kat would agree. She was so proud, always unwilling to ask for help. Always wanting to do everything on her own. He loved and deplored that about her.

And if he stood here one minute more, ruminating like some jackass, he'd run his sword through himself.

A hand on his arm stopped him before he lurched out the front door to figure out why the sirens were sounding.

"You leave her now, and I don't care how much you outweigh me, I'm gonna kick your ass."

He turned to face Jade. "Leviathan's got to be the reason for Kat's failure to thrive around me. I need to put this threat behind us."

"Are you nuts? You can't take on an archdemon by yourself. Why don't you call on some of the other Guardian free agents?"

"I already have. But most of them are assisting in areas more vulnerable than Waikiki. Since the Seam opened, Leviathan is the only one of Satan's five offspring and their attending legions who hasn't laid siege to a Guardian stronghold yet. Other free-agent Guardians will be here as soon as they can."

"What about Nate and Jessie? They got rid of Asmodeus."

"Yes, but they've still got their hands full with the fallout. Asmodeus is back in Hell, but now they're dealing with his demon horde."

"Well, okay, but leaving Kat when she needed you is why she lost trust in you three years ago. I thought you finally realized that."

He shoved a hand through his hair. "When I brought you here, I thought she'd see it as an act of commitment."

"Leaving as an act of commitment? Come on, Grimm," she scolded, eyebrows pulled low. "Her past wired her brain to believe that everyone always leaves. She didn't ask you to find me, but you seem to think that because you did, she should automatically forgive you and get over her fear of abandonment. Well, think again." Jade poked him in the chest. "Why couldn't you stay in the first place? Were you afraid of Kat's grief...and maybe your own?"

Ridiculous. And these fucking sirens were driving him batty. He raised a hand to create a sound barrier around him and Jade. "Vikings have no fear."

She folded her arms in front of her chest. "Are you really that stupid? There is no shame in feeling afraid. It's what you *do* with that fear. You're afraid of being stuck, and instead of dealing with it, you're being a heavy-handed douche."

"What's that supposed to mean?"

"You don't know what it's like to stay in one spot. More specifically, you don't know how to find happiness staying in one spot. Even though you and Kat were together for many years, you guys hardly ever stayed in one place longer than a few months. You *know* Kat doesn't prefer that kind of lifestyle, yet she did it for you. Now, if you love her as much as I think you do, you'll figure out how to accommodate her needs as well." She looked up and acknowledged Maddox from across the room, adding as she walked away, "Just because you don't know 'the how' of something doesn't mean it can't be done."

Ari watched Jade depart without really seeing her. She made it sound so easy, but he was coming to realize his and Kat's situation was anything but simple. He was a man of action. He didn't know what to do while standing still.

The sirens stopped suddenly. The silence was almost more

worrisome than the blaring. He glanced over to the DJ stage where Kat was reaching out to touch Makoa's arm. "Kat, no! I'll do the exorc—"

Ari streamed toward her as fast as he could, catching her before she crumpled to the floor. "Christ. Enough, you hear me? *Enough*," he whispered as she turned her face into his chest. He gritted his teeth at the sign of her yielding in front of her staff, then he faced her team. "Reinforce all the exits, especially the terrace doors, with salt, holy water, and chrism oil. Use all we have if you need to. Get a few trusted priests to exorcise Makoa and help us ready more holy armaments. I'll wipe minds if needed afterward. Unless you find yourselves in an unavoidable emergency, leave us alone. We'll be back down...when we're down."

It would have to be enough.

He left Kat's team and streamed to her private quarters upstairs. He had to figure out why she was so sick. He entered her office and went straight through to her shuttered, shadowy bedroom with its soothing wood and ivory linen textures. With her still silent in his arms, he sealed the doorway, the vents, and all the windows with wards. Whomever had set off the alarms—Leviathan, her hordes, Siolazar—they'd all have to wait.

The island needed its Guardians whole.

He sat her at the end of the bed and began removing the pins from her hair. Her eyes soon drifted shut, her pulse settling into a rhythm that matched his own. With all the pins removed, her hair fell down around her shoulders. He ran his hands through it, the fragrance of it reminding him of happier times. "Remember when I told you that every time you feel the wind in your hair it meant I was thinking of you?"

She nodded, her eyes opening. "I'm in over my head right

now, so I'm grateful for your help. But you need to know that I can't do this with you, Ari."

"*This?*"

She looked down at her hands. "The bonding. I'm attracted to you. I can't hide that, but...the rest isn't there."

His chest tightened, but he sat down beside her anyway. She was lying. Again. He wasn't wrong about their connection. What they had went beyond attraction and lust. But right now, he didn't have the energy to convince her to drop the walls. She stiffened when his hand went to her hair. "It's longer now," he said quietly.

When she swiveled to face him, her gaze was tired. "Who knows what new madness is unleashed on the city, and you want to talk about my hair?" She tried to stand up.

He pulled her back onto the mattress and rolled on top of her, using his knees to nudge her legs apart, wishing she was wearing a dress instead of these tailored dress slacks she'd changed into after the white-light bomb. "I don't want to talk at all." His lips found her neck, her quick intake of breath the perfect encouragement.

"Take me home."

Yes. He'd been waiting to hear those words from her lips for three years and eighty-five days. Ari leaned up and away, pulling her with him so he could dispatch with her flimsy blouse. He tossed it across the room, stripped off his own shirt, and then pulled her against him to feel her skin on his.

He groaned satisfaction. *You feel so good, elskan.*

She began pushing away from him.

He leaned back, keeping his hands on her upper arms. Everything in him stilled when he noticed tears forming in her eyes. "Did I miss something here?"

"I want to go *home*-home. As in, not here. And I don't feel...I don't want to take the time to drive there."

Meaning, she wasn't strong enough to stream there.

He had them to her house across the island in seconds. His vigor was steadily returning simply by being with her. After a quick check of the grounds to ensure no demons lurked in the area, he carried her to her bedroom.

Her quarters here were vastly different than the ones at Aqua. Both were comfortable and polished, but this bedroom was done in shades of gray and white. More streamlined and modern. Glamour and glass. Mirror and shine. Each bedroom reflected a different side of Kat. Her choice to be here told him much about her current mood. She needed the facade of strength to bolster her until she'd rediscovered her center.

He came up behind her at the dresser, watched her remove her diamond earrings, grateful that she no longer seemed ready to weep. He brushed his fingertips across the nape of her neck, then leaned down to breathe in her ear. "Tell me what I can do for you, my..." *Love.* "...lady." He forced a smile into his voice.

Her hand paused on the velvet nesting box for her earrings, her lips quirking infinitesimally. "You may remove my necklace." She tilted her head slightly forward. Delicate goose bumps ran the length of her arms.

"I am ever at your service." His fingers lightly traced the line of her shoulder as he released the clasp. The gold slid down between the lacy cups of her bra before she caught the precious metal in one fist. He eased forward, pressing her into the dresser, his eyes tracking up every delicious inch of her exposed skin until they met hers in the mirror. His erection burned against the denim of his jeans. Her fingers flexed on top of the dresser. His palms came to rest on the hips of her gray slacks, not that she was going anywhere, but because if he didn't put his hands somewhere semi-safe, he'd move way too fast.

"And now?" His voice was gruff, his throat dry. His hand

cupped her chin. "No, don't look away. Look me in the eyes when you tell me what you want, Katherine."

One eyebrow rose. "*Now* it's Katherine?"

"I'm trying to get you in a more agreeable mood. You owe me a month, remember?"

"That was only if *you* got rid of Siolazar. You didn't. Leviathan did."

"In case you forgot, the terms of my deal were 'if we get out of this.' And we did. Doesn't matter how," he replied. His fingers crept along the front of her waistband, her stomach jumping with each advance as he unbuttoned her slacks. When they puddled at her feet, she lifted first one foot, then the other, freeing them from the fabric. Then she stood there in nothing but her bra, thong, and high heels. *Bond. Make her mine.* His gaze fixed on her navel in the mirror to find a center of control. To go slow.

His eyes closed. *Breathe.* Her body shuddered slightly, and a rush of electricity arced through him. His eyes snapped open to find hers in the mirror.

She'd reopened their intimate pathway.

"I'm too tired to fight or play games. And I'm damn tired of being alone. Care for me once last time so I may face death with strength and honor."

He turned her around and lifted her in his arms, wrapping her legs around his waist, staring deep into her faded blue eyes. "You will not die while I have breath," he whispered.

Skin against skin, his blood sang. Her fingers threaded through his hair, the sweet sensation making him groan against her lips. His fingers curled into the soft skin of her bottom, moving her up and down in a slow, delicious grind against the front of his jeans until she was breathing heavily.

"Your jeans have to go."

Helvete, her voice could slay him. "Not yet."

She slid down his body, slow like molasses upon a wall.

They were both shaking by the time her heels sank into the carpet. "*Ari*," she protested.

He settled her into the wing-backed chair, placing a pillow behind the small of her spine. "You'll get everything you want and more. I promise, *skjaldmær*—my shield-maiden."

His chest felt so tight he could hardly take a full breath. He knelt between her legs, her skin an almost surreal shade of rose in the height of her arousal. She leaned up and reached for him then, vanquishing his control. Their mouths met, hot and seeking. Her fingernails scored his back. He unhooked her bra, then cupped her breasts. "So perfect."

Her hands bracketed his face, pulling him away to look at her. "Y-you can't say that."

"What?" A rich blue-green was returning to her irises. "Your eyes are the color of *Sognefjord* on a foggy morning. Have I ever told you that?"

She blinked at him. "No. I...no."

"It reminds me of my family in happy times, and of all things that have a good soul in this world."

"Really?"

The naked vulnerability in her expression was so at odds with the polished, acerbic side of her. "I would never lie to you, Kat."

She laid her forehead against his, wrapping her arms around his neck. "I know. But calling anyone perfect is too much pressure."

Of course she would think that. "Okay, no more perfection." He eased her back against the gray cushions to nuzzle her belly. "No more thinking either." His fingers slid the edges of her lace thong down, his lips following his fingers to press open-mouthed kisses along the way. "No thinking. Just pleasure."

Her hands tunneled through his hair, her sighs weaving around them. His shoulders pressed into her legs as his tongue sought her softness. She squirmed on the chair, her hips shifting, rolling against his mouth with increasing strength. Sweat beaded at his temples, slid into his eyes. He hooked her legs over his shoulders and sucked harder, then pulled back before she lost control, blowing and kissing her swollen labia. Up and back down that erotic slide he took her, over and over until she was panting, cursing at him, demanding release, the claws he craved fully unsheathed.

He loved her in all her facets, but he hungered for this raw side. The way she threw off her cold veneer. So rare. But she did it for him. Came...

Undone.

"Yes, Ari. God!" His head rang with her intimate scream. His mouth, his fingers, his arms holding her in place. Riding out the orgasm with her. So beautiful.

"You are mine. You can't deny me anymore, Kat." A shadow passed through his mind. *Don't let her think.* He scooped her out of the chair, pivoted toward the bed, and laid her diagonally across the covers. He studied her as he unzipped his pants, erection pulsing when she leaned up on her elbows to watch him. He pulled her up to stand, kissing her mouth when she opened it to complain. He swept her into his arms once more, then turned and sat himself on the edge of the bed, bringing her spread legs around him to hook about his waist. *Let her lead.*

She didn't make him wait for long. She accepted him, then took him deeper into her body on successive grinds. Each motion of her hips brought them closer together, hearts beating in rhythm, breaths stirring each other's hair, sweat mingling.

"Lean back into my arms."

The freedom—the power—she felt with this man was a gift.

And a blade.

So much pleasure. So much pain. So much life.

So much *everything*.

Ari.

Everything was so dark without him. He brought the light.

How she'd missed him, the effortless vitality he wore like his own skin. When they were together like this, she could almost forget something tainted was inside her, consuming her.

Tears sprang to her eyes as ecstasy rose up. She grasped at her Viking's broad shoulders and buried her face in his warm neck, the forceful pulse of his life echoing the ripples of the orgasm rolling through her. His arms banded around her, his deep voice whispering ancient words in Norse and Latin as his body continued to claim her.

She could feel his spirit reach for her. Her soul jumped in response, but she blocked the connection before they could merge.

She held on to her Viking's shifting back muscles. Wishing...

I'm sorry. If only you could stay, it might be different.

CHAPTER 15

K at came awake with all her senses online—the murky and curious pre-sunrise energy suffusing the atmosphere beyond her windows, the waves eternally crashing against the rocks outside her bedroom, and the cool ambient temperature of the room contrasting sharply with the heat radiating off the body beside her.

Ari. The way he moved, the scent of him, everything about him...so full of mystery. Exuberant, dauntless, free.

Everything she was not.

He would tire of her so quickly.

Yes, he would be drawn back to her over and over because of their artificial pairing. Maybe she could have lived with that if she had the lifespan of a mortal woman.

But an eternity of watching him leave?

You don't have an eternity. Sure, she felt good right now, but this vigor would fade as the sickness inside her came creeping back. She could sense it during quiet moments like this. Feel it under her skin and in her mind. Watching. Waiting. For what, she didn't know. It had gotten worse since her first meeting with Leviathan. Maybe the archdemon had cursed her with the dark sleep? But an archdemon had to be powered up by a holy relic to infect a Guardian, and she hadn't heard of any relics going missing. Neither from her Unholy Inc partners or from any free-agent Guardians.

Then again, maybe she was simply losing her mind. Going insane like her notorious father.

Alexios would eventually be forced to end her. Or maybe Michael would blitz her into nothingness. That would probably be the most merciful way to go.

Whatever was causing her physical and mental malaise, it was already coming back—an awful heaviness thickening her blood, making her heart work harder to pump vital oxygen through her body.

As ardently as he'd tried, Ari's healing was becoming less effective.

She blinked back the moisture rising in her eyes as he rolled onto his back, naked and spread-eagled on the bed. Then he went completely motionless again. His lips parted slightly, soft in repose. He slept the sleep of the guileless. Lucky bastard. She'd resisted him for so long now. Once she'd thought he was hers.

Silly girl.

Silly, sad girl.

She ached to brush the sun-kissed locks from his brow. To wake him with kisses along each glorious, sculpted plane, and start the healing all over again. But one person—especially one full of shadows like her—couldn't expect to hold a lightning bolt like Ari. He was laughter on the wind, a shout of triumph standing on the bow of a warrior's ship, a living example of *fight hard, play harder*.

If only he could stay.

Stay, stay, stay.

She shivered and touched her lips, remembering how his

skin had warmed her through the long hours of the night. She never thought she'd have another experience like that again.

All that focused attention was overwhelming and magnificent.

Her heart drummed against her chest, her legs shifting in the sheets. He would probably try to stay. Might even be able to by sheer force of will. But his spirit would die like a bird with clipped wings.

She wouldn't change her restless Viking. She probably wouldn't even lov—

She snatched back the hand that had nearly caressed his face. *Oh, you stupid girl.*

She would always love him.

He didn't think she understood why he'd left to find Jade, but she did. His pride refused to accept that he couldn't fix her grief. And the Viking code that forbade any show of weakness denied him the solace of acknowledging his own grief. He did the only thing he knew. Went in search of a salve for both of them.

She loved him all the more for it even as it broke her heart to realize that what he needed, she couldn't give: her soul, bonded eternally.

The connection they both craved would eventually rip them apart.

Stop thinking about it.

And she needed to stop looking at him.

She rolled carefully away and slipped from the bed, quickly dressing in yoga pants and a thin cotton shirt. She froze when he turned and reached toward her side of the bed, but he only grabbed a pillow and pulled it to his chest. She stared at him for a few more bittersweet moments, then grabbed her phone off the nightstand and quietly left her big, beautiful warrior slumbering alone.

5:17 a.m.

She stepped onto the tiled lanai, skirting around the pool toward the beach. She needed sand between her toes. The spray of surf on her skin, the wind in her hair.

All permanent things. Things she could count on.

She kept her distance from the waves, gathering shells that gleamed milky white in the hazy light, trying to block thoughts of Ari.

And Mary. Her sweet face. How she'd loved her younger sister.

How jealous of her she'd been.

The ugliness of it twisted and burned in her belly even now.

Father had loved Mary best. No, Father had loved *only* Mary.

"Enough!" She crushed the shells in her fist and threw them back toward the ocean. "I don't care! Do you hear me, Father? I can't keep doing this." She plunked down onto the dry sand, staring at the waves.

So tired of it all.

Tired of keeping the wall fortified. Keeping the bad memories away.

The few good ones, too.

Nothing felt right anymore. All of the pieces were torn, and she didn't know how to fit them back together. Maybe she could try to take happiness where it came. Would that be so bad? Her heart had been broken before, and she survived.

A sound reverberated above the thrash of the surf. She focused her auditory senses to the south where the muted noise originated. A woman in distress?

Kat stood and moved along the beach where the sand broke to rocky outcroppings, keeping well away from the water's edge. The rising tide surprised her ten yards from the cliff, swallowing her ankles in shocking wetness, shifting the sand around her toes as it retreated. She backpedaled, skin crawling, sweat beading between her breasts. *Go back.* She turned toward home, but a woman screamed louder this time.

Kat swallowed and tested the potency of her water element by pushing the tide out further into the ocean, away from her. The surf foamed, curling back upon itself. She exhaled shakily, knowing she shouldn't use up her resources like this for long. *I'll just check it out, then go back.*

She climbed the slippery boulders. It wasn't long before she saw the source of distress. A Rephaim—his back to Katherine and his red bodysuit obscenely tight over his musculature—stood over a body on the rocks, holding something in his arms. *Siolazar.* She couldn't tell if his prey was human or demon.

The being on the rocks screamed once more. A black mist swirled above it, waiting to invade its body. The Rephaim son of a bitch. Why couldn't he sense her presence? And how dare he help another demon possess someone so close to a Guardian bastion?

She marshaled her power element, feeling the expansion inside her body, but then...

She tempered it, frowning.

If she used her powers now, she might not have the strength to face off with Siolazar and the untethered demon. Siolazar continued to stand with his back to her. Something in his arms was big and lumpy, but she couldn't make out what it was from this angle.

A great gust of wind surged around her, lifting her off her feet briefly. *Ari.* No sooner had his air element tracked her, he was behind her.

"The next time you want to go for a dawn adventure, nudge me. I profoundly dislike waking without you beside me, North," he whispered in her ear.

She looked up at him. "North?"

He smiled, the stubble on his cheeks shadowy in the

glom. "Tell you later." He looked at Siolazar. "Now, what kind of mischief—"

Her gaze darted back to the Rephaim at Ari's arrested words. Siolazar had turned to the side to focus on the ocean, holding a limp creature with a hunched back and a smooth, white bulbous head.

What the hell? A dead Nephilim? The Rephaim and Nephilim avoided one another, gravitating toward different forms of evil.

Ari's body had gone completely still except for the tensing of his fists. "I don't sense Leviathan anywhere around here, but this has something to do with her...and what's going on with you."

"How would you know?"

"The Rephaim and Nephilim have no reason to go to war with each other. In a thousand years, I've never seen anything like this." He bracketed his hands around his mouth. "Let the human go," he yelled out, "otherwise we're going to have problems, demon."

Siolazar's attention finally snapped toward them. He smiled as he dumped the Nephilim's white body to the ground. "Tell me, Guardian, just how useless are you going to be today?"

The air pressure built around Katherine. "What do you want me to do?" she asked.

Ari started to respond until Siolazar grabbed the human woman by her hair and forced her to her knees in front of the crumpled Nephilim.

"*Fy fæn!*" Ari materialized his ax, body shifting to lunge.

"Ari, wait!" Katherine streamed forward and latched onto his back pocket. Siolazar yanked the woman's head back, opening her lips in a wide yawn. The black demon mist spun into a long, tall funnel and shot down her mouth while the Rephaim laughed.

Ari raised an arm to send his ax wheeling through supercharged air manipulated by his element. Siolazar raised his left hand with a snarl and the ax thudded to the ground. "Ah, yes, quite as useless as I suspected. How disappointing."

The hairs shot up along Katherine's arms. Jesus, now what? They needed to get the woman away from the Rephaim while they could still exorcise her. Katherine took a step away from Ari's side so she had room to manipulate her water element, but he pulled her back. *"Something's not right,"* he said, telepathically.

"No shit, Ari."

"We need to bail. Now!"

"Wait!"

But he'd already gathered her into his arms as the Possessed shrieked and sunk her teeth into the dead Nephilim's neck.

CHAPTER 16

Fucked. Up.

This was so fucked up.

But at least now he understood why Kat was so sick. And since he knew, he could fix it.

Please, Thor, Freya, Jesus, and whichever other Gods are listening...help me fix this.

Ari tore around Kat's house, warding the windows and exits on hyper-speed after streaming the two of them out of the Rephaim's presence. He wasn't one to run from a fight, but watching a newly possessed human cannibalizing a Nephilim corpse was one of those situations that required a clear head.

Kat grabbed him out of hyper-speed, spinning them head-over-heels to the sofa in her living room. When they landed, her head was at his crotch, her sweet ass inches from his mouth, and just like that he morphed into a horny bastard, imagining her hair in tangles, her head thrown back, her lips wet, open, moaning for him...

She pawed and swiveled on him, trying to sit up, but only managing to make his cock stiffer than his forged-iron sword.

"North, stop. For the love of Odin, just *stop*," he ground out, gripping her arms and rolling her to her feet.

She placed her hands on her hips. "That's what I was trying to get you to do, you big oaf. Let me help you set these damn wards."

He readjusted himself as much as he was able to without unzipping his pants, then looked up to see her smirk. "I don't want you using any of your resources. You're getting sick because of what we saw. Doesn't it make sense?" But he could see she wasn't connecting the dots. "When Healer Guardians exorcise humans, we draw their entire essence into our bodies, flush out the evil, and then return their souls back intact. Or at least as intact as they were before the possession. Now think about the consequences of exorcising humans who've drank Nephilim blood."

Her lips parted and eyes widened. "I've been mainlining poison."

He nodded, beating back the urge to go berserk. "Exactly. I couldn't understand why you weren't regenerating. I mean, even without bonding, you should have been able to rejuvenate to moderate levels and then maintain that for days."

He finished setting the wards, then broadcast a message to all Guardians about their discovery. "The Rephaim are badass motherfuckers, but Nephilim are even more pernicious to Healers. Usually they're solitary, but I worked with a group of Guardians to round up several dozen of them during the Thirty Years War in Central Europe in 1647. Made me nauseous just being around that many. None of the other Guardians were affected, but then, none of them were Healers. At the time, I thought it was because I was already running on empty, being it was close to the end of the conflict. But in light of what we saw just now, and the shitty way I felt after healing that child when I first arrived at Aqua a few days ago...this has to be the problem."

All those centuries ago, he'd been brutally ill without actually internalizing Nephilim like Kat had when she exorcised humans who'd likely drank Nephilim blood. How much sicker was she from repeated exposure to Nephilim toxin? Could it kill her?

He sent out an urgent call to Alexios, but the Guardian leader didn't respond.

Ari rubbed his chest. He needed to keep calm, for fuck's sake. *Breathe.*

Kat twisted her hands in front of her. The little tell made him want to hold her. "Back then, how'd you heal when you were so depleted?" she asked.

"Alexios put me into an ether sleep, then suffered greatly when he channeled my pain."

Her lips compressed. "Do you have any lingering effects all these years later?"

He shook his head, exhaling, trying to slow his heart rate. He pretended to examine a bird figurine on her coffee table while he waited for Alexios to link up telepathically.

"Why the 'North' nickname?" she asked quietly.

He set the figurine down and turned to face the woman he loved beyond life. He walked to her and pulled her into his arms, curling himself around her, wishing he could absorb everything ugly and evil that had touched her soul. "You still mumble in your sleep."

She wriggled and shifted to get more comfortable. "Well now, that explains nothing."

He tried to smile, pushing fears of her dying aside. "Don't get your thong in a crevasse."

She snorted. "That would be 'panties in a bunch,' hotshot. Might I suggest the Urban Dictionary for all your modern slang references?"

He kissed the top of her head. "Sarcasm's your degree, not mine. In any case, you say we're polar opposites. You're right, but that's our strength, not a weakness." He tilted her chin up. "I also finally realized that while we're different, my needle always points to you. You'll always be my true north."

She froze, then blinked, moisture suddenly floating in her eyes. She spun away and walked to where her phone sat on the kitchen counter. He could feel the zipping of her blood echoing the roar of his emotions.

"Grimm, your distress is disquieting. Have you discovered more dead Nephilim?"

Alexios, thank God. *"Can you heal, Kat?"*

"Expunging Nephilim toxin will require more than ether sleep."

"What about using her relic?"

"I thought of that, but if she has a preponderance of evil inside her, there is a possibility the relic could kill her instead of healing her if she has contact with it. I would advise that you take over her duties of guarding the Chains of St. Peter."

Ari pounded the side of his fist against the wall. Kat looked up, her shoulders dropping as she set her phone down carefully. Ari began to pace. *"What can we do then? She cannot die."*

The Guardian leader remained silent for a few heartbeats, then, *"I will attempt to consult with Michael, but don't be surprised if we are left to figure this out on our own. In the meantime, bond with her. It should have been done decades ago. And don't leave her side."*

There was nothing else to say—no encouragement to be found—so Ari closed the mental pathway. He stopped pacing and pierced Kat with his gaze. "You cannot go anywhere near your relic. Alexios thinks it might be a danger to you with the infection."

"But then how can I protect it?"

"I will take over the responsibility."

She frowned fiercely, but nodded.

They stared at one another a few moments. "Will you not bond with me to save your own life?" he finally asked.

She moved toward him until there were only inches between their bodies. "Did Alexios say that was the only way I could be cured?"

He should lie and say yes. "He doesn't know. He said he'd consult with the archangel. But *I* know it would help." It had to. He couldn't lose her. "Please, Katherine."

Her eyes were luminous in the diffused light of the room. "I can't give myself to you in order to save myself. That would defeat the purpose of the ritual, don't you see? The sacred joining of souls, by nature, is a loss of self. I cannot come to you—the connection will never truly work—if I'm not whole to begin with." She laid a hand on the pounding wall of his chest, and his fingers slid into her hair.

"No."

"Yes, Ari. You know I'm right. I don't know why it's taken me so long to realize it, but I can't give myself to you because I'm broken." Her voice caught. "I've been broken so long I don't know what it feels like to be whole."

"Then we'll fix you."

She smiled through her tears and laid her cheek against his forearm. "You can't do it for me. I have to do it myself."

She would have pulled away then, but he held on to her. "Then do it. Love yourself like I love you. See yourself through my eyes."

"If only it were that easy."

"Kat, just tell me what I can do..." God, this helpless feeling...

She lifted to her tiptoes to plant a kiss on his lips which he deepened until they were both breathless. She broke away first, touching his lips, watching the trail of her fingers. He brushed away her tears. "Kat..."

She brought her gaze to his. "I will try. But I have to do this on my own. It's the only way, okay?"

Everything in him rebelled at the thought, but it was true. She had to learn to love and forgive herself. "Okay, but don't push me away. Even Alexios said I shouldn't leave your side."

She brushed the remaining wetness from her eyes, then mock-glared at him. "Fine, but only if you call me Katherine."

A laugh wrung from him, the pressure of his fear relieving slightly. "Deal, but don't get pissy if I forget from time to time."

Her eyes crinkled. "Oh, I'll get pissy, all right." She kissed him quickly once more, but pushed him away before things escalated.

He stared at her, trying to bring his emotions into stasis. She said she'd try, so he needed to trust her. "I believe in you."

She blushed, and tried to scowl at him. "Enough with the mushy stuff. We have work to do. I've asked Nate to send us his rock-star exorcist, Father Angus. He's in the field right now, but as soon as Nate makes contact with him, he'll let me know. Hopefully my team will bring in a few more priests we trust from various islands. In the meantime, though, what ideas do you have for healing the Possessed?"

"You have to stay away from the relic, but I can use it. I did that once with great success."

"No way. The Chains should never leave the sanctorum. The wards protecting them are some of the most layered I've ever woven. I don't know if I'd be able to recreate ones that complex again, even if I were at full strength. I'm afraid to even bring them out of the reliquary."

"I can add my wards to yours. Playing it safe sometimes prevents living fully and without regrets."

She frowned. "I've lived with regrets for so long I wouldn't know how to live otherwise."

Anger flushed through him. "That's a total cop-out. Is this

the toxin speaking or have you become a coward in the years I've been away?"

She stiffened, eyes flashing. "Know what, Ari?"

He leaned toward her, uncertain what she would say, but eager to spar, to release some of this awful tension that had sprung up between them.

He watched her lips as her mouth opened. What came out...

"Whatever."

Oh, hell no. He hooked his finger in the waistband of her yoga pants when she started walking away. "Not *whatever*," he bellowed. "Say what you want to say, goddammit. Don't hold back from me. That's the worst thing you can do."

She shimmied out of his hold. "Sometimes discretion is the better part of valor, Viking. A concept your forebears didn't comprehend."

"As much as you enjoy it, insulting me isn't productive."

She blew out a heavy breath. "I'm trying to concentrate on the immediate problem, not the mountain of issues between us. The fact remains that we're still very different, and I'm not entirely convinced that if you stay with me you won't end up feeling trapped and grow to resent me. Concentrating on *that* makes me angry, and I'm afraid it might come out in the most insignificant ways. Like being mad because you have chest hair or something else absurd like that. So yes, discretion and focus are pretty important right now."

He was speechless for a moment. She didn't like his chest hair? "I'm not that hairy."

She rolled her eyes. "I know. It was just an example, but surely you get my point."

No, he wasn't sure, but admitting that would probably upset her more, and he certainly didn't want to keep going down that road. So...appeasement. "Okay, so we'll keep the Chains in the reliquary."

Her stance relaxed slightly. "Do you think the Rephaim are more powerful than the Nephilim? I mean, how else are they killing them without a big show? And how are we going to stop the possessed humans from cannibalizing the Nephilim?"

"The only thing we need to worry about is stopping Leviathan. Once we take care of her, everything goes back to normal."

Her brow furrowed. "You want to blame everything on her, but I'm not convinced. She saved us from Siolazar."

"Probably to buy herself time to do the double cross. Come on, you can't be serious about giving her the benefit of the doubt." He went to the refrigerator and withdrew items to make sandwiches. The action calmed him. When he glanced up from his task, she was chewing on her bottom lip.

She'd never done that before.

"Maybe there's an unknown relic out there powering up the Rephaim. One that a Guardian's never been responsible for. Siolazar wouldn't be able to touch it, but he could command it, right?" At his raised eyebrows, she continued, "Don't look at me like that. I don't hear you sharing any hypotheses."

"Fortunately—or unfortunately, depending on how you look at it—there haven't been enough relics stolen by fallen angels to know how they interact with holy relics."

"But religious medallions, holy water, and crucifixes burn them. It only makes sense that they wouldn't be able to touch a holy relic."

"Right. I agree with that, but I was referring to their ability to command relics to act on their behalf. That we don't know. Nor can we speculate on any unknown relics not under the protection of a Guardian. The only certainty is the archdemons' desire to ferry them to Hell for Lucifer."

"It's unrealistic to think we have every single relic accounted for. All religions like their tangible objects. Christianity's no different. There's probably dozens of holy objects still waiting to be discovered." She sat on a stool at the counter. "And if that's the case, it's only a matter of time before a demon sets Lucifer free."

"Or, it buys us *more* time because there are more keys they have to find in order to get the right one—if only one is needed. Which I believe to be true in Lucifer's case, though not all Guardians agree."

"Why do you think it'll only take one?"

He shrugged and slid a plate with a turkey sandwich in front of her. "I had a philosophical discussion with the Dalai Lama about keys. Keys to the Kingdom, Keys to Happiness, key to my heart. That sort of thing. But think about it. When you unlock something *in particular*, does it usually take multiple keys?"

Her eyebrows lifted and her face paled. "No. That's actually...alarming."

He shouldn't have brought it up. The last thing she needed was extra worry. He came around the counter to put his hands on her shoulders. "Who knows if it's true. If it is, they'll have to go through a lot of relics to find the right one."

She shimmied away. "Or they'll get lucky right away."

He shook his head. "We can only do our best with what's in our control." He stared at her as she looked around the room, again wishing he hadn't brought it up. "Kat. I mean, *Katherine*."

"What?" she snapped, bringing her gaze back to his.

"We can only do our best with what's in our control."

She compressed her lips. "I heard you the first time."

"Good." He pointed to her sandwich and moved back

around the counter. "Now eat. Forgiving yourself burns loads of calories, I've heard."

While he made a few more sandwiches, she swiveled her stool to look out the window, eating. He exhaled quietly and rolled his shoulders. After a while she leaned back in her stool. "Logic says relying on Leviathan would be a bad move, but we have to think outside the box."

"Outside the box, yes, but gambling on an archdemon's ability to be honest is insanity."

"Michael and the other archangels won't help us, the rogues."

"Archangel involvement equals Armageddon," he reminded.

She rubbed her eyes. "I know. But...maybe it's time."

For Armageddon? Whoa. He set his sandwich down and moved toward her, holding out a hand. "You definitely need more rest if fatalism is overshadowing your propensity toward sarcasm. While you sleep, I'll check in with your staff and the relic."

"Doom and gloom is the perfect diet for sarcasm." She stood and avoided his grasp. "Knowing what's happening out there, it's irresponsible to sit here doing nothing. Siolazar is probably watching this house waiting for the right time to annihilate us. Leviathan is likely plotting her next move. Demons are eviscerating Waikiki Beach tourists and locals alike..."

"You can't do any more exorcisms until the humans are cleared of Nephilim toxin."

"So, what then? We let more humans lose the fight to the invading demons?"

He wished he had the answers, but he'd never encountered anything like this before. "I'll summon Alexios for his thoughts. In the meantime, you need to focus on returning to full strength."

Kat pulled a protein shake from the fridge. "We could convince Leviathan we're ready to work with her, then use her to control things."

Stubborn woman. "Good luck with that. You ever heard of holding a tiger by the tail?"

"Being a Guardian is dirty work, Ari. Existing almost twelve hundred years should have made that abundantly clear to you. I'm not suggesting we trust her. I'm saying we use her game against her."

He stared at Kat. She wasn't being honest with herself. She was still holding out hope that Leviathan was who she was claiming to be. An innocent victim of bad public relations via her evil daddy. But Ari didn't want to fight anymore. He just wanted to take care of his soul mate. "Nate and Jessie beat Asmodeus without consorting with demons."

"Well, good for them," she said. "But unless you have any other ideas, I think making up new rules might be in order."

Meaning play Russian roulette with Leviathan.

Well, that was definitely not happening. He tamped down a surge of guilt to concentrate on the telepathic link she'd left open to him. He honed in on her metal barriers to break them down, chastising himself as he seized her neurons that were responsible for action and wakefulness. As an old-as-dirt Guardian, it was almost as easy for him as turning off a light switch.

He caught her the instant she dropped into unconsciousness.

His heart pounded as he looked down at the woman in his arms.

This was selfish. He knew it.

He didn't *like* knowing it. He'd rarely ever worried about what was self-serving. He squeezed her to his body, twin sensations of guilt and relief raising his core body temperature. He had told her he didn't want to control her or do anything that made her uncomfortable. Now here he was, forcing her to sleep. Controlling alpha jackass move for sure.

He gritted his teeth. When she woke, she'd be understandably cross. But...he'd rather deal with her fury than her corpse. Consorting with an archdemon definitely qualified in the fear-for-her-life category.

Ari streamed them back to her private chambers at Aqua, still questioning his heavy-handed move. He laid her down on the bed, then went to the closet to look for an extra blanket. His fingers tunneled through a pile of fur throws he'd once given her.

She'd kept all of them.

He brought three of the blankets to the bed and gently wrapped her in them. He kissed her forehead and paused by the door to look back at her, his pulse still bumping erratically. He'd check on her staff, watch over the relic, and try to figure out what the hell they were going to do while she slept.

Maybe if he had a plan together by the time she woke up, she'd forgive him for taking away her self-determination.

CHAPTER 17

K at woke alone with midafternoon sunlight on her face. She opened her eyes and stared at the wood beams in the ceiling of her Aqua bedroom. *You. Have. Got. To Be. Kidding. Me.* She let out a yell, slamming her fist ineffectually against the bed covers.

That son of a bitch had put her to sleep.

She lay there for a moment, breathing through her anger and embarrassment, sending out her senses to detect if there was any immediate jeopardy beyond these walls. Encountering the typical energy pattern of her team and no unusual malevolence in the vicinity outside, she brought her focus back to her bedroom. Her twisted emotions sent a new rush of blood into her face. She rolled to her side and curled her knees to her chest, closing her eyes against the welling, angry tears. Yes, horrors awaited them with Leviathan's demon horde. But Ari had taken away her choice, damn him.

Damn him.

That could not go uncontested. Did he think so little of her Guardian abilities or her mental capacity to handle the situation?

She never would have done the same thing to him if she were in his position, would she?

Would she?

It was hard to know. Ari seemed so...invincible.

She wiped her eyes on the pillow and gathered the soft blankets to her nose, allowing herself a moment to indulge in his scent—a self-injurious tradition she indulged in once a year on the anniversary of their first night together. He'd acquired the furs for her in Quebec.

Now he knew she'd never gotten rid of the blankets. Wonderful. She blinked up at the ceiling for several more moments, resisting the answers to her questions. But when it came down to it, yes, she'd do anything in her power to protect Ari, too.

And, no, he didn't discount her capabilities. To believe that of him was unfair and unkind. She knew on a strictly rational level that he respected her. He was too damn honest to lie anyway.

Why, then, was it so hard to let herself accept it? To believe she was worthy of his esteem?

"Baggage, baggage, and more buggery baggage," she whispered to the empty room.

She was tired of carrying it. Unpacking it was going to prove messy and time-consuming, so for now she'd have to settle for off-loading it.

Glancing out the windows at the ocean side of the club, everything sounded and appeared normal. No city sirens or scary fallen angels and archdemons trolling for their next soul. Instead, tourists strolled along the sunny beach snapping pictures while surfers paddled out to catch the next wave.

It was a relief to finally know why she'd been so sick for the last few weeks. If Ari hadn't been here, she probably wouldn't have figured it out. Or it would have taken her a long time.

Time she might not have had.

She yawned and stretched, then grabbed her phone, which Ari had had enough sense to bring when he streamed them back to the club. *Three p.m. Lordy.* She'd slept a deep, uninterrupted sleep for hours. Incredible.

Feeling this good, she could almost excuse his heavy-handedness.

Almost.

You'll always be my true north.

For better or worse, love and fear were the greatest motivators of all.

One side of her lips tipped up. Wasn't she so mature now?

The next trick would be actually learning to like herself.

She grimaced and strode into her closet where she stripped out of her day-old yoga pants and T-shirt and slipped into a pair of dark jeans, white blouse, and tailored, navy blazer. If she was going to die facing off with demons today, at least she'd do it looking put together.

She rolled her shoulders as she emerged from her closet, but stopped mid-stride to the bathroom when she suddenly heard water running. Why hadn't she heard or been aware of it before?

She sent her senses through the woodwork. When she connected with Ari's unique essence, a slow wave of desire rolled through her. Visions of his powerful body, warm water sluicing down his shoulders, sliding over the ridged planes of his abs, dripping off his—

"You're welcome to come in and touch the real thing," his bass voice rumbled from behind the door.

She wrinkled her nose, her face heating. *You ninny.* If she could feel him, of course he'd be able to sense her as well. She shivered. *Do* not *open that door.* "I have work to do, but first I need to use the facilities, so you need to scram, Grimm."

"Come in here. I'm not talking to you through a closed door—your head is thick enough."

How annoying could one man be? She barged in and stopped, heart skidding to a halt, her breath hitching in her throat.

Her gorgeous Viking was buckass naked...

Shaving his chest hair.

And smiling that sexy grin that imploded her brain cells.

He'd always been immodest. The man could walk around naked all day long and not care who saw him. And he absolutely loved to bathe. Whoever started the myth that Vikings had been unkempt had it wrong, wrong, wrong.

Yowza. Five, ten, fifteen seconds ticked by... The longer she stood there taking in that hard, golden body, the more she could almost hear her brain cells whimper.

He smirked like he knew—*just knew*—what she was thinking.

"Permission for verbal admiration granted, North. And hey, I'm feeling generous today, so monosyllabic vowels count. *Ooo* and *aaah* are perfectly reasonable, considering your present awestruck condition."

Her face burned as she swiped her watch off the counter, watching his powerful forearms out of the corner of her eyes. "I couldn't sense you in here. How did you do that?" Maybe it was a Guardian trick she hadn't learned.

"You needed sleep so I dropped the air density in the bathroom to prevent the sound waves from transmitting."

That was sweet. Truly. And the physics of his air element were fascinating. Still... "If you ever put me to sleep like that again, I will hurt you."

Solitary confinement would probably be the best way to torture him. Solitary confinement with no windows and no

light. "Would you get some clothes on? You look ridiculous."
Ridiculously sexy. Gah! God would surely dispatch his warrior
archangel to smite her for her ludicrous insult to such
magnificent manflesh. Particularly if God was a woman. Or at
least bisexual.

Actually, was God pansexual? That made the most sense.

"I'd rather be completely ridiculous than completely
boring," he drawled. "The ethereal Marilyn Monroe said that.
I'm sure you've heard of her. Lovely individual. Raj asked me
to fill in as her bodyguard for a few days when you announced
to the worldwide Guardian contingent that you'd had enough
of me back in the nineteen fifties, remember that? You
returned my red roses. Spray-painting them black was a nice
touch, by the way."

Katherine's whole body tensed. Bodyguard to one of the
world's most enduring sex symbols? What was that
expression her English partners, Nate and Spencer, used with
such aplomb? Ah, yes...

Bloody hell.

She snatched a towel and threw it at him. If it was
possible, he looked even sexier covered by the towel. And
that bulge...

She slapped a hand over her eyes to keep them shut, but
the image of the tented towel was seared in her brain.

Why did she even care who he thought was ethereal? She
was the one who kept pushing him away. If she rejected him
long enough, of course he'd seek out more hospitable women.

And who wouldn't be hospitable to—she parted her
fingers to peer at him—*that.*

Dumb, dumb, dumb. Just DUMB. She was jealous over a
movie star who'd been dead for decades. Marilyn Monroe had
been a sad, lonely woman, ever scorned by jealous bitches like
herself. It was more a depressing commentary on herself than
anything the breathy-voiced actress had ever done. "Ethereal

is not a descriptor for exorcists like me, so, just...whatever. Go on and get out of here."

She moved toward the vanity, but he held her in place with a warm, firm grip on her upper arm. His other hand caressed her face, his eyes twinkling. "I am humbled and greatly pleased by your possessiveness."

"*Pfft.* Why would I be jealous? Remember the black roses? I swear, Ari, you don't have a humble bone in your body."

"You'd never want a man whose machismo wasn't bulletproof." He backed her into the sink and hoisted her up onto the cool Carrera marble, his eyes suddenly somber. "I am much aggrieved for taking away your self-determination."

"Good. Then don't ever do it again. I mean it, Ari. Now scram. I need to get ready so I can get back to work."

"Everyone is accounted for downstairs, supplies are stockpiled, repairs are underway, and the demons are obviously licking their wounds. My main concern right now is your physical and emotional well-being." His lips traced her ear and a delicious warmth spread through her belly. "How are we doing with that self-love thing?"

"*I* am doing fine. Now really," she tried to push him back, but he wouldn't budge, "I must see to my staff, Ari."

"Are you pleased that I am now hair-free?"

She pulled her lips to the side to forestall a smile. "I never objected to hair on your chest." But it was quite endearing that he'd worried over her earlier comment.

"But you said..."

"It was an off-the-cuff example to illustrate a point. Anyway, you're getting me off topic. Please, Ari. Seriously, I want to check on everything."

"Alexios brought Father Angus, as well as another Guardian-friendly priest a couple of hours ago. They've been knocking off possessions like special ops forces. And we now know how to clear the Nephilim taint in the Possessed, so there's no reason why you can't take another hour to rest. I'll help you fix your hair."

He removed her blazer instead. Then his hands found the buttons on her blouse. She sat there, letting his fingers work their magic until every last button lay undone, her blouse gaping open in silent welcome. He unhooked the center clasp of her bra and slid his rough palms along her waist, his thumbs coming up to caress the undersides of her breasts. "You feel so good, North," he breathed in her ear.

She inhaled deeply to clear the lust haze clouding her brain. "Wait, how will you clear the Nephilim toxin from the Possessed?" A single thought flashed in her mind, and when his eyes widened, she realized she'd linked up with him. "Using my relic? No way. It would probably kill them, the same as it might kill me. We are not taking the Chains out of the reliquary. Besides, Alexios would never agree to that."

"Under normal circumstances, no, he wouldn't. But these aren't normal times, North. The two priests are doing great so far, but they can't do all the exorcisms. There's just too many. And relics have been used on possessed humans innumerable times with great success."

So she'd heard. Still, she couldn't imagine their Guardian leader agreeing to let the Chains of St. Peter out of the special inner chamber she'd built for the holy object. "You're sure Alexios gave his okay for this?"

"Since when are you so concerned about following orders?"

"I'm—" He hoisted her off the counter and peeled her jeans down her thighs. When he set her back on the marble counter top she realized her thong had somehow managed to hitch a ride with her jeans, so she was...quite exposed. "Grimm."

"I liked seeing you wrapped in the furs I bought you..." His hands drew up to cup her breasts.

She cleared her throat, unable to stop her fingertips from exploring his back and obliques. "I forgot those were still in my closet."

"Liar." His whisper raised gooseflesh all over her body though it was still warm and humid in the room. He ran the backs of his fingers down from her clavicle over the swell of her breasts peeking between the opening of her blouse. "But I like you better in—" She watched his eyes darken as his hands slipped her blouse and bra straps from her shoulders. "—*skin.*"

Damn you, smooth seduction.

She was an intelligent woman. She could rationalize what was happening. See it for what it was.

She should stop it.

Check on her people.

See to her responsibilities.

But...

That one word.

Skin.

His called to hers. An elemental longing that reason couldn't appease.

She held eye contact with him as she unpinned her hair, the fall of the tresses like a cleansing rain on her soul.

She ran unsteady fingertips from her neck to her areolas, down her belly to slip between her legs.

Then she reached for him.

※

She was going to kill him with that look in her eyes.

He would tear apart any other man who happened to see it.

A hundred lifetimes. A hundred lifetimes walking alone across a barren desert would be worth that look. He couldn't suppress the low growl that rumbled up his throat as her nails scored his back. He looked down at her, the V of her parted thighs open to him, her narrow landing strip of tawny hair slightly darker than the silky strands floating around her shoulders. He hardened to the point of pain beneath the towel.

His hands advanced from her knees up to the fleshy, delicious part of her thighs, then skated his thumbs over the plump, pink skin he ached to bury himself in. Kat moaned and leaned back against the wall-to-wall mirror, one hand over her head, her fingers clearing paths through the misty fog on the glass.

He brought her to the brink, then eased the pressure, not ready for her erotic sighs to stop. Her eyes were pools of stormy aqua. *Perfect.*

"Ari."

He reached behind her ass to yank her flush with his body, lifting her up and down slowly to grind against the soft, textured towel covering his erection until they were both breathless. When he pulled back to drop to his knees, she grabbed his face in her hands, keeping him on his feet. She kissed him like she'd never let go. His stomach jumped when her nimble fingers went to the towel at his waist. When the towel dropped, he sprang free and one thought...

Mine.

Nothing else.

She hooked her feet against the backs of his thighs and shifted her legs wider on the counter. He watched their bodies come together. Something dark and dangerous moved through him to see his body fill hers, her lithe limbs so accepting, her darkness so hungry for his. He pulled out, pressed back in—*fuck, yes, home*—setting a steady rhythm that tested the limits of his control. His air element fired up, banging the Roman shades at the window in his ache to bond with her.

"Meld with me."

She closed her eyes, nuzzled his neck where his pulse hammered, then not-too-gently bit the fleshy part of his ear. "Ari, I want…"

"Want what, North? This?" He hitched her up against his hips, grasping under her thighs as he rubbed her against his pelvis and seated himself all the way. "Bond with me. *Say it*."

She moaned. He pulled out and drove back in, her breasts bouncing with the force of their lovemaking. He shook his head, sending water droplets flying until he realized she was making them bead all over the room. He felt them gather across his body—like her hands touching him everywhere. "I'm not going to last much longer if you keep that u—"

Her orgasm rocked the room in a blast of warm water that sluiced down their bodies, ran down the mirror, and dripped from the counter. The exquisite convulsing of her body pulled him over the edge to follow that sharp blade of pleasure.

She ducked her head to his chest, wrapping her arms around his trunk, making tenderness swell in the wake of their passion. He hoisted her into his arms and carefully made his way over the wet tiles of the floor to the shower.

He set her on her feet, tilted her chin to look up at him, then kissed her softly. Her eyes were now a gray blue, uncertain.

And afraid.

She opened her mouth to speak, but his fingers pressed against her lips. "Shh. Don't say anything now. I won't pressure you anymore. Let me care for you a little while longer. Then we'll go down and face the monsters."

CHAPTER 18

Ari's regret and ensuing apology had seemed sincere. Even more heartening, he seemed to be focusing on what she wanted, instead of what he thought she wanted. And of course, the sex was still amazing so...

The hell with it.

She was going to enjoy him—and work side by side with him—for whatever time he was hers. His love and support strengthened her. She'd be a fool to deny it.

A greater fool to deny herself of it.

And perhaps it was time to return some of that love and support. Honest emotion and a new priority would maybe dampen her father's awful voice in her head. She didn't want to feel guilty anymore. Wanted to move on from the blame of her sister Mary's death. Her mother's murder. Her father's suicide.

If only Ari hadn't been called away so suddenly. He and Alexios had left Aqua a few minutes ago to assist at Spencer's San Francisco club, where the Rephaim had somehow managed to blow a hole in the wall of his reliquary. *Not good.*

Katherine stood before her apartment closet, staring at

the designer clothes she'd accumulated from shopping trips all over the world. Her other closet at home was even more extravagant. The carefully hung, color-organized ensembles, shoes, and jewelry weren't just a hobby she enjoyed.

It was more pathetic than that.

It had been a desperate attempt to replace—or at least forget about—the man she loved far more than any liberated, independent woman should. She'd been as lost as Stark in his desire to erase the pain of his past. But instead of heroin, she self-medicated with shopping. Using objects and outward trappings to prove to others how worthy she was.

The pity was, looking the part never made her feel it inside.

But if she was worthy of Ari's love, maybe she was okay.

If she only knew how long he'd be around this time...

She frowned, hopping on one foot while she zipped up her ankle boots, and then hurried downstairs. With each step, the tenderness of her groin reminded her of Ari's loving. Her top-of-the-line vibrator was definitely a poor substitute.

"Your desire is desperately distracting, North. You'd better be alone and thinking about me, not eying another male."

She paused at the foot of the stairs so the others wouldn't see the goofy smile on her face at her mate's mental growl. That he could so effortlessly reach through the ether to connect with her was actually more comforting than she cared to admit. *"I'm not good at reassurance, Viking. May I interest you in a sarcastic comment?" And hurry back*, she added, speaking only to herself. His telepathic chuckle was like a caress. *"Just be careful, okay?"*

"You, too," he said. *"I hate to be away from you, especially with Leviathan suspiciously off the radar. Be on guard for anything, and whatever you do, do not touch the relic."*

"I've been fine without you for the last three years. I think I'll survive."

He didn't reply, but she could feel his unease. She sighed as she came down the newly repaired hallway, remembering the unfortunate altercation with Siolazar. She bypassed the tall potted palms to approach the wide bar where Jade was lining up new chrism oil bottles. The priests had clearly brought extra supplies with them. Thank goodness.

Jade whistled. "Damn, girl, you're glowing. But with a sex-god Viking taking care of you, I shouldn't be surprised. Seriously, you look great, honey."

"Thanks." Katherine examined the bodies in the Devil's Trap on the dance floor. Only six of them. Her heart rate sped up. "Where's Makoa?" She turned back to Jade. "If he's not healed by now..."

Jade chuckled without looking up. "Put your claws away. Ari made Father Angus exorcise Makoa first. He's in the break room grabbing lunch with Nani and the priest."

"What about the other priest—Father Murphy?"

"Alexios and Ari took Murphy to San Francisco to help with the shitstorm there."

"As they've done the exorcisms, have either of the priests shown any ill effects from the Nephilim toxin?"

"Ari was really careful about that, but thankfully, no. Looks like it only affects Healers because of the way you guys suck the essence into your bodies, unlike the priests who use the sacred ritual."

"Good." Katherine exhaled, her neck and shoulders relaxing as she moved past the tables toward the dance floor where the Possessed watched her approach with shifting gazes. Usually the newly Possessed were a noisy lot, flocking to nightclubs where the normal chaos of the setting made it easier for them to hide their crazy. But during the low-key hours before the club's opening, this calm behavior on their part was eerie.

She glanced back over her shoulder at Jade. "Why are they so quiet?" she asked.

"They must've worn themselves out when they watched the priests work on the others," Jade said. "I 'spose they're conserving their energy to fight Father Angus when he comes back from lunch."

It sucked that they had to do all the exorcisms the old-fashioned way, but she and other Healers couldn't afford constant tainting by the Nephilim blood. So, time to stop gawking at these freakishly quiet possessions and get to work.

She'd almost reached the break room when a well-built man with a steel-colored beard and spiked hair emerged from the kitchen wearing pink jeans and a short-sleeved gray clerical shirt and collar. And behind him...Makoa.

Katherine smiled at the young Hawaiian, her heart easing when he nodded with an answering smile. His color looked good, and though his warm brown eyes didn't quite project that peaceful serenity she'd yearned to bottle a million times in the last decade, his comportment was calm.

She held out her hands to the priest. "It's about time you two stopped stuffing your gourds. You've kept me waiting."

Father Angus bypassed her hands and went in for a sturdy hug. "Happy to see you, too, lass." He stepped back and thwacked her shoulders, his sleeve tattoos shadowed in the darkened hallway. "Seems like ages since we stuck it to Asmodeus's bastards at Mirage."

Her lips twisted in a wry smile. "Indeed. Maybe because we both almost died."

"Och, that hard chaw Viking wouldn't ever let that happen to you. What's the story on you two anyway?"

She decided to let the Viking inquiry pass as much as it made her stomach swirly. "Not much juicy gossip around here."

He chuckled bawdily. "That's not what I heard with my own ears a couple hours ago."

Her face heated as the priest stepped aside to bring Makoa into the conversation. The men shared some unspoken communication that had her glancing between them.

"Katherine, may I have a word in private?" Makoa asked.

His soft-spoken words made her heart begin to pound. Had she missed something in his demeanor? She stared at him for a moment before she turned and led him down the hallway to the business office she shared with Jade. Once the door was closed, Katherine reached for Makoa's hand, the gesture making her feel exposed, but unwilling to let it stop her.

She hadn't been much of a mother figure to him these past ten years, but she'd done her best to clothe, house, feed, and educate him and his older sister. He'd been a boy of eleven, Konani just fifteen, when she'd found them. She'd probably always feel they were hers—even when they were old. The thought of them not being around someday...

She swallowed past a hard knot in her throat. "You had us worried. How are you feeling?"

His other hand came up to sandwich hers between his two palms. "I'm grateful to be free of the demon, but I feel awful that I've been living a lie. I believe it led to my possession. I could've hurt you, my sister, or the others."

Katherine shook her head. "But you didn't. You fought the demon and were ready to kill yourself to prevent that. And if this is about you coming out, you have nothing to fear. I've known for a while."

Makoa's eyes widened. "No."

She smiled and nodded. "For about two years."

He looked down at their joined hands, then quickly back

up at her, trying to read something in her steady gaze. Finally, "You're not ashamed of me?"

His whole body was shaking. She dropped his hands and pulled him in for a hug. "God, no. I'm the one who should be ashamed for making you wonder. You are the gentlest soul I've ever known. Being gay is not what made you vulnerable to evil. It was your guilt. It's a poison that eats away at your insides." She should know. She held on to him until his quivering ceased, then brushed at her eyes and pulled back. "Love is a gift no matter who it comes from. All I want for you is to be happy."

Makoa squeezed her again, rocking her side to side. "Where would Konani and I be without you?" When he stepped back, his smile shone like diamonds in the snow of Ari's homeland. "You gave us new life when we had no hope. Now, I feel like I am reborn once more. Thank you, *'ānela kia'i*."

She couldn't imagine anyone finding those children and not doing anything. "Just so we're clear, the next time you have such a huge weight on your mind, don't wait so damn long to tell me. And no more guilt. Got it?"

He nodded with twinkling eyes. "That 'no more guilt' also applies to you, you know. As my role model, you're obliged to take care of yourself, too."

Katherine snorted. "Your role model, huh? That might be the biggest lie you've ever told, brat."

"I love you, Katherine. I also want you to be happy." He leaned down to kiss both her cheeks, then walked out of the office, quietly closing the door behind him.

Katherine stood, staring at Jade's bulletin board filled to the brim with notes and pictures that called to mind happy times. How had she managed to have such wonderful people in her life?

They even loved her.

She thought about that—really thought about it—for the first time as she slumped down into the sumptuous white leather chair she'd bought for Jade after seeing her admire it in a catalog. Jade had cried when it was delivered, going on about how thoughtful it was. Katherine had imagined it was only because of the price tag.

Yet Jade had also cried when Katherine had brought her her favorite flower, which she'd picked along the side of the road on her way to work.

Katherine sat in Jade's chair and ran her fingers along the buttery-soft armrests, smiling as a strange new lightness settled in her chest.

Maybe it was finally time to let go of the past. Time to believe she deserved the love of the special people in her life. They hadn't stuck around for no reason, right? She paid well, but so did a lot of other places where they wouldn't have to deal with demonic horrors on a near-daily basis.

And of course, there was her Viking.

She reached into the ether to find him. To tell him she wanted him back as soon as possible. When she found his essence at Spencer's club, there was a startle and a sudden disturbance, which meant he was engaged in battle. She gathered her strength and sent as much power as she could through their connection, praying to the God who'd given her this second chance that Ari would prevail and come back to her.

That she would overcome the evil that was currently on her own doorstep.

And inside her.

She stood and was on her way to gather all her staff so they could devise a strategy for dealing with Leviathan, Siolazar, and the rest of their problems when a knock sounded. She opened the office door to find Father Angus. "Is everyone okay?"

"Aye, rest easy, lass. Jade dispatched me to find you. She figures you'd be the least surly with me since I haven't had much chance to annoy you."

"Don't worry, priest, the day's young yet. You'll have your chance." They both laughed as they walked down the hall toward the dance floor. "I hear you've had a full morning of exorcisms. I feel terrible that I'm not able to assist in my usual manner. You'll have to refresh my memory on how to do things the old-fashioned way."

"We'll do fine. Things aren't as bad here yet, not like what Spencer's dealing with against Archdemon Baal. For whatever reason, your archdemon is acting the maggot with you instead of going full-court press."

She stopped and turned to him. "Then you should be in San Francisco fighting Baal with the others."

The priest hooked his arm through hers to continue walking them toward the Devil's Trap, where the Possessed broke their silence to strike up bone-jarring shrieks. "Life is going on as usual here on Oʻahu for most everyone, but something is brewing. I'm sure you feel it," he said.

"But—"

"Someone has to do the exorcisms. Plus Michael instructed me to remain here. That's all I need to know."

Interesting. Or unnerving. "Is the archangel appearing to you?"

"Well, not exactly. But trust me, the scary bugger's getting his message across."

Katherine nodded. *That* she knew all about. She looked at the bedeviled humans, feeling her unease about Ari's absence fade. This was her purpose. To heal humans for as long as she could. It didn't matter if they deserved it or not. That piece of the puzzle wasn't hers to judge. "How do you want to do this? Each one together, or divide and conquer?"

Father Angus assessed the writhing mass of bodies and

cracked his knuckles. "I think we make a go of 'em together. They've had a chance to perk up, and I'm not liking the look of that gouger on the right."

Katherine agreed. The man was built like a wine barrel, and his eyes had already started blinking in and out of that black, soulless gaze. She narrowed her eyes and smiled. "Let's do him first."

"You have a streak of the devil in you as well, do you not?" He returned her smile. "But then, I suppose you Guardians have to have a little black in your marrow to carry your yoke."

Katherine signaled for Stark before turning back to Angus. "Are you saying you don't, Father?"

"What, have a touch of the devil in me? Of course I do. More than a touch, I'd wager." His eyes probed hers. "You still feeling the darkness inside? Ari mentioned the Nephilim toxin because he thought it might be important for me to know."

She chafed at the thought that others knew of her vulnerability, but she supposed he was right. She nodded. "The sense of waiting and watching in my blood is there, but physically, I'm much better since I'm no longer exposing myself to the poison over and over. I'm trying not to think about it. There's too much to be done."

Angus put a hand on her shoulder, saying a prayer of protection in a loud voice. When he finished, he squeezed her shoulder. "Let me know if the exorcisms get to be too much."

"I will," she replied.

Stark's heavy boots scuffed the dance floor as he approached with his usual swagger. Katherine lifted her brows, but didn't say anything for once. There was a time when she'd have made him get down on his hands and knees and buff the marks out with the shirt on his back.

And he'd have sported attitude the whole time, then

retaliated in a more private fashion later. Like leaving her to deal with a catty staff member instead of taking care of those little dramas like he usually did.

She appreciated his irreverence and discreet rebellion.

He liked that she wasn't up in his business all the time.

They understood one another.

"Stark, bring the iron chains." He started to turn away to ignore her when she added, "Please."

He raised a brow, and she grinned, tickled that she'd thrown him off guard with unexpected civility. When he returned with the chains from the storage room, he ignored her outstretched hand and presented them to Father Angus. *Insurrectionist.* She glowered at him.

His lips turned up in a patently fraudulent all-American-boy smile.

Katherine raised her hand and used water from one of the pools to shoot a forceful, carefully aimed water spout at the side of Stark's head after he transferred the chains to Father Angus. "Rock, paper, *water.* I win."

Stark shook his head like a wet dog, then sulked off, muttering, "I'm gonna drain those fuckin' pools."

The trapped fiends began wailing and tearing into each other. Father Angus lifted the chains cautiously. "These aren't the apostle's now, are they?"

"No, St. Peter's Chains are safe in the sanctorum's reliquary. These are regular old iron chains. Stark should have made sure you had them earlier." She threw a withering look at her head of security where he was tipping his head back to drain a shot at the bar.

"Very good. Ready then?" Father Angus asked.

"As I'll ever be." She nodded to Jade and Konani, armed with holy water and chrism oil, who'd moved onto the floor. "When the demon's shade leaves its host, don't let it get out of this room alive. Do you guys know what to do?"

"Yep," Jade assured her. "Holy water on the colloidal form to stun it, then a drop of chrism oil to vanquish it. No more than absolutely necessary. We've been over this a million times."

"Good. Don't muck it up."

Jade smiled brazenly.

Father Angus transferred the bultk of the iron chains to one forearm and pulled a crucifix out of his back pocket. "How you wanna work this?"

"You mind getting a little wet?"

The priest winked at her. "You're talking to a native Dubliner, lass. Bring on the rain."

Katherine built up her aqua element, borrowing more water from the terrace pools to spew horizontal geysers at four of the possessions. She knocked them to the opposite side of the Devil's Trap, away from her and Father Angus's first mark. The stocky man they planned to exorcise first bellowed and launched toward her position where she stood outside the circle.

"I've seen visions of your death, Guardian. Alone. Drowning. The water filling your lungs, dragging you down into the cold, dark water," he yelled.

Katherine shuddered. Her element faltered, the water restraints suddenly failing to hold off the other possessions. They scrambled up from the floor, one of them grabbing the stocky man by the ankles.

Father Angus tossed the chains and caught their quarry on the left shoulder with the iron weights, taking him down. The crazed human screamed, the whole left side of his body smoking where the iron made contact with his skin. The priest lunged into the circle the same time as Katherine. "Stark, Maddox, get over here!"

With the two men's help, they pulled their target out of the Devil's Trap so they wouldn't be accosted by the other possessions while they worked on him. The first set of chains and a second set produced by Jade were looped around both of his arms, legs, and crisscrossed over his chest and pelvis. He shrieked and bucked beneath the chains.

Katherine dropped to her knees beside Father Angus and used her palm to press a St. Benedict medal again the fiend's forehead as her voice joined his. *"Exorcizo te, omnis spiritus immunde..."*

The man's body smoked, the tips of his hair catching fire so often that Katherine conjured a dense mist in the room to prevent burns for all involved. This process was different from her regular method, requiring so much more physical strength. Her Guardian process was almost purely spiritual. And this way took much longer.

She dared not move her hands, but she glanced up at Father Angus, his brown eyes clamped shut as his lips moved with the old words, his gray priest's shirt clinging damply to his toned shoulders. She caught movement beyond, where Jade and Konani stood at the ready to touch the demon's shade with chrism oil.

Katherine extinguished the artificial mist and squinted at the club's entrance, where a form hovered in the shadows. She didn't have time to reroute another wayward tourist looking for a drink. What was wrong with these humans? Couldn't they tell something was off? Obviously most of them had no self-preservation instincts. Or they didn't pay attention to them.

Sometimes she wondered how the species made it past their elementary years.

"Go back to your hotel, we don't open until eight!" she yelled toward the doorway. The possessed man roared, still more beast than man, his head shifting back and forth on the wooden floor, his mouth filling with foam. *Almost have you, you evil bastard.*

From the corner of her eye, she saw the form slip behind one of the potted ferns.

Great. She did not need a freaked-out human to contend with on top of this crap. "I said we're closed! We have to practice our skit privately, or it won't be any good for the paying customers!" She glanced at her security head. "Stark, deal with this." She tossed her chin the shadow's direction. Stark nodded. He turned as the shadowy figure stepped out from behind the plant. Katherine's gut dropped.

Leviathan.

Katherine lurched to her feet, the St. Benedict medal burning in her palm as she took in Leviathan's new look. Shoulder-length bob, subtle makeup, khaki pinstripe suit, navy designer pumps. She looked beautiful, human, and...harmless.

Yeah, right.

Katherine's heart slugged at her chest. She sent a telepathic message to Ari letting him know the archdemon was here. "Everyone to the safe room!" None of her team moved. "Now!" she barked, keeping her gaze on Leviathan, praying she wasn't wrong about the archdemon's lack of interest in her staff.

Jade was the last to leave. "Kat—"

"Everything will be okay." It would. She just needed to focus and keep Leviathan's attention on her while the staff got to safety and Father Angus completed the exorcism.

As Jade made her way down the hall to the sanctorum, the possessed man screeched and headbutted Father Angus, knocking his body so hard the priest slid across the floor and slammed into the DJ stage, where he crumpled to the floor. Katherine ran to him, using her senses to detect his heartbeat. It was stable, but he was bleeding badly. She gathered energy and pressed her fingertips to the priest's skull to cauterize the wound.

The Possessed rattled his chains, prostate on the floor. His deep, echoing growl raised the hairs on the back of Katherine's neck. Now that the exorcism had been interrupted, it wouldn't be long before he was able to throw off the chains if they didn't get him back into the Devil's Trap in time.

Katherine stood in front of Father Angus, keeping both the possessed man and Leviathan in her line of sight. The archdemon still hadn't spoken, her eyes filled with humor as she watched the Possessed thrash on the floor. Katherine took a deep breath. "If you really have good intentions, now is the time to prove it."

Leviathan raised her gaze to Katherine, the emotion in her eyes shifting from amusement to warmth. It was the sort of look Jade had given her hundreds of times. Intimate and honest. What was she supposed to do with that? Believe it? Why wasn't this black and white?

Katherine's muscles bunched, instinctively preparing her water element as Leviathan raised her right hand. The body of the possessed man on the floor began to levitate. He ceased his struggles as his body rose, the chains shifting across his frame, sliding down to crack as they hit the floor. Leviathan slowly opened her fist and the man's mouth gaped in sync with the motion. Black mist seeped from his mouth, nose, and ears until it coalesced above his body, seeming to tremble before the daughter of Satan. With a whisper Katherine couldn't comprehend, Leviathan closed her fist, and the black mist was gone. No sound, no sulfur smell, no discomfort.

Katherine brought her gaze back to the exorcised man, whom Leviathan was gently lowering to the floor beside the chains. His eyes were closed, but Katherine could detect a stable heart rate.

When the man turned to his side and tucked his hand

under his cheek with a slumbering sigh, Katherine looked at Leviathan, wanting to trust her, but not knowing how. "Thank you?"

Leviathan nodded, but remained silent.

Katherine swallowed, wondering if she should even ask. "Why have you returned?"

When the archdemon opened her mouth to speak, a cold, dry wind swept across the dance floor, raising gooseflesh up and down Katherine's arms.

"I have found your sister."

CHAPTER 19

I *have found your sister.*

Leviathan's words resurrected old aches and desperate desires. *Wrong. She's wrong.* "My sister's dead," Katherine whispered.

Father Angus groaned and scooted up to a sitting position, his pupils dilated. "Don't listen to the demon's lies, lass. You know better."

Leviathan's cheeks reddened, her eyes glowing silver. Liquor bottles burst on the bar shelves. "You know nothing, priest!" Then she blinked, looked at Katherine, and the rage was gone. "Mary's here on the island. I can take you to her, but you must come now."

Katherine looked at the archdemon's outstretched hand, feeling Jade's presence move behind her next to Father Angus. The priest's lips moved, but his prayers sounded like a buzzing that grew louder and louder until Katherine wanted to scream. *What's going on?*

"North, I'm coming!"

Ari's voice, his entire connection, communicated conflict. He was obviously in the middle of a battle of his own. *"We're okay here. Come back when you're finished at Inferno,"* she projected back.

"You said Leviathan was there."

"She is, but we're just talking. It's only her, no one else." She wanted to tell him about Leviathan's claim to have found her sister. But she knew what he'd say. Don't trust or make deals with devils. So she wouldn't. *"If you don't trust me, this will never work."*

There was a pause on his end. She could almost feel the blows he was taking and delivering. Leviathan was walking around the dance floor, as though waiting for Katherine to make up her mind.

"By 'this,' you mean, our bonding?" Ari eventually asked.

"I'm disconnecting so you can keep your inflated head attached. Go fight. Bye."

Katherine cut their connection before he got himself killed, her gaze following the archdemon's leisurely pace toward the pool terrace. Like she hadn't just dropped an emotional bomb in Katherine's life.

The low-level buzzing renewed in her head. She rubbed her temples, trying to clear her mind. Leviathan had to be lying. Even if Mary had survived the drowning, she'd be more than one hundred and sixty years old.

What game was the demon playing, and how could she counter these cat and mouse moves? In her wildest imaginings, she'd never thought an encounter with an archdemon would be like this. She'd visualized carnage and devastation, blood and pain.

Instead, this felt like a slightly off-tune lullaby.

Lulled to death by polite warfare. Her lips curled self-mockingly as she followed the archdemon outside where the sunshine glinted off Leviathan's honey-brown hair. Father Angus's renewed prayers were close behind.

Leviathan hissed and threw a venomous look over her

shoulder at the priest and sped with supernatural haste to the opposite side of the largest pool. Katherine halted with Father Angus at her side, a cold tingle spreading through her torso as the pool bubbled and steamed.

Don't leave me heeeeeerrrrree.

A muted voice was calling, as though traveling through water. Katherine's body temperature dropped as the buzzing ratcheted higher. Teeth chattering, she crouched down to scan the water, sending her element through the hydrogen and oxygen molecules of the pool.

Nothing there.

What had she expected? She rose to her feet, her hands pressed against her temples to dull the drone and resist the darkness that seemed to be expanding inside her head. She locked eyes with the archdemon who trembled as though as cold as she. "Why are you doing this? Stop these games and get on with it!"

Find meeeee.

Father Angus put a comforting hand on Katherine's back and pulled out his rosary, holding it in front of him toward the roiling water as his lips recited the Hail Mary, the Glory Be, then... "Oh my Jesus, forgive us our sins, save us from the fires of Hell..."

Leviathan screamed, her hair standing on end as she sent an electric shock across the water, headed for Father Angus. Katherine shot energy from her hands, a counterforce in the water to shield the priest. When her energy met Leviathan's darkness, searing pain poured through her, sending her to her knees.

Pleeeease, Kitty. I'm so c-c-cold!

A quiet sob wrenched from Katherine. Nausea rose up in her belly until she wanted to vomit. She rocked back and forth on bloody knees. "Mary," she whispered. No one else had ever called her Kitty.

Father Angus crouched beside her, laying his hand on her back once again. "Stand and say the prayers with me. *Say them*, Guardian, and call your soul mate!"

Yes. "Ar...Ari...I need—"

"Katherine!" Maddox's voice penetrated. She turned to look as he and the others poured onto the terrace, demon weaponry of all sorts clutched in their hands. She stood, her mind still fuzzy, afraid to take her gaze off the archdemon for long. Leviathan would kill them all, and there was nothing she could do about it. If only she could think. Why couldn't she think?

She pressed her fingers into her temples harder, yelling to hear herself over the awful ringing in her head. "Make it stop!"

Maddox, Jade, Stark, Konani, and Makoa launched Molotov cocktails across the pool at the archdemon. Leviathan froze all five bottles midair, a small stream of chrism oil from Makoa's bottle burning the flesh on her cheek before its airborne arrest. The smell of sulfur carried across the pool on the breeze, and the demon's eyes blazed silver above her putrefied, smoking cheek. She circled her hands, launching the bottles far out into the ocean. Makoa and Nani joined Father Angus in his prayers.

"Time after time, I have come to you in peace, yet you continue to scorn and assault me!" Leviathan cried. "What do I need to do to get you to believe that I am only here for connection?"

Katherine held up her hand to halt her team from making any other attacks that might further provoke the archdemon. "I want to trust you, Leviathan, but I don't know how."

The archdemon laid her hand on her smoking cheek, closing her eyes as her palm absorbed the fire. "Will finding Mary be enough?"

Katherine's chest constricted. She'd never heard of a

demon being able to resurrect a deceased body. They could only use a live human as a host. "You don't have the power to do that."

"I am more powerful than you know."

The ground shook, the once-sunny sky now birthing murky, restless clouds that pulsed with lightning. *Ari.* Leviathan yelled something in the Enochian language as a shrill sound preceded a massive rush of wind. It sucked all the water out of the pool, and spat it out in a twisting cyclone aimed at the archdemon.

Ari landed as a shield in front of Katherine, crimson blood streaming from a jagged gash bisecting his entire back. Katherine moved around him in time to see Leviathan shoot up into the sky. Sensing Ari gearing up to meet her in mid-air conflict, Katherine grasped his arm. "Wait!"

He turned to her, his eyes full of war and vengeance. "No more waiting! She's slowly killing you, lie by lie. I won't have it!"

"She found Mary. *I heard my sister's voice, Ari.*"

"*She's waiting for you on the beach at your house.*"

Katherine gasped, eyes probing the clouds, as Leviathan's voice filtered through her mind. How? How could she do that —be in her head like that?

Ari grabbed her shoulders and shook her. "Don't be a fool, Kat! She's manipulating your deepest vulnerability. Why can't you see that?" He glanced up, then cursed wildly when he found the target of his fury gone. "This has to stop. She's spoon-feeding you nothing but deception, yet you lick your lips and wait for more. Why, North?" A cold rain fell, drenching them both, creating bloody puddles on the concrete from Ari's wounds. Her team scurried inside. "Why would you trust her more than me?"

Maybe it was the pain in his voice and the fact that they were finally alone that made the tears come. "I don't know."

She wrapped her arms around his waist, placing her hands over his torn flesh, sending healing through their connection to make his tissues knit together faster.

He squeezed her tightly, his chest rumbling beneath her ear. "You do trust her more, then?"

She shook her head, wiping her eyes against his chest. "I don't know anything right now. I don't...I don't know what's wrong with me." But she wanted her sister back. Right?

Or did she just not want to feel guilty anymore?

That was sick. And she was awful.

She eased out of Ari's arms. What if she infected him with what was still inside her?

She had to get home to check if Mary was really there.

No! It's all lies. She was losing her mind. Everything seemed so twisted up, her confusion snowballing with each encounter. When Leviathan was standing in front of her, she so much wanted to believe the archdemon. When Ari spoke, of course she believed *him*.

Why would she believe the archdemon over Ari? It made no sense. He loved her. Had always loved her.

He took her hand, pulling her rapidly toward the club doorway. "It's the Nephilim blood. It's creating an artificial bond between you and her," he said, as though he'd been reading her thoughts. "Come inside now, let's get you some dry clothes, some food, and some *me*."

"What?"

He scooped her closer to his side, walking her inside the club, past the bar where everyone stopped talking to stare at them somberly.

"I come back to see you ready to sell your soul to a devil, so in the aftermath, yes, you're damn well going to succor me, woman."

"No, not that, you really think the Nephilim blood is

playing with my head? That she's manipulating me through the toxin?"

He nodded. "It's Raj's theory. Alexios and I agree."

She stopped midway down the hallway. Ari paused beside her. It made sense—the weakness, the inability to recharge, the confusion.

Still...what if Mary was really back? If she was, would Katherine ever be able to forgive herself for not checking? If Leviathan was lying, at least she would know once and for all.

She looked at the only man she'd ever truly loved. She'd always thought that love made her weak, but perhaps not. Maybe it gave her strength she never knew she had.

She tried to smile to put him at ease. "I need to retrieve something at home. Will you stay here with the team? I'd feel much better knowing you were here." When it looked like he was going to argue, she rushed to reassure him. "I won't be long. And I'm sorry. I never should've doubted you."

"We can both go and be back in moments."

She shook her head. "I need some time alone, okay? Trust me. Please."

He stared at her. She tried not to blink or show any of the uncertainty that was pummeling her from the inside out.

Finally, he spoke in a firm voice. "Twenty minutes. You take longer than that, and I'm coming for you. Don't make me regret this, North."

She was gone before he could change his mind. Or her own.

CHAPTER 20

Katherine streamed directly to the beach at her house. The salty sea spray coated her face before she made it even halfway to the water. Finally there, she stopped, her breath coming fast and hard. The ocean called to her, but even for her sister's memory, she could go no further. The wind plucked at her bun, gouging one of the pins into the base of her skull. She didn't remove it, so the pain could orient her to what was real. Her eyes scanned the horizon and surrounding area for a young girl, which would prove Leviathan wasn't lying.

It was late afternoon, the sky darkening with each roll of the waves. They curled forward, one after the other, their frothy tips burbling as they propelled onto the wet sand. Then, a fuzzy blur of white approached on top of the surf.

Katherine's pulse pounded in her throat, making it difficult to swallow.

A blur of white light. A lantern—held by a shadowy figure that seemed to float on top of the water. A girl in a long-skirted dress with two layers of lace near the hem. The figure continued toward Katherine, her face still in shadows, but that dress...

She'd worn it until her younger sister decided she must have it. Father had forced her to pass it down. A cry slipped from Katherine's lips. The shadowy form stepped onto the sand and lifted the lantern to illuminate her face.

Oh my God.

Old emotions shuddered to the surface. Katherine's vision blurred with tears as her hands crept to her neck where her skin burned. "Mary?"

Her sister. The light brown hair, bright blue eyes, the dimpled chin and smooth skin. Another sob broke from Katherine's throat, but she couldn't move.

The water.

The waves lapped over Mary's feet. Climbed up her ankles and washed over her slim calves. Katherine broke into a cold sweat. Mary's lips quavered as she held out a hand. "Help me, Kitty."

"C-come onto dry land, Mary."

"I'm scared. I need you to make me whole again."

There was no way she could go into the water. She was already closer than she could hardly stand. "How is it possible you're here?"

"This is your chance to overcome your fear and save me."

God, her sweet voice. Katherine's legs shook. Her toes left grooves in the sand as she took one step and then another. *Can't...can't breathe.* Katherine's knees buckled, dropping her hands-down into the sand. She sucked air into her mouth, trying to focus on her sister through bleary vision. She held out her hand. "Mary, run to me!"

Mary's eyes widened as the waves crested higher. "Please, Kitty, I can't move! Don't let me drown!"

How the sun sparkled on the ocean! It was the most beautiful thing Katherine's eleven-year-old eyes had ever seen. The water felt like heaven, cool and alive against her skin as it push-pulled at her body and made strands of kelp dance in the surf.

Katherine giggled and yelled at her little sister, who watched worriedly from the blanket on the busy beach. She was always so timid when Mother and Father weren't around. "Come in, Mary, it feels amazing!"

Mary shook her head, the golden tips of her light brown hair shining in the sunlight. "They told us to stay on the beach until they come back. It's not safe. They'll be angry, especially Father," Mary yelled back.

"Balderdash! Look at these other kids. If it wasn't safe, their parents wouldn't let them do it. Besides, Father could never be angry at you."

A slash of something ugly swept through Katherine.

Lately, Father's words had been especially harsh. She could do no right, while Mary and their six-year-old brother Paul could do no wrong. "Don't be such a chicken, Mary! Mother and Father will be back soon. I'm sure Paul is fine."

He'd fallen off the merry-go-round at the park, out of sight behind the lined-up bathing machines that weren't used much anymore. Paul's wails had brought their parents running. Katherine glanced toward the park, but with the bathing machines in the way, she couldn't see her parents or Paul.

Katherine wondered if they would have made such haste had it been her cries.

When Mary finally gave in to Katherine's taunting, it happened so fast.

A rip current swept their feet out from under them, severing Katherine's grip on Mary's hand.

Katherine came up, gasping, gagging from all the salt water she'd swallowed.

Mary! Mary!

Don't let me drown! Kitty, help!

Katherine kicked her legs, her arms flailing to keep her head above the water. A chorus of screams sounded from the beach and from the panicked people in the water. A young man, his green eyes wide, his lips babbling incoherent words, grabbed her head and shoved her down, trying to climb her like a ladder. Pain, burning. Her lungs. Her eyes, open underwater, seeing blue and silver fish zoom and dart among the thrashing legs.

Then, brown strands of hair like silk ribbon. Mary! Katherine struggled to swim toward her sister's limp form, her chest ready to burst. Mary, please, please, please!

She grabbed her sister's lilac muslin dress and pushed off from the sandy bottom. She broke the surface of the water again, sputtering, pulling her sister by the hair so her face would crest the waves.

Don't give up.

But the water was so cold, and they were being forced so far from shore. Help!

Crying. She couldn't stop.

Swim parallel to the shore, Mother had said. But she couldn't swim and hold Mary.

Another wave. Water poured into her nose and open mouth. She let go of her sister's hair for a moment.

Her arms grew numb from the cold and exertion.

Her body...heavy.

She couldn't live if her sister died.

She reached again for Mary's dress, her fingers grasping the lacy hem. She gathered her sister's body to her as they both went under, floating down, face up, jostled by an unseen force, slow, like they had all the time in the world for drowning.

Silver fish. Sea kelp. Bubbles sparkling like the gems on Mother's fanciful ball gowns.

Savage sounds of the liquid underworld faded. A pregnant darkness wrapped around Katherine like the light dimming as her father closed the closet door as she sat huddled inside. Alone. Arms wrapped around her knees for hours.

All because she'd broken Mary's doll.

Echoes of her father's words...You're only here to protect Mary and Paul. Never leave her. No matter what.

No matter what.

Father had told her.

And so she didn't.

I'm sorry, *she thought as they sank further down into darkness.*

They were supposed to have died together.

Instead, Katherine had been thrust out of the rip current and washed ashore by the breakers, her dead sister tied to the sash on her dress.

The vision faded from her eyes. Katherine sat back on her haunches, then managed to stand despite her trembling. Mary was now waist-deep in the churning water. Katherine brought her hand to her mouth, then thrust it toward her sister. "Mary, *come!*"

She tried settling the water, but her mind was racing, too manic to control the waves. *What good is my element if I can't control it when I most need to?* Thunderclouds built and then flattened, glowing with jolts of electrical energy articulating her wild jumble of fear.

A loud wind roared over the water. Katherine staggered from the force, shielding her face with her hands as a new form rode a wave toward her.

Leviathan.

Katherine shook her head against a creeping fog that confused her Guardian energy and made it hard to concentrate on the demon walking the last few yards on the water. Leviathan held up her hands nonthreateningly, and Mary's form winked in and out like she was a superimposed image against the ocean's backdrop.

Katherine's eyes snapped fully open. "Oh God! No! What are you doing?"

Leviathan stopped, her hands coming up placatingly. "Shh.

I'm not here to hurt you or your sister, Guardian. I felt your pain. It drew me."

Suddenly Mary's form was gone. Not sucked under by the waves, just...

Gone.

Katherine's whole body shook. She tried to form words —*bring her back!*—but she couldn't get her voice to work. Leviathan pivoted slowly to stand a few feet from Katherine, looking out to sea.

"So, that was Mary's ghost. Your greatest tragedy. I'm so sorry, Katherine. I know you blame yourself, but you were only a child. Your parents never should have left you and Mary alone by the ocean. They should have taken you along when they hurried to attend to your brother."

Sweet words of redemption. How she longed to believe them.

You are an evil child. Mary would have never gone in the water without you. Now your mother can't function, and I don't know what to do. You will carry the shame of your sister's death your whole life. It's all your fault.

She should have died instead of Mary.

It would have made everyone happier. She could only imagine how much blacker her father's hatred would have been if she'd had the courage to tell him she'd pressured her sister to join her.

Katherine was hiding under her bed when the gunshots shattered the numbing silence of that big, sad house.

She flexed her fingers, overcome by the sharp memory of the dark crimson blood pooling on the hardwood floor. She gagged, remembering the rawness of her screams and the awful coppery scent of the blood welling past her palms as she covered her mother's bullet hole. She looked at her hands, now seeing Mary's pretty hair twisted in her fingers.

Her ears ringing with her sister's cries for help each time her head broke the surface of the waves.

Two memories colliding as she stared at her hands.

Hands responsible for not one, but three deaths. Sister, Mother, Father.

Paul was the only other one of the family who'd survived, Jade his beautiful legacy.

Katherine's arms dropped limply to her sides as she drove her torments back into the shadows in her mind. She returned her attention to the beautiful demon who was patiently waiting by the water's edge. "Did you make her?" Katherine whispered.

"The ghost?" Leviathan turned away from the ocean. "No, I don't waste my time with ghosts. But I can bring her back for real."

CHAPTER 21

Leviathan was lying. Playing on Katherine's deepest wound to create an artificial intimacy. "No one but God can resurrect humans."

Leviathan's eyes smiled. "Oh, but you're wrong, Guardian."

"Why would you do that for me?"

"We are different sides of the same coin. Reviled and abandoned by the ones who were supposed to love us unconditionally." Leviathan looked off into the low-slung gray clouds that pulsed with lightning, her face filled with pain.

"Most of the world never knew, but I was born a twin," she continued. "I had a brother. Your leader Alexios killed him long ago, but the misogynistic pricks in history decided to write me off instead, whispering stories of the great and wicked Leviathan—male. Always male. God forbid a woman be more powerful or cunning than a man. Neither of us have done anything wrong, but still our fathers took out their disappointments on us."

Don't trust her ploy to relate. Katherine took a deep breath. "Tell me more about Mary, or I'm leaving."

Leviathan regarded her quietly. "Mary's ghost appeared because your misery called to her. Just as it called to me." When she paused, Katherine's gaze returned to the water, not certain if she wanted to see the ghost again, or if she hoped it would never return.

"Together we can bring her back," Leviathan continued, "but it requires use of dark arts. You'd have to keep Ari far from here because he'd detect its power almost immediately since he's so fucking old."

Katherine didn't know much about dark arts other than they entailed surrendering yourself to Satan's influence. A ball of lead formed in her gut. "If Mary really came back, how long would she stay, how old would she be, and would she be...mentally stable?"

"She'd be as you saw her ghost just now—nine—her age at time of death. You'd be responsible for her until she became an adult."

Katherine's legs trembled and her pulse rose. The archdemon made it sound normal when it should be anything but. Was she supposed to sacrifice everything—her soul, even —to atone for Mary's death? "Would she remember everything?"

Leviathan folded her hands in front of her. "You wouldn't want her to, would you?"

No. But that would be dishonest and cowardly. Still... "Can you have her remember only the good parts?"

"Yes."

Do it.

"You didn't answer if her mind would be intact."

"There might be some...glitches, but I'm confident she'd be fine."

Glitches. That wasn't comforting. Ari's warnings filtered through her mind. "If I damn my soul by practicing dark arts to bring Mary back, what do you expect in return for helping me?"

Leviathan's eyes glowed silver. "I want a companion of my own."

CHAPTER 22

K atherine pressed her lips together, trying to hide her disquiet. Dark arts. A companion for Satan's daughter. Holy Hell.

It's time for you to show up, Grimm. Her eyes searched the horizon briefly before bringing her gaze back to Leviathan, who hovered calmly where the specter of Mary had been only moments before. She needed to stall until Ari could get here. "A companion of your own. What does that mean, exactly?"

"Someone with whom to share my life. Isn't that what every human desires?"

But you're not human, Katherine wanted to say. Instead, she folded her hands in front of her to stop them from shaking. "And this companion...you want it to be me."

Leviathan smiled, and the ocean calmed.

A shiver crept up Katherine's spine. "A true companion can't be forced. You *must* know that."

Leviathan's lips drew down, her blue eyes doing that silver thing again. "I don't have the luxury of time to build trust with you. I thought our instinctive connection would be enough for you to take a leap of faith. I'd hoped we could help each other grow. Help one another heal." She brushed at her eyes, and Katherine's heart nearly stopped.

Has a demon—much less, an archdemon—ever wept? Could a natural-born demon rise above her nature and environment? Humans did it all the time.

Sure, but always with tremendous struggle, came a voice inside. *You're exhausted. Why work so hard to get what you want when there's an easier way?*

Dark arts. Hadn't she already been riding that line for her entire, artificially long life? Her stomach rolled as a new sequence of memories assaulted her in slow motion. Highlights of her selfishness, her need for control, her quest for power. All of it, defensive weaponry she'd honed to awful perfection.

Katherine's stomach tumbled so viciously she sank to her knees and retched on the sand.

I'm sick. A hundred years of fighting to become invulnerable to abandonment, all for nothing.

Ari, I need you.

"It's time for you to choose, Guardian."

Katherine wiped her mouth and looked up at the archdemon, whose eyes gleamed with hope. She wanted to trust.

Leviathan held out her hand. "Will you take a leap of faith with me? Or will you continue to let others decide how our story should be written?"

Join with her. One who'd been born in evil through no choice of her own. Katherine sat back on her haunches, fighting the heaviness in her limbs, the white noise in her brain. "I am open to a journey of self-healing. I will even share that road with you, Leviathan, since God knows I need it, too." She gasped, struggling to hold the toxin's effects at bay. "But dark arts can play no part in self-healing—mine or yours."

Leviathan stood motionless. "So, you reject me?"

Katherine shook her head. "No, not you. Only the dark path. There's a difference."

"I am born of darkness. I see no difference."

"We are the sum of our choices," Katherine said, and a wall came down inside her, revealing another's presence, which cleared more of the Nephilim toxin from her mind. *Ari?*

Her heart was beating so fast. She rose slowly to her feet and took a step toward the water, which had begun to ebb and flow once more. "Life has been difficult for both of us, but good and evil are products of free will. We can choose to make life-affirming choices. And so far, you've demonstrated that you have the power to make good choices. All you need to do is keep making them." She held her breath as Leviathan stared at her.

"If I can't have you, I want Ari."

What? Katherine's gut clenched, her skin tingling painfully. Of every possible scenario, she hadn't expected this. She shivered. "He's not a doll to be fought over, Leviathan."

The demon raised her arms. The waves lengthened, and the sky filled with gauzy, charcoal clouds that pulsed with a deep red light. "I could've made you happy."

Katherine staggered back from the furious water, thunder ricocheting through her chest, filling her with dread. If Leviathan chose this moment to strike, she didn't stand a chance. Katherine looked down at her hands once more, this time envisioning Ari's strong fingers engulfing her own.

No matter what, there was always a choice to be made. Always a choice to love. To forgive. To do the right thing.

Until you were dead, you had a choice.

Her gaze wrenched back to the demon. "Leviathan, please listen. You can choose to be good. I believe in you."

Leviathan lowered her arms, her eyes alert, her body calm.

Katherine swallowed, taking a step toward the archdemon, her heart bumping against her rib cage.

Suddenly, the air molecules shifted as Ari and two other Guardians soared through the sky. Leviathan shouted an Enochian curse as the three ancient Guardians landed on the beach. Raj and Alexios flanked Ari, whose face was a mask of anger, his body covered in blood and sweat. "Katherine must learn—like the rest of us—how to make herself happy. You are no one's path to joy, demon." Ari opened his arms, marshaling high humidity and competing air masses to wind together with enough force to develop a low-pressure center.

Katherine raced to the edge of the ocean. "Wait! She's not entirely evil like the others."

Raj and Alexios raised their hands, thrusting power into Ari's typhoon before Leviathan's water shield was at full strength. The tearing winds ripped through her wall of water, enveloping her in a twirling, twisting mass of air and sea water.

"No! Please, give her a chance!" Katherine screamed. Ari grabbed her arm, adrenaline and violence pumping through him. Leviathan was wailing, but whether in fear, pain, or rage, Katherine couldn't tell. She tried to wrench herself from Ari's grasp, her gut somersaulting to feel the water swell over her ankles. "Give her time to make the right decision. She was on the cusp of it!"

Alexios's features seemed carved from stone as he turned to pin her with a fierce glare. "This has all been an elaborate ruse, Katherine. You are still under the influence of Nephilim toxin. Stand down. *Now.*"

Ari's gaze was nearly as aggressive as their Guardian leader's. "This will be over soon."

Her hands covered her mouth, her shoulders quaking with her sobs. "But this is wrong."

Wasn't it?

Katherine pressed her palms against her temples to quell the horrible sounds of battle. She watched, helpless, as it took three of the oldest Guardians in existence working together to control the archdemon. How was she so strong?

Katherine backpedaled from the turbulent water as Leviathan rose up in the tsunami and battled back the waves. The three Guardians were pushed back, blood dripping from their ears and noses. Katherine tested the mental pathway to the men's power chain until the razor-sharp pushback from the archdemon made her double over in pain. Raj bellowed ferociously, his black hair lighting on fire as he launched himself toward Leviathan.

But the archdemon disappeared with a shriek that felt as despondent as it was ominous. Suddenly the sea and skies calmed. Raj fell limply into the ocean as Alexios, Ari, and Katherine collapsed on the beach.

Katherine stared up at the still-swirling clouds, matted pieces of her hair whipping in her face. Pain rode every muscle in her being. Still, it wasn't nearly as sharp as the stabbing in her soul.

The lines had been drawn in the sand, and now she'd never know if she'd been right about the demon.

There could be no Mary.

No more choice.

And no more hope.

CHAPTER 23

A ri lay unmoving on the beach, catching his breath. The sun emerged from all those ominous clouds, baking his blood crusty all over his body. He'd been inside Kat's head as she'd relived her near-drowning while trying to save her sister.

Horrific.

He'd known about the tragedy, but never the particulars. It had been the one thing Kat had never shared with him.

Fuck.

Fuck, fuck, fucking *fuck*.

She'd been a little girl. In the long history of the world, what sibling hadn't engaged in silly taunts? Kat hadn't wanted any real harm to come to her sister. And then for her parents to blame her for her sister's death...

And then *their* deaths.

How could the universe allow something so awful to happen to a child? To carry that weight all her life was inconceivable.

A knot worked its way into his throat as he sat up and crawled over to Kat. When a broken sob choked out of her, he gathered her in his arms, pulling them both back onto the sand. He held her body on top of his as she feebly fought against him, the Nephilim poison in her body continuing to confuse her.

"What if I was right? Now I'll never know. Damn you, Grimm."

There was no heat to her accusation and no use arguing with her in this state. Until they found a way to clear the toxin inside her, she wouldn't be able to see things for what they were. He squeezed her in his arms and willed love and healing energy into her soul. He would give her everything, every last drop of his essence if he could. "I've got you, North. I'm here, and I'm not going anywhere."

She laid her head on his chest, her fingers relaxing on his shirt. "We should have given her more time. She might have chosen the right path," she whispered. Her submissive tone and behaviors increased his urgency to find a cure for this goddamn poison.

Ari sat up, pulling Kat with him as Alexios and Raj approached, battered and bloody. They looked as battle-weary as he felt. "Thank you. I never could've managed Leviathan on my own," he said.

Raj nodded, running a hand down his body, replacing his wet clothes with dry ones. "We got lucky. When she shows up again, we won't have an ambush advantage. I will watch over the Chains of St. Peter until you return to Aqua."

Alexios frowned at Kat, though she continued to stare at the sand. "Ari will fill you in on what we've learned. For now, take comfort in each other." When his gaze returned to Ari, the Viking could see his concern. "I'll see if Nate can spare Dorian to stand guard with Raj at the club. Make haste."

The two Guardians vanished in a geyser of sand that would've rained down on Ari and Kat if not for Ari's air manipulation. He lifted Kat to her feet. Her hands came around his midsection, sliding up his back, her palms cool and healing against his wounds.

"I don't know if I'm right about the demon...or if I'm losing my mind. I don't want to be like my father."

She'd reopened the gate to their telepathy. Relief poured through him that she was communicating with him, and that she was having moments of clarity. He leaned back, his hands grasping her upper arms. "You are nothing like your father, *elskan*. You are under the influence of Nephilim toxin, that is all. You will overcome. And I'll be by your side the whole way."

Storming in and controlling the situation was how he'd always done things.

And how he'd always messed up with her.

Then, when he didn't know how to fix things, he'd run, saying he had responsibilities to fulfill elsewhere.

It always left him empty.

No more.

He stared into her aqua-blue eyes. "Do you trust me?"

She nodded, *thank the Gods*. He exhaled heavily, the pressure in his chest easing.

"I do trust you. More than I trust myself at the moment. But I'm still angry. Angry about a lot of things."

He kissed her forehead, then took her cold hands in his own. "I know. That's fair. I've done many things I regret. I'm sorry for hurting you most of all. Before I was summoned to Inferno, I went to the ruins of my old village. There's not much there along the coast anymore, except crumbling blocks of stone and the voices of ghosts. I had to go back to my beginning to leave something there."

Her eyebrows furrowed. "What are you trying to say?"

"I buried my shield next to the bones of my baby sister who died when she was six. My father gave me that shield on my tenth birthday. With it, he said, 'A cowardly man thinks he will ever live, if warfare he avoids; but old age will give him no peace, though spears may spare him.' All these centuries, I thought I knew what he meant—never stop exploring, fighting, conquering. That was the Viking way. The path to honor. Anyone could see that those who never went raiding would perhaps live longer, but they would be haunted by their cowardice." He looked down at her hands resting in his own. "Now, I believe I've been thinking too narrowly." He smiled as he brought his gaze back to hers. "I think my father was trying to tell me that everything precious is worth fighting for. The bigger the risk, the greater the reward. And so today I buried my shield to lay to rest my old ideas. I want a life with you, North. More than anything—no matter how long we have together. I love you."

Her eyes darkened as he linked in with her emotion. Deep, beautiful, combative. There was also a touch of something dark he didn't recognize. *The toxin.*

He picked Kat up and carried her toward her lanai, then upstairs into her modern kitchen. He set her on a stool, then turned to her fridge.

After a moment, her fingernails started drumming on the quartz countertop. "We just had a near-death experience with an archdemon, I told you I think I'm going crazy, then you bared your heart, confessing your love, and now you expect me to eat?"

When he turned back, she was wiping her eyes.

"Are you laughing or crying?"

She picked up a decorative orb and threw it at him.

He caught the blown-glass piece of art, then brought out all the ingredients for steak sandwiches. He was almost too amped to eat, but they had arduous hours ahead, for which they needed replenishment of all sorts. "What? You expected me to take you to bed right away? I know you can't get enough of my body, but we actually have to eat sometimes."

She leaned her elbows on the counter, rubbing circles on her temples with her fingers. "What was Alexios talking about? What news do you have?"

He set a sandwich in front of her. "Does your head hurt?"

He could tell she was deciding if she should tell him or not. That meant it did.

"It's not bad. It's just...static. Makes it hard to concentrate."

Ari pressed his palms on the countertop to mitigate a rush of agitation. "Let me take you to bed for real now. Maybe that will help."

She raised an eyebrow. "No."

"Fine, then eat. We need to get back to Aqua as soon as possible to relieve Raj and Dorian."

She took a bite, and then another. He finished his sandwich in half the time she did, then went behind her to rub her shoulders. "You remember Pepper Jackson, one of Spencer's trusted humans at Inferno?" he asked.

"She's a strong psychic who can remotely view things, or something on that order."

"Yes. She can project herself anywhere in the world as long as she's already been there or has the exact coordinates."

"What about her?"

"Spencer tracked down one of Baal's lairs and sent the coordinates to Pepper. She was then able to project herself to the archdemon's location. She learned that the Nephilim are working with Baal to come after Leviathan after Inferno falls and they take Spencer's relic."

"Well, I suppose that's somehow helpful for Spencer to know, but I don't see how it helps us. Or how it means Leviathan is lying to me. I believe she was being honest with me about her feelings of abandonment. I mean..." She fiddled with a fork. "She knew what I was feeling because she'd felt it herself."

"I hardly think you can compare your situation with that of the Devil's daughter."

"But how do you know? Demons have souls, too, which means they can feel everything we do."

"Their souls are black, North. They may be able to feel emotion, but they have no remorse. They're not sorry, and they feel no guilt for their wrongdoing. That's why they're in Hell. I don't get why you're so conflicted about this. It's not complicated."

"But she didn't make the choice to go to Hell. She was born there. There's no free will in that."

"Maybe not, but now that she's been unleashed, she has the power to make good choices, but she's not making them."

Katherine threw up her hands. "I disagree! The only things I've seen her do are positive actions. She saved us from Siolazar, cast out a demon from a possessed man in the club, and several times now has turned the other cheek when we've been the aggressors."

Ari took a slow breath. He wasn't sure how exactly the toxin was affecting her judgment, so he wanted to proceed carefully. "All Guardians know the Nephilim and the Rephaim don't like each other, but they stay out of each other's way because their method of terrorizing humans differs. They have no reason to go to war with each other when there are so many humans ripe for the picking. So think about it. Why would the Nephilim help Baal take down the Rephaim, who are in league with Leviathan?"

She shrugged. "Maybe the Rephaim pissed the Nephilim off after all these years? I don't know, though, it seems unlikely since the Nephilim are so solitary."

She had it, but just wasn't seeing it. "The Rephaim are using Nephilim blood to poison Healer Guardians, right? To do that, they have to kill Nephilim. That doesn't exactly sit well with the Nephilim."

"Okay, but that doesn't mean Leviathan is involved. This could just be some civil war between the fallen angels."

He shook his head. "It doesn't add up. The Rephaim have nothing to gain by starting a war with the Nephilim. They also have nothing to gain by courting your attention because then you're up in their business. They'd rather fuck with as many people as they can while you're busy with demons in your club. Think about it, North. This is going down on your island; therefore, the end game of the Nephilim toxin is your defeat. The Rephaim wouldn't just decide to do this on their own. So why would they want to take you down? Or more specifically, who's higher up on the demon food chain *ordering them to take you down*, and why is that so important?"

Finally, understanding dawned on her face. "To take my relic."

He nodded slowly as she walked to the wall of windows overlooking the crystalline waters of the Pacific. Her deep sadness hung in the air between them. She'd really wanted to believe Leviathan had benevolent motives. Her desire to believe that the demon was a misunderstood creation reflected her own need to be represented that way.

He moved to stand behind her, loathe to disappoint her further. She sighed and turned to look up at him. "That could have been Leviathan's original plan, but I really feel like I was reaching her. Helping her see she could choose to walk a different path."

She was more of an optimist than she ever wanted anyone to know. He loved that about her, even more so because she tried to hide it. "It's the toxin, clouding your judgment."

He took her shoulders, holding her when she tried to wrest from his grasp. "No, don't get mad. Listen. If Leviathan could somehow miraculously rise above her evil nature, she wouldn't continue trying to poison us. And even if this was a rare war between two groups of fallen angels, the archdemons wouldn't get involved. Pepper heard Archdemon Baal and Maeprix, one of the older Nephilim, talk about skewering Leviathan for ordering the Rephaim to brutalize the Nephilim."

Ari hesitated momentarily, letting go of her shoulders. "And Baal wants Leviathan taken out of the equation because she stole something he'd recently 'acquired.'"

"Are you serious? A relic?" Kat sank down onto the edge of the windowsill.

Ari ran a hand through his hair, not wanting to expose her to this ugliness. Especially after that shit she'd relived on the beach.

"There's more. I can feel it in you. Just spit it out, Grimm."

"You remember meeting the Guardian Hector Alvarez?"

She held her breath, nodding slowly.

"A few weeks ago, Baal found Hector's compound, caught him by surprise, and tore him apart. Then he took possession of his relic." Ari started pacing, rage resurging at the loss of one of their own.

"Oh God, the Rod of Moses."

Ari nodded and forced himself to stand still. "You know how things have been quiet around here? You thought Leviathan wasn't like the other archdemons terrorizing your partners' nightclubs, but in fact she was plying you with lies while she orchestrated a coup of a different kind." He paused and let her fill in the blanks.

Her face paled. "Leviathan took the Rod of Moses from Baal."

CHAPTER 24

T otal nightmare.

Katherine gritted her teeth and took down her disheveled hair to repin it into a severe bun. If Leviathan was honestly trying to walk a different path than her evil family, she wouldn't need to collect holy items. Katherine had believed the demon was minding her own business and staying out of trouble, when in fact, she'd been marshaling the Rephaim army to do her dirty work and poison Healer Guardians with Nephilim blood.

As the offspring of the Dark One, her powers were already more fearsome than either the Rephaim or the Nephilim. But now she had the Rod of Moses. No wonder she controlled Siolazar so effortlessly. And no wonder her entire horde could walk about in broad daylight with such ease.

Katherine moved to the sofa and sank down into the soft cushions. Everything seemed hopeless. Like all their efforts were merely delaying the inevitable. She leaned forward, rested her elbows on her knees, and put her head in her hands. *Think, Katherine. Think.*

A fresh wave of static ran through her mind.

Ari's big booted feet came into her line of sight.

"Get up."

His voice held an undercurrent of steel. Katherine blinked at the jute rug, ignoring his boots.

"I said, get up."

Katherine dropped her hands with a loud sigh. "What do you want me to do? I'm trying to think of something, but really, do we have a chance? If Leviathan has a relic, how can we possibly defeat her?"

Ari pulled her up, frowning fiercely. "So you want to just give up now? Come on, North, give me some of that fire that makes me want to simultaneously tie you to a bed and pitch you into the deepest part of the ocean."

"I hate this. I didn't sign up for this."

"Yes, you did. Every one of us Guardians would have been sent to Hell, but when given the choice, we picked this existence. *You* picked this. Now Guardian-up, water woman."

He turned away and stormed to the door. He opened it and walked out without even looking back. He never did that.

She didn't like it.

She followed him down to the beach, her skin sparking, her body electrified by the friction between them and her proximity to the water's edge. He used his powers to strip away his boots, socks, and shirt. All that remained on his body was a pair of rolled-up white linen pants that he'd materialized to replace his jeans. They hung low on his hips, revealing the deep V of his obliques and the golden hairs trailing from his belly into the waistband of his pants.

Thank goodness he hadn't shave that off.

His shoulders and back muscles shifted as he proceeded to enter the ocean, the water pulling at his shins, then his knees.

She grew more light-headed the further out he went. She

spread her stance for balance and cupped her hands around her mouth. "W-what are you doing?" *Please come back.* "Leviathan could be out here." Probably was. Watching. Waiting. Biding her time to use the Rod of Moses to unleash a new holocaust.

And right now her Viking was up to his shaved, but still gorgeous, golden chest in ocean scariness. "Ari, please come out!"

He turned to face her and held out a hand.

Yeah, right. He had to be joking. No way in hell was she stepping foot in the water.

He knew that.

And that actually made her mad. Why would he do that to her? To make her feel even more like a coward?

She took a step back when the intense look on his face indicated he wasn't messing with her. Acid washed up her esophagus.

"Come. It's time to overcome your fear, North. I will die protecting you and the relic, but if something happens to me, you need to know how to control all aspects of your element as well as your fear. It's the only way to best Leviathan."

No.

No!

Can't.

Her hands grew cold, then warm, then started to shake. The shakiness spread to her thighs. *Going to throw up.*

Ari materialized by her side. She could feel the warmth of his body radiating toward her even though she knew the water was cold. He'd always been warm blooded. She loved that about him. Remembered all the times he'd shared his warmth with her. All the times he never minded her cold feet on his legs in bed.

She blinked up at him, lost in the past. Uncertain of why he was here now, and where they would go from here if they somehow managed to make it out of this alive. *I want him.* Wanted him even if it was in slivers of time. He would go, but he'd always come back.

And it would be enough.

"Don't make me do this," she whispered. "If you love me, you won't make me do this."

He began pulling the pins from her hair, dropping them into the sand. The wind whipped her hair into her eyes, and, heavens, it felt scary and exhilarating.

"I am making you do this *because* I love you."

He slid a warm palm into her hair, grasping her by the hip with his other hand, and brought her into the shelter of his body. His lips settled on hers, confident and soothing, arousing and calming all at once. His tongue rolled against hers, a slow dance mimicking their bodies last night as they'd slid against one another. Her hands climbed up his back, marveling anew at the warmth and velvet power of the muscles beneath his skin. The bulge in his pants pressed insistently against her pelvis. She moaned when his lips trailed hotly downward to press open-mouthed kisses where her shoulder met her neck.

He lifted one of her legs, pulling her hips tightly against his erection as he rocked into her softness. His blue eyes burned into hers when she lifted her lids. She brushed his blond hair out of his eyes. "Let's go back inside," she managed.

"You think to distract me from what needs to be done, but don't forget how on-task I can be when your safety is at sake."

She shook her head, feeling desperation rise up. "Ari, I— put me down."

"If you run, I will catch you."

She knew he would. "F-fine." *Bastard.*

When he set her feet on the sand, goose bumps broke out

across her arms. Her mind spun with possibilities on how to avoid the unthinkable. *Aquaphobia.* She hadn't been in the ocean—or any collective body of water, including a bath tub —since she was eleven years old.

That was in 1863.

Sweat rolled between her breasts, and sharp pains shot through her chest.

"I'd like to relieve Raj and Dorian before dark. Let's go, North. Dragging your feet like this gives your fear more teeth."

There was so much truth to that. Okay, okay.

Okay.

But then again, no.

"Can you carry me?" she squeaked, mortified at how weak she sounded.

The first smile since they'd come outside spread across his rugged face. "That would be cheating. You need to walk into the water of your own volition. But I'll hold your hand." He brushed another quick kiss against her mouth, then rubbed his thumb across her bottom lip before threading his fingers through hers. "I won't let go."

She nodded, then tore her gaze from his to stare at the curling ocean waves. Ari took one step. When she followed, he took another. And another. Soon they were standing on the wet lip of the sand, and it was all Katherine could do not to scream, to loosen some of the tremendous pressure in her chest. Her sweaty fingers twined death-grip-tight to Ari's, her other hand curling around their joined hands, her body turned toward his.

Maybe if she didn't look at the water...

They took another step, and the water lapped at her toes.

She hopped back, her heart pounding so hard it hurt. "Oh God, I can't!"

Ari let go of her hand to grip her head between his palms.

"Yes. You. Can. Water is your element. It's part of the very fabric of your existence. You can direct it. Control it. It's your gift. Your weapon, you hear me? Fuck this fear, you own the ocean! You *own* it."

She gritted her teeth and nodded rapidly. Don't think, don't think.

Dontthinkdontthinkdontthink...

She turned and reclaimed her Viking's fingers, looking out into the horizon as she did it.

Then she walked into the water.

She panted through parted lips as the ocean pulled and sucked at her shins.

The unfamiliar liquid strength of the waves pulled her off balance, but Ari was at her back, supporting her with his whole body. Something brushed against her feet, raising the hairs all over her skin.

"It's only debris," he said earnestly into her hair. "Sand, shells, plant material. You're doing perfect. You're so strong, North, I love you so much."

Tears welled up, sudden and hot. They scalded her cheeks as they fell. She turned around to face her *One and Only*—she knew that now—with the big scary ocean at her back. Trust, so hard to give—so awfully hard to yield—given.

Handed over to this one man, come what may. "I love you, too."

He groaned and wrapped her in his arms. Their lips met, hot, electric as the waves churned at her knees. She gasped against his lips and pulled back to look down, but he captured her chin, bringing her gaze back to his to smile into her eyes. "The water is translating your energy, North. You win."

Her lips quivered only slightly as they curled up. "We win."

He laughed freely and grabbed her hand. They waded in further to their hips. The water was...

Vast, mysterious, alarming...

"Breathtaking!" she telepathically gushed at him, unable to suppress her wonder.

"It is, isn't it? I love it when you're breathless." His eyes were hot, leaving her no question as to what he was fantasizing about. "Dip down a little for me, North. I want to see that white T-shirt get all wet, your nipples beckoning me to put my mouth on them, sucking... Whoa, fuck yeah, come here."

As he lunged for her, she released his fingers, laughing, and dove down into the water. The disorienting underwater echoes suddenly brought the panic back full force. Her eyes snapped opened. Her lips gaped in a scream, bringing a rush of salt water into her mouth. She flailed harder when something grabbed her from behind. Mary's face in the bubbles, raw terror clawing at her chest. Katherine struggled, sputtering and crying as her face broke the surface of the water, which had turned choppy, the skies a baleful gray.

"You're safe. You're in control, North. Command the water to calm. Do it. Do it now."

Ari. Ari's steady voice.

Water. She was in the water. Oh, God, the water was not steady.

But she was in Ari's arms. She shuddered and stopped struggling.

"Good. Now calm the water." Ari's heart beat against her back as he lowered her feet to the sand once more.

She searched for the quivering thread of power deep within and plucked at it. Began to knit it to her essence, weaving her Guardian elemental power with her soul. She dug her toes into the sand, burying them, feeling the ocean around her start to energize in a new and completely different way than she'd ever felt. Like it was gathering toward her.

Ari's laugh rang out. "That's it. I feel it! The water wants to please you."

The power built, heady and intoxicating. She raised her arms, and the water split, rising up twenty feet on either side of her and Ari where they stood on instantly dry sand. Ari whooped, clapping his hands. "You did it! You fucking did it, North!"

Katherine's heart swelled. She swung to kiss Ari, and in her peripheral vision saw a tsunami building a half mile away. Moving fast. "Ari!" She pointed, heart in her throat, and sent a surge of power to meet the turbulent mass of water. It shattered against the wave in a plume of spray, which gathered into a huge cloud. The sky darkened further, lightning flashed, and thunder concussed the sky like a giant shaking a box full of magnets.

And still the sea swell bore toward them.

And riding the crest of the waves...

Leviathan.

CHAPTER 25

Ari's mind spun with possible solutions. Leviathan had no doubt observed that Kat was overcoming her fear of the water, and was on the cusp of being able to exert the full force of her liquid powers. He was also sure Leviathan knew her time to sway Kat with lies was coming to an end. Which meant she would be more desperate.

And a desperate archdemon in possession of a holy relic was bad all the way around.

The best chance they probably had right now was to use relic against relic. Which would either turn out excellent, or it would be catastrophic. If they brought the Chains of St. Peter out of the sanctorum's reliquary and failed to beat Leviathan, the relic would fall into her keeping.

Ari stepped closer to Kat, but kept his eyes on the wave Leviathan rode. "Let's get back to Aqua."

"You want to retreat?"

The disbelief in her voice almost made him reconsider. "We need time to plan, plus I'm not sure what level of power an archdemon has when shot up with holy relic juice. Let's go."

"I don't want to bring more danger to my staff."

"For all we know, she already has the Rephaim beating down the doors while we're here."

Thankfully that was enough motivation to get her to stream with him to the nightclub. When they arrived, Jade was preparing more holy weapons while Maddox and Raj were patrolling the poolside terrace, the roof, and the sidewalk outside the entrance. Makoa and Stark were helping the priests with new exorcisms. The club didn't open for another hour, but human clubbers, mostly Waikiki tourists, were already lining up behind the velvet ropes, chatting animatedly about what an experience tonight promised to be.

Poor bastards. They had no idea how right they were. He hoped he'd be alive at the evening's end to wipe the minds of those whose survived.

Dorian, a rookie Guardian from Nate's club, was supervising Konani's etching of a new Devil's Trap in the ceiling plaster. Ari smiled and waved him over. As he made his way toward them, Kat grabbed a bottle of chrism oil off the back to the bar. "Alexios summoned an eternally promiscuous, teenage Guardian to look after my relic?"

Ari's gaze shot to Dorian before smiling. "Well, Raj is here, and he's almost as old as Alexios, so he has lots of Guardian babysitting experience. And on the bright side, if Dorian gets an STD, at least it won't kill him."

Kat pulled a box off a shelf. "I'm not worried about him."

Dorian wrinkled his nose at them. "Yo, I heard all that."

Ari leaned down to Katherine's ear. "If you need an outlet for your anxiety, beat up on me. Dorian's doing us a favor. Cut him some slack."

Kat pursed her lips momentarily. "I guess you're right." She raised a sassy eyebrow at Dorian. "Thanks for your assistance, *lad*."

Dorian's dark eyes twinkled back at her. "Hey lady, I can't

help it if I'm not as elderly as y'all. Wait, you want me to talk slower? How about louder? CAN. YOU. HEAR. ME. N—"

"That'll do, Dorian," Ari warned, watching to make sure Kat didn't do anything they'd both regret.

Dorian's broad shoulders shook with mirth as he raised a hand to high-five and bro-hug Ari. "Hey man, we're cool. I told y'all you had nothing to worry about. I know Lady K's crusty on the outside, soft and goo—"

Ari flushed a rapid pulse of air up Dorian's nose to put a stop to that incendiary comment. As Dorian wheezed and coughed, Ari slung a friendly arm over his shoulders. "Unlike a few of our snooty Guardian brethren, I don't mind a little youth in our ranks. You must have half a decade under your belt now, right?"

"Hell yeah, man. I'm no greenhorn anymore. I'm hoping Michael will be giving me my own relic to guard in a year or so. I've been building quite a badass rep among the incubus. Those fallen angels don't scare me at all."

"Too bad stupidity isn't painful," Kat muttered, moving off to converse with Stark, Makoa, and Father Angus near three dazed-looking humans they'd picked up off the streets. They must've been recently exorcised. Score three more for Team Good.

"I'll do the mind wipes. Just give me a sec," Ari told Kat telepathically.

She shook her head without bothering to look back at him. Fine, he'd let her do it without interfering, but he'd definitely be on watch to make sure she wasn't overtaxing herself. She needed to be as close to full strength as possible when the showdown came with Leviathan.

"Any Rephaim activity around here in the last couple of hours?" he asked Dorian.

"No. I almost wish they'd poked their heads around because I've been itching to try out my dragon-scroll dagger I bartered with Jinx for. That little ninja piece of ass drives a hard bargain."

Ari swatted him on the back of the head.

"Ow, what the hell, man?" The younger Guardian slid the dagger back into his waistband.

"If you think it's okay to call a woman a 'piece of ass' and have no fear of what fallen angels can do, you're a long way from being entrusted with your own relic. Besides that, you won't be alive much longer if Jinx hears you call her, or anyone else, something so disrespectful. Now, how many exorcisms has Father Angus performed since we left?"

"Eight. Raj mind-wiped two of them before he and Maddox went out to do another patrol of the perimeter. Of the six more that need to be done, three are on the floor there"—he pointed to where Kat was placing her hands on a young woman's forehead—"and the other three are sleeping in the employee lounge. Mind-wiping isn't my strong suit yet, but I got the Sandman powers down pat."

"I'll take care of the rest of the mind wipes. You head outside with Raj and Maddox, paying particular attention to the ocean side."

"I'm on it."

"Dorian."

The young Guardian swung back, his hand already on the door. "Yeah?"

"Fire's your element, right?"

"Damn straight. I light 'em up and burn those bitches down, Grimm."

Good. Elemental diversity for the coming fight would be important. He had air, Kat had water, and Raj possessed the rare ether power, like Alexios. Their various energies would work synergistically against Leviathan. *Hopefully it will be enough.*

Once he and Kat had wiped the remaining human minds

of what they'd experienced during their demonic possession and sent them home, Ari pulled her aside.

She spoke before he had a chance. "Why hasn't she come yet? She was obviously ready for a confrontation back at my house. And she had to know we'd come here because of the Chains. I don't understand what she's waiting for."

"She knew it would have this effect on you. Remember, she lives for manipulating people's emotions. The more rattled she can make you, the more your power diminishes."

"I can't take this waiting, plus we have to get the Rod of Moses back. Why don't we go after her?"

"And face her Rephaim army on their turf?"

Her shoulders sagged as she slid onto a barstool. "Well, what do you suggest?"

"How long will it take to unward the Chains?"

"The minute that relic comes out of the reliquary, it becomes vulnerable. Look what happened to the Rod of Moses."

"We're about to go toe-to-toe with an archdemon, North. We have to pull out all the stops because we only get one chance when this shit finally goes down. Right now, with you, me, Dorian, and Raj, we have all but the earth element represented. That's definitely in our favor, but consider the opposition. An archdemon alone is bad enough, but she has who knows how many Rephaim *and* a holy relic in her corner. I relish a challenge, but even I don't like those odds. Using the Chains of St. Peter would help balance the battle."

She ran a hand through her hair. He realized then that she'd kept it down after their time in the water. Maybe that's why her staff had been looking at her with an unusual amount of interest. He kissed her forehead and squeezed her shoulders. "Let's get this over with and get on with our lives. I want to adopt a house full of children with you."

"Oh Jesus, are you kidding me? I'd make a horrible mother. I own a nightclub. And we hunt demons."

"So we'll be unconventional parents—we'll teach them how to do it, too!"

The ground suddenly quaked with such force Kat tumbled into Ari. As they stumbled, they locked eyes.

She's here.

Screams poured into the building from the crowd gathered out front. Ari ran to open the door, letting the people flow inside to safety. "Earthq-q-quake! We c-can't be inside!" stammered a coed in five-inch platform heels, caught up in the massive current of bodies streaming into the club.

"Everyone's okay," Konani yelled over the melee. "Aqua's earthquake resistant!"

Ari wasn't worried about earthquakes either. And not just because Aqua's inner skeleton had extra steel bracing, giant rubber pads, and embedded hydraulic shock absorbers designed to withstand shifts in the earth's crust.

Leviathan's power was water-based, not land-based, so this land movement was probably about as severe as it was going to get. She didn't have the juice to cause significant damage using terra plates. What was troubling, however, was that she'd likely generated an underwater disturbance to create a—

"Tsunami!"

The Civil Defense sirens blared, and people screamed louder. Kat's hand pressed against Ari's back as she shouted orders to her staff to get everyone to the upper level, lock down the cement shutters, and sprinkle salt along the perimeter of the rooms. She grabbed his shirt in her fist. "Can you calm them down? They're safe from the elements in this cement bunker, but they're going to kill each other in their panic before the demons even get to them."

He raised both hands, palms outward, to emit a massive

pulse of energy to stimulate serene alpha brain waves in all the humans. Then he grabbed Katherine's wrist before she could spin away from him. "I don't want you out of my sight."

"That's not practical right now, Grimm. We have work to do. But first..." Her eyes blazed into his. "We need to find an unoccupied closet so we can bond, then we'll unward the Chains."

Whoa.

Had she really said what he thought he'd heard? He watched a flush creep up her neck.

She glared at him. "Do we have to light candles and be horizontal to make it official, or can we drop our pants, say a few sappy words and, presto, we're good to go?"

Ari put his hands on his head and pulled his hair to make sure he wasn't dreaming. She wanted to motherfucking bond.

"For chrissakes, North, you want to do this *now?*" He could hear and feel the wind howling outside, banging detritus against the side of the building. A wall of water traveling at four hundred miles an hour was bearing down on Waikiki, and she picked now to bond.

"It will give us extra mojo, won't it?"

"Well, yeah, but this isn't something you do just because you need an edge."

Something exceptionally large and metallic—a car maybe —slammed into the side of the building, raining plaster dust from the ceiling onto the floor. Stark ran to the Devil's Trap with a broom to make sure the circle of protection wasn't marred or covered.

"Can't think of a better reason to up my edge than when facing sudden annihilation," Kat cried.

She wanted to bond not because she wanted to finally join her everlasting soul with his, but because she wanted extra juice to fight Leviathan.

As much as he wished it would be for the right reason, he

couldn't deny the cold reality that they needed every advantage. He grabbed her arm and steered her toward the men's bathroom, trying to tamp down the racing of his pulse and the anger simmering in his veins at the way this was going down.

"I don't care what you have to do, but keep the demons the fuck out of here for five minutes," he barked at Dorian and Raj, not even waiting to see the looks on their faces as he shoved the bathroom door open.

Three people cowering in the stalls ran out after one glimpse of his face. When they exited the room, he flipped the lock and passed his hand over the door, adding a ward to keep unwelcome guests out.

"Ari, I—"

He unzipped her pants, pulled her jeans and thong down her body and hoisted her to the cold countertop. Everything inside him protested what was happening. But death was knocking on their door, and her protection as his bonded mate mattered more than her pleasure or whatever fantasies he'd had about this moment of their joining.

He wanted to give her languid whispers and, hell yes, candlelight. A long body massage followed by a sensual meal, then a bubble bath and roses.

Instead it was fluorescent lights and a goddamn quickie.

He couldn't even look at her as he unzipped his fly and brought his swollen erection to her softness.

It was over in less than sixty seconds. The sacred words exchanged in a place where people washed germ-filled hands and vomited excess alcohol.

They were well and truly mated now, but as he watched her fix her clothes and race from the room without looking back, he knew he'd never forget the tears rolling down her cheeks as he'd climaxed.

CHAPTER 26

Desperation could make even a cold heart do foolish things.

Katherine wiped the wetness from her cheeks, ignoring the people's cries to deliver them from something they instinctively knew was worse than their nightmares. Their fear clawed at her, but she had to shut them out to do this. The bonding energy she'd tapped into when she'd joined with Ari pulsed under her skin in every vein and sinew. *So much power.*

She didn't regret bonding with Ari. It was awful and beautiful and inevitable with the perfect mortifying rightness she'd imagined.

If only she hadn't hurt him.

Focus, Katherine. None of that would matter if Leviathan annihilated the island.

Get the Chains. Take her down. She could do this. *They* could do this.

As long as the Chains didn't kill her when she touched it and it sensed the remaining evil inside her.

It was a chance she had to take. If she didn't, thousands

could lose their lives. Their souls, even. That was worth the risk.

If she lived, she'd tell Ari how she really felt about him.

Katherine streamed to the sanctorum, her mind stumbling over the Latin words of the unwarding spell to unlock the door. When she finally got the words right, she looked over her shoulder and stumbled into the room, pulling the door closed behind her.

She looked around the room with its lovely, but eerie darkness—the low, tray ceiling, the expensive antiques, the imported floor tiles—all to honor a relic.

A loud boom her made her heart skip a beat and restart on a gallop. Had the first wave struck the building? Were the Rephaim here? Had Leviathan been able to breach the building's wards already?

Her throat squeezed. She breathed slowly through her mouth to calm the panic. She'd worked through that. Her Viking had showed her she could control her fear. Could control the very thing she feared. Water was hers to command. *Remember*.

She ran to the dark mahogany paneled walls and shoved the Louis XVI chair out of the way so hard the priceless antique splintered. She pressed the right series of raised panel moldings, trembling, whispering the words that would unlock the sanctorum's inner secrets.

The impenetrable wood slid away, revealing the ornate gold and glass reliquary containing the heavy iron chains. The chains that had shackled the Apostle Peter when he was jailed in Jerusalem. An angel had come, broken the iron bonds, and led him out of prison the night before his trial.

The entire room was lit from the glow of the relic, an unmistakable hum of power thrumming in the space. Katherine's stomach quavered as she lifted the massive gold cover of the container.

A fine sheet of perspiration coated her body as she set the lid on a velvet stand. Her hand shook, her fingers poised above the old iron shackles. If the Chains didn't kill her, Ari probably would for attempting this. *The greater the risk, the greater the reward.* She hoped his words would prove true.

She listened to the rush of her blood—and something else. A low reverb that made her shiver as it faded away into the darker hollows of her body. A bad taste rose in her mouth, black licorice and tar. Katherine gagged, shook her head, then inhaled and exhaled slowly. "You know what's inside me," she said aloud to the Chains. "Help me do what needs to be done to rid this island of evil."

She blew out one last shaky breath and wrapped her fingers around the Chains.

Dense and warm, they vibrated against her skin, mainlining healing energy straight to her Guardian life force. She stiffened suddenly, so filled with light there was nowhere for the toxin to hide. She dropped to her knees, hanging on to a section of the Chains in one hand, the back of a chair with the other as she vomited a black, oily soot that lit on fire and then disintegrated on contact with the Chains.

She shifted to plop down on the floor, waiting for her trembling to abate. She rubbed her hands on her arms as she closed her eyes and drew inward. Observing, probing. But there was no more static. No darkness hovering at the edges of her consciousness. No desire to appease the archdemon. No muscle weakness or fatigue. No defeatism.

Well, maybe a little of that, but that was all *her*. She came by her cynicism naturally.

She was cured.

No. More. Toxin.

She laughed more freely than she had since happier times so many years ago with Ari. Laughed until her belly hurt, and she realized she owed a debt to the relic.

She'd never held this, or any other relic, before. But as she stood and draped the Chains over her shoulders, she understood for the first time why they were so critical in the battle between good and evil. Could finally comprehend why the Guardians were created to protect not only humanity, but relics such as these.

They were a symbol of light overcoming darkness.

They offered hope in times when it seemed so out of reach.

They should be placed in public instead of hidden away in dark rooms—safe, yet available for all to see and benefit from.

Katherine chanted a canticle ward—the most powerful, yet risky, magical shield in a Guardian's arsenal. She sliced her palm with the small dagger she'd tucked into her blouse, using a few drops of her blood to metaphysically link the Chains to her body. If a demon wanted to take the relic, it would have to kill her to sever the relic's connection with her.

A soft squeak behind her made her spin toward the door. She froze when she saw the small figure standing in the doorway. "M-Mary?"

The girl held out her hand, then let it fall, tears gathering in her large, blue eyes and slipping down her pale cheeks. "Kitty."

Chills shot down Katherine's spine. Another of Leviathan's tricks. She could see it for what it was now. Thank heavens. How she could make Mary look so real? Katherine rushed to the apparition, expecting to be able to walk through it. But two feet from the ghost, the Chains burned Katherine's shoulders, halting her progress. What was this?

"Why didn't you help me? Don't you love me?" ghost Mary said.

An enormous knot settled in Katherine's throat. *Don't answer. She's not really here.* Mary had been an innocent child.

She was in Heaven with all the other children, animals, and good people who'd passed from this life to the next. If that was not the case, Katherine would give up right here, right now. Forsake all her duties and just say to hell with it all.

She attempted to open her pathway to Ari, but found only silence. Same when she tried to send out a general call to the other two Guardians in the building. The humidity climbed to uncomfortable levels, making sweat gather at her hairline. She swallowed hard and attempted to move forward once more, but the Chains burned her shoulders again, rooting her feet in place.

"Lay down those chains," the ghost pleaded. "Take me home so we can start over. I forgive you. Leviathan will, too, if you only ask."

It's not Mary. Her sister would've wanted to see the Chains, not tell her to put them down.

Katherine put a hand to her chest and looked around the room, searching for another way out. The screams and wailing outside the room likely meant the possessions had begun. She tried telepathy again, but couldn't reach anyone. All she registered was water smashing large objects against Aqua's exterior walls and...

The rush of fluid in the ghost's body.

Odd. A shade typically had only a small percentage of water contained in its form. She focused on the ghost's respiratory process to latch onto the water molecules in the body. *Sixty point three percent.* A water ratio compatible with a living human's.

Dark arts were being used to reanimate someone.

Sick laughter in the hallway. The Chains jostled on Katherine's shoulders, the edges of the iron slicing into her skin. Mary looked over her shoulder, her lips pulling back into a snarl.

That's not my sister. Katherine thrust her hands in front of her and closed her fists, savagely extracting water molecules from the ghost's membranes. Mary's form sagged to the floor, her skin shriveling, eye sockets sinking, chest rising and falling rapidly with the instant onset of extreme dehydration.

Mary's desiccated form shifted, lengthened, changed at the cellular level. The form congealing and curling up on the floor was...male. Before she could identify the new figure, the lips cracked as its mouth opened into a wide maw, spewing out red colloidal smoke that indicated archdemon.

The red cloud ejected from the desiccated body and circled behind Katherine. She spun, grasping the links of the Chains which hung down over her torso. The demon smoke swooped at her with a shriek so shrill her eardrums expanded and then collapsed with a rush of fluid and pain.

She swung a segment of the Chains, connecting with the tail end of the red cloud. The smoke sparked brilliantly, twinkling in a kaleidoscope of reds, yellows, and blues. The demon's pain-filled roar shook the walls, rending a crack in the door's head jamb as the cloud shot out of the room, gone, but not vanquished, even though it had touched the relic.

Because it was a red smoking mist, that had to have been Leviathan. Ordinary demons spewed black mist from their hosts. Also, they would have been destroyed on contact with the holy object much the same way the Nephilim toxin had been when she'd expelled it. She and the others thought contact with a holy relic would have the same effect on archdemons.

Apparently not.

Katherine's upper body sagged as she leaned her butt against the wall and resettled the Chains across her shoulders. Then she glanced down at the body on the floor. "Dorian, good God!"

She dropped to her knees, ripped open his button-down shirt, and put her hands on his bare chest, rehydrating his body with as many water molecules as she could sift from the room.

Seconds later, her gaze shot up to meet Siolazar's as he sauntered across the doorway.

"Bravo, Healer. I see you worked through your pathetic guilt tendencies to see through Leviathan's attempt to manipulate you. Even I have to admit, glamour-possessing a Guardian as your dead sister was a rather brilliant and intimidating show of dark arts, was it not?" Siolazar's cultured voice did not match his leathery, gray-striated skin and red eyes.

Katherine stood to position herself in front her dazed, but rehydrated and demon-free fellow Guardian. The Chains shook and rattled. With the mojo from the relic, she'd likely be on an even playing field with the fallen angel. The only problem was, she wasn't sure she could stream both the relic and Dorian from the room. Either the relic would make it easy, or it would be a huge power suck. And she only had one shot to get this right. "Let me pass from here, or I'll make sure you don't fare as well as Leviathan did against these Chains."

The Rephaim crossed his arms over his powerful chest and cocked his bald head with an indulgent smile. Her heart rate climbed higher. That he wasn't concerned about the Chains was a bad sign.

Unless he was bluffing.

"Aren't you curious about why I fucked with the Nephilim?"

Time for talking is over. In one swift motion, she lifted the Chains from her neck and swung one of the ends at Siolazar. The Rephaim ducked and let out a howl as his left ear melted from proximity to the iron. He thrust an arm out at Dorian, metaphysically pushing him across the floor till the young Guardian's back slammed against the far wall.

Dorian brought his hands to his neck, making choking gestures.

Katherine held the Chains in front of her body and sprinted to place herself in front of the energy stream suffocating Dorian. Her hair stood on end as sparks flew off the Chains, but Siolazar's hold broke. Dorian slumped down on the tiles, coughing violently.

"Leviathan is going to rip you apart, piece by piece, you stupid bitch. And after I consume your friend, I'm going to pick chunks of him from my teeth with slivers of your bones."

Time for Plan B.

Katherine focused her energy and tapped into the power of the Chains to initiate the epic demolecularization process required to stream her, Dorian, and the relic. *Please, please, please work!* Siolazar raised his arms in classic Rephaim pre-attack mode.

Light fixtures fell, and more plaster and wood paneling detached from the wall and ceiling as competing power sources swirled and exploded through the room. With no windows, the room plunged into darkness except for the light filtering from the hall. Backlit in the doorway, Siolazar suddenly dropped his arms and spun away from her. Then he demolecularized and vanished.

She heard it milliseconds later.

Water.

Hundreds of thousands of gallons of water.

Katherine cried out and clawed in the dark for Dorian, pulling his body into her arms as she made for the doorway. The water roared down the hall, bouncing foreign objects against the walls as it careened toward them.

No, no, no. It wasn't going to end like this. It couldn't.

Katherine struggled to hold Dorian and herself upright against the rush of water, taking huge gulps of air to forestall the panic that threatened to make her curl into a ball and just give up.

"Ari, please answer me!"

Where was he? Shouldn't their mind connection be stronger now that they'd bonded? She grasped Dorian tighter as the water rose to her hips. *Find the thread of power. Command the element.* She said it over and over in her mind. She'd done it earlier with Ari. She could do it again. Had to.

But she couldn't ignore the pull and suck of the salt water, up to her neck now. She tilted her neck back to keep her mouth and nose above it. She couldn't shut out the screams of the humans beyond the hallway. The horrible sounds rushed over her as furiously as the water. She tried to swim, but with Dorian and the Chains, it was too much weight to keep her afloat for long. And streaming them was out of the question now because that required a quiet, focused mind.

Her feet slipped when a dead body barreled into them. Her arms tightened reflexively around Dorian as they plunged beneath the surface. Opening her eyes, the water was cold and opaque with pollution from the tide rushing unnaturally over the wave breakers and city streets. She swam in a circle, blowing out the last of her air, suppressing her body's natural urge to inhale for life-sustaining oxygen.

A dead woman's hair caressed her face, and Katherine's mouth opened in a scream as her feet pushed off something soft. She broke the surface of the churning water, gasping. She kept one hand on Dorian, grabbing on to a sconce in the hallway with the other. She caught her breath, lungs on fire, arms and legs trembling.

Why wasn't Dorian coming around? She closed her eyes and clenched her teeth, begging the water to part. It vibrated and separated in a bizarre two-foot-long crevasse in front of her before crashing back together. Caught in the water's backflow, her fingers slipped off the sconce, and she and

Dorian were flushed backward and underwater, careening them toward the floor by the weight of the Chains.

North!

Her knees scraped on something sharp. Dorian's body floated up. Dead? Her fingers strained through the dirty water trying to recapture him.

Head foggy.

Need...air...

Hang on, North! It's coming.

It? The water was frigid, but her whole body burned with the need to inhale.

She clawed up toward the ceiling, seeking the narrow strip of open air when a bubble slammed into her, encircling her head. Her mouth opened on an aggressive inhale, bringing oxygen to her vital organs. Panting, her fingers curled under the ceiling tile seams as she moved forward, searching for Dorian.

There. She grabbed him, bringing his head into the large, artificial air bubble Ari had created. Then she concentrated on flushing the water from all the wrong places in his body. "Come on, breathe!" She rammed him up against the wall and compressed his chest. Dorian's body seized furiously, then he coughed until Katherine thought he'd spew out the lining of his esophagus.

By now there were only weak rays of dirty light slicing through the cold, swirling currents. Before long, the water would be too deep to escape, and Ari's artificial air bubble might not be enough to save them.

"She's going to kill everyone on the island." Dorian's thready voice made Katherine's heart stutter.

"Calm down, you're not helping."

"She was inside me, Lady K. We're not gonna make it. She's too strong."

Katherine shook him once more. "If I want your opinion,

I'll give it to you. Do you see these Chains around my neck? They are a holy weapon. We're as strong as she is. Do you understand?"

When he nodded, she swiveled in the water toward the dance floor, still clinging to the ceiling tiles with one hand. Swimming against the current would wear her powers down faster than she could recharge them, which would leave her seriously underpowered for her confrontation with Leviathan. *I need to think.*

First, she needed to part the water and get the hell out of here.

Yeah, right. She'd already tried that.

"I'm almost there, North. Calm your mind and use your element."

Katherine exhaled heavily, relieved to hear Ari come back online. *"Hurry. I don't know how."*

"Yes, you do. More innocent people are going to drown—right now—if we don't get this water under control. Focus. I'll keep feeding you fresh oxygen. You can do this."

She gritted her teeth and looked at Dorian. "When I release you, hang on to me so I can concentrate on getting us out of here."

He swam around behind her and placed his hands on her hips.

The air bubble around them quivered. *"Beware my wrath, rookie."*

Dorian's hands released her immediately, but Katherine replaced them. *"Survival mode here,"* she pushed on the frequency Ari used between the three of them.

She felt Ari move faster.

The water continued to surge into the hall, the powerful rush of the ocean consuming the entire building. Katherine grabbed onto a ceiling light, praying it would be enough to anchor her against the tremendous force of the water push-pulling against her, banking off the walls, and surging into any available space. Then she closed her eyes, trusting Ari's air bubble to keep her safe. She focused on the warmth of the ancient iron around her neck. Warm, it was surprisingly warm, in spite of water so cold it made her teeth chatter.

Saint Michael the Archangel, defend us in battle...

The Chains burned and hummed. Behind her closed eyelids, a soft blue light expanded. The sound of crows. Hundreds—thousands?—of them, cawing. The rough vibrations wrapped around her, energizing, comforting and mysterious. The blue light faded with the sound of wings taking flight. A moment of silence. Then,

A sky ablaze with the vivid poetry of twilight. Two men standing on the edge of a craggy cliff beyond a city's high, shadowy stone walls. The details were extraordinarily clear even though she stood below the men on a dusty plain halfway between the cliff and the city walls. One of the men—a bent, bearded man of advanced age —wore a long tunic, his feet in sandals, his ankles and wrists bloody, the lines of his face indicating struggle and exhaustion, but his eyes were filled with an unmistakable hope.

The taller one, young, unsmiling, dangerous. He, too, wore sandals, but a warrior's scarred greaves girded his shins. Something dark dangled from his grasp. He raised a powerful arm and opened his hand. Iron chains dropped from his fist, falling from their great height and shaking the ground far more than they ought when they hit, stirring up choking clouds of dust.

When the debris finally settled, the chains were at her feet. She shivered, glancing back up at the cliff. The soldier gave her a cold look before unfurling midnight black wings.

She fell to her knees beside the holy iron shackles that had imprisoned the Apostle.

"Rise, Guardian, and fight."

Katherine's eyelids flew open as the deep voice flowed around and through her consciousness.

Michael. The archangel stood before her, lit by the glowing Chains around her neck.

"You are humanity's first line of defense. Do not fail."

Michael's body filled the entire hallway, seemingly untouched by either the water or detritus. His blue eyes burned like the hottest part of a flame, his lips a cruel slash on his hard features. In his hand, he held the deceptively simple sword she imagined he'd used in his most epic task at the beginning of time.

He'd escorted Lucifer to Hell. And he'd released the apostle from these chains.

"Why did you let me see you and Peter on the cliff?"

He stared at her for another endless moment while she became conscious of every biological process in her body. Individual cells regenerating, electrical currents racing along her nerves, the rush of her blood through every chamber of her heart. Was the archangel creating this awareness? He was a strange, frightening being. Did he ever feel—authentically *feel*—anything?

She glared when he remained silent. "Well, are you going to help us, or stand there and watch us flounder?"

Michael raised his chin, bringing the sword in his fist to rest against his chest as though he were offering a pledge. "I let you see because love and hope are powers which darkness always underestimates. Unleash them, and you will overcome."

Then he was gone, and everything—the amplified underwater sounds, the push-drag of the frigid currents, the dead bodies floating grotesquely through the water, even the city's emergency sirens—everything came back online, loud and scarier than ever.

Katherine wanted to scream. Talk about vague. How was she supposed to "unleash love and hope"?

"Makes no damn sense, Michael!" When she didn't get a

reply from the archangel, she took a deep breath in Ari's bubble, trying to regroup. At least now she wasn't in the dark anymore, since the Chains shone as brightly as spotlights.

When Michael spoke of not failing, did he mean he knew that she wouldn't fail, as in a pre-knowing sort of thing? Or did it mean, she'd better not fail...or else?

All Guardians knew what the "or else" meant.

If they botched things up, the archangels would have to get involved. If that happened, Lucifer would be automatically released from his cage, and those horrific trumpets would blare, indicating the start of Armageddon. And as much as they despised their existence at times, none of the Guardians wanted to be responsible for the end of the world. They had way too much pride to let that happen.

Well, that, and they knew what fate awaited them if they were unsuccessful.

A tug at her waist. "Boss, can we get the fuck outta here?"

Clearly Michael hadn't let Dorian see him or hear their conversation, otherwise the young Guardian would've had questions. "Shush, I'm concentrating."

She continued pulling them along the ceiling tiles until she'd wedged herself and Dorian in the nook between the kitchen and the storage room. Then she shut everything down—the fear, the uncertainty, the guilt—to turn inward, touching the hot metal links around her neck.

Heat and a popping sensation—like little bubbles at the bottom of a pot right before it begins to boil—started to simmer in her solar plexus. She summoned that energy, pulling it through her vital organs, streaming it up her spinal cord, wrapping it around her heart, weaving it across her shoulders. Heat licked around the edges of her power, growing into a fiery dance that brought together points of conflagration that built inside her, more potent than anything she'd ever experienced. Katherine hurried away from the wall and jerked her hands in front of her, commanding the water to retreat before her.

A giant sucking sound erupted as the water frothed, barreling backward, out of the hall, beyond the dance floor, and out into the poolside terrace as though in a movie rewind.

"North, whoa!" Ari's strangled gasp told her exactly was happening.

She pushed her hands apart to force a channel through the water where Ari was making his way toward her. Dorian released her and abruptly sat down on the wood floor. She'd driven all the water from the building by the time Ari ran the rest of the way to her, his black T-shirt and jeans plastered to his body. His eyes widened, his body tensing when his gaze fastened to the Chains. "What the hell?" He quickly looked into her eyes, assessing. "I should give you an ass chewing for this risk. You're okay?"

She nodded as he curled down around her, his wet hair dripping on her face and neck. "The greater the risk, the greater the reward," she whispered.

"Touché," he whispered back. The Chains hummed between them—a low, comforting ring like from a Tibetan singing bowl. He pulled back to assess her one more time before his muscles finally relaxed and one side of his lips curled up. He stared at the still-humming relic. "I think it likes me."

She slapped his hands away. "Of course you do." But she was likewise pleased by the Chains' response to her soul mate. When she turned to survey her devastated club, her stomach dropped. She hurried to the first group of bodies lying in unnatural positions over the short wall that separated the first-row seating from the second. Three young women and two men, their whole lives before them.

I couldn't save them. Families would grieve.

A hand on her arm. She looked up through a blurry lens.

"I couldn't get here fast enough. I'm sorry, North. Siolazar proved more difficult than I'd hoped. We'll take the time to feel all of this later, but we don't have that luxury right now."

She brushed at her eyes and refocused on him, turning him around like he'd done to her. The back of his shirt was torn and bloody. "You're hurt."

He shrugged. "Already healing. Leviathan's outside. We have to do this now before she destroys the entire island. Are you ready?"

"Michael was here."

Ari's eyes sharpened. "I know. I felt him."

She wasn't surprised. "He doesn't do reassurance well."

Ari smiled grimly. "Sounds like him. What was his counsel?"

"To 'unleash the power of love and hope.' I have no idea what that means."

"You will when the time is right. Trust your gut and the angel. Let's roll. You, too, Dorian." He grabbed Katherine's hand, and together the three of them ran upstairs to the upper terrace where Stark, Jade, Konani, Makoa, Maddox, and Raj were keeping the clubbers corralled.

Up here the roar of the winds and crash of the waves against the building was much louder. Stronger. Shaking the foundations of the building so hard people reached out to grasp onto railings, countertops, and anything else that was cemented or bolted down. Father Angus mingled in the middle of everyone, his energetic singing voice weaving calm among the group.

From her position on top of the bar, Konani saw them first. She waved, jumped down, and ran toward them, talking a mile a minute. Katherine wanted to hug each member of the team, but was afraid to let them touch the Chains.

"Is that what I think it is?" Jade reached out to touch the relic, but Katherine put her hands up and moved back.

"Yes. But I can't let anyone touch them. It's fused to my body with a ward, and I don't know how it'll react. Sorry." The last word felt awkward on her tongue. She turned back to where Ari spoke in rapid undertones to the other two Guardians. Raj's eyes widened as he considered the relic around Katherine's neck, but made no move to touch or comment on it.

"Any possessions or demons in the near vicinity?" she asked. If so, they'd need to be exorcised ASAP, otherwise Leviathan would be able to exert some measure of control over them. What the hell was the archdemon up to, and where had she gone? Katherine felt like she'd lived a hundred lifetimes in the twenty minutes since Leviathan's colloidal form had exited Dorian's body and Siolazar had cornered her in the sanctorum.

"No demons up here. Father Angus finished the exorcisms with Stark's assistance, and we've safeguarded the area the best we can," Raj replied.

Katherine turned a startled look at Stark. He returned her gaze with a half-smile. Since he didn't look too worse for wear, she said nothing. "Nice work." She inhaled hard and walked away from everyone toward the door that led to her private quarters. She felt Ari at her back. She left her door open behind her when she walked into the library, going straight for the windows to look outside at the dark, wreckage-strewn water streaming over the grounds.

She removed her shoes and paused, raising her gaze to her Viking. Her heart was pounding. Never had she ever felt so responsible for the well-being of others.

Not even when her sister had drowned.

Ari walked to her and tried to take her hands.

She folded and then unfolded her arms, fighting not to

put up a wall like she always did. She finally placed her hands on his chest. His heartbeat was steady. "Is there anything that rattles you?"

He didn't say anything for a moment. "The thought of losing you. I love you, North."

"Even after everything I've done?"

"Your eyes are telling me everything I need to know right now."

She blinked fast, the urgency of the moment—what was inside her soul and what was outside these walls—making everything so raw and honest. Like she was finally waking up from a long dream. "You're too good for me. You always were. I'm sorry for the way we bonded earlier."

He shook his head. "I understood. We can talk about all this afterward, okay?"

Her pulse pounded furiously in her neck under the heavy Chains. She looked into his beautiful eyes, touched his face. "I need you to know something in case this goes bad."

A bone-chilling wail seeped through the walls. Out on the upper terrace, the humans began to scream. Ari's rough hands palmed her cheeks, bringing her gaze back to his. "We will make it. We *will*."

Her lips trembled, her soul wanting to hide. "But if we don't, you need to know you've always been my true north, too."

CHAPTER 27

The wind, the storm, the world with all its pressures, obligations, and ugliness faded away as Ari looked into Kat's teary eyes. "I don't need the words, North, but I love you for them anyway." Complex emotions pulsed inside her, ricocheting through their connection into his own system.

It was more than he ever imagined he'd be able to share with her.

Her gaze skipped to the windows that groaned from the battering elements, then quickly back at him. "You are the best thing that ever happened to me. I don't know why you love me. I've tried to push you away not because I don't love you back, but because I was always afraid I'd fall apart every time you need to leave to be whole."

"Oh, no, *elskan*, I—"

She pressed her fingers to his lips. "Let me finish. I want to face whatever comes next with a clear conscience and an unburdened heart." She clutched his hands to her chest, her face so uncharacteristically earnest his chest squeezed. "I love your restless soul. Your sense of adventure, your need to explore distant shores. It's so opposite of me, but I long to have your sense of freedom. I'd never, ever want to change that about you. These last few days, I've come to realize that I'll take you whenever you're here." She smiled slightly, though her eyes remained somber. "I think you would be too much to have underfoot all the time anyway."

He couldn't believe it. This was everything he'd ever wanted to hear from her, though she was definitely overstating his wanderlust. His extensive travels had been a means to fulfill his misunderstood promise to his father. And, after their breakup, a way to occupy his mind so he didn't go crazy thinking about her rejection.

She'd learn about all of that soon enough.

"Release the Chains into our joint care. Let me share your burden."

Kat paused. "It would put your life in jeopardy."

"If something happened to you, I wouldn't want to live anyway. Think of this as extra insurance for the Chains."

She nodded, then chanted a new canticle ward, including him in the Chain's protection. Now, even if they were separated from the relic, Leviathan would have to kill both of them in order to take it.

He reached for the relic when suddenly the air pressure deadened. A split second later, a gargantuan-sized cannon of water barreled into the window. He took Kat down to the floor as the balcony door shattered inward. The influx of water and glass ripped Kat from his grasp and stole his breath, somersaulting him until he slammed into the far wall. He reached outside himself to establish an air bubble and spun in a circle underwater, looking for the bright light of the Chains to find Kat.

Water continued to pour in, but Kat had managed to hold

the water back so she was dry. She didn't need his air bubble this time. And she still had the Chains around her shoulders. "That's my shield-maiden!"

She didn't smile. "Let's take this outside. I'm tired of this bitch."

He followed her out the window to stream to Aqua's rooftop. Up here the devastation Leviathan had unleashed on the city was even more apparent. Water had surged into the harbors, the debris of broken docks piled in drifts with ruined boats, uprooted trees, and the twisted metal of cars. All around, buildings were swollen with water, the ground floor damages especially extensive. Glass doors and windows were blown out, patio furniture wedged into their empty frames. The skies were dark and wet, but no lightning threaded through the moody clouds overhead.

"It doesn't seem like Leviathan can control the atmosphere. Just the water," he said.

Kat nodded. "Hopefully, she's not saving it as a secret ace in the hole. Do you see anyone who needs help?"

Ari looked around, then closed his eyes, going inward to try to sift through the noise to detect cries for help in a three-block area. He shook his head. "I can't detect anything close by. Only a wandering Nephilim and a few demons. Raj and I sent out pulses of mind control to direct people to emergency tsunami shelters. Hopefully there's enough room for everyone, and they'll stay put."

"Do you suppose Siolazar is with Leviathan? And what about other Rephaim? I'm sure she can control as many as she wants with the Rod of Moses."

He had no answers for her. He looked around at the crowded structures along the narrow strip of Waikiki Beach, then turned his gaze out to the massive waves still rolling miles out in the ocean. "All I know is, we have to stop this soon or the whole island will be underwater. Do you remember how we tried to fuse our elements together that time we faced a succubus at Spencer's club?"

"I don't want to remember. We tried and failed." Kat pointed to the left toward Diamond Head, the iconic natural monument rising 762 feet above the ocean. Water was crawling up the extinct volcanic crater in a freakish manner as though pulled upward by some unseen force. The hairs on the back of Ari's neck tingled. "She's got to be over there somewhere."

Kat rolled her shoulders, her knuckles whitening as she gripped the Chairs. "Why is she hanging back? She could have attacked when Siolazar had me cornered in the sanctorum."

"I wish I knew, but we're both stronger now than we were in San Francisco. Joining our elements will work this time."

She swung to look at him, her face tight. "I have the Chains. We can come at her from different angles. I don't want to try knitting our forces again."

He opened his mouth to argue. Then shut it. Her turf, her choice. Unless she was about to die. In that case, all bets were off. "Okay. But let me know if you change your mind. I hope you do."

"Fine." Kat turned back to Diamond Head. "Oh, shit."

Ari glanced over, and his gut dropped. The water wasn't scaling Diamond Head any more. "Get ready!"

The growing wave was the largest wall of water he'd ever seen. When it broke on shore, it rolled over buildings and streets, sweeping along everything but cement structures in its forceful wake. Katherine thrust her hands toward the water, pushing back the deep gray lip of the advancing edge, curling, churning and spraying the water in all directions as it found itself sandwiched between Kat and Leviathan's opposing forces.

Ari moved beside her and began to build and rotate low pressure in the atmosphere to try to get the water to evaporate, fueling energy for a cyclonic storm. Once he had the winds swirling, he recondensed the water into clouds and guided the mass in tune with the earth's rotation, flowing the heavy, wet air inward toward the axis of rotation. The Chains made it easier than it had ever been.

"Yes, that's brilliant," Kat yelled over the crush of the humid wind. "Do you want me to add to it?"

"No, it's a careful balance. Keep pushing the ocean back as hard as you can. Try to stop any more from coming inland. I'll gather the remaining inland water into the cyclone and send it out to sea."

She nodded.

"If this works it will only address the elemental portion of the problem. It won't take care of Leviathan," he said.

"Yes, but think of all the people we'll be protecting. We have to start somewhere."

She was right. And sometimes beginning was the hardest part of all.

The water shivered and frothed, violently churning against the competing directives. Palm trees bent and waved their fronds like a woman's hair streaming in the wind. The air vibrated seconds ahead of Leviathan's bellow of rage. The sound ran up Ari's spinal cord, chilling him from the inside out. He gritted his teeth and dug deep into the power of the Chains, his element, and his bond with Kat, rotating the low pressure counterclockwise even faster, building a second spiral.

He glanced over at his soul mate, his skin growing clammy at the strain on her face. How long could she hold Leviathan back?

"S-stop your damn worrying, Grimm. Viking up."

Ari smiled grimly as he shook the water out of his eyes.

He reached for the warm ambient air temperature in the center of the dual swirling masses, feeding its power and his own need to rage and fight. Screams of the Valkyries sounded in his mind as his blood circulated furiously through his body.

Skål, motherfuckers.

CHAPTER 28

Katherine's entire body was afire—her bones the kindling, her skin the accelerant. The Chains were melting her skin. Burning down past the multiple layers of dermis in excruciating waves of pain. Never had she deployed her strength so potently, jacked up like she was with both the Chains and Ari's bonding energy circulating in her system.

Leviathan suddenly appeared on the roof of the building next to Aqua, her body now clothed in a flowing white shift, her face unnervingly calm. Was the archdemon that confident in her ability to defeat them, or was it another tactic to throw the Guardians off-kilter?

Katherine closed her eyes and focused all her strength and the energy pulsing from the Chains to push the water back into the ocean. Ari had directed his twin cyclones off the surface of the water into the air, and was getting the swirling masses into position on either side of Leviathan. Still, Satan's daughter seemed unconcerned. Katherine's heart pounded so hard she felt almost light-headed.

"Dorian will stay with the others inside, but let's get Raj and drive her out to sea. We'll finish this there," Ari said.

It was the best way to minimize casualties. But the thought of going into the water with Leviathan...

Katherine shivered. "Don't let me lose the Chains."

"I'm right beside you, North."

A black-eyed demon in a black pinstripe suit was crawling up the side of Aqua. Katherine yelped as Ari unsheathed his sword and ran it through. More full-fledged demons began scaling the walls of the cement buildings around them. Ari commanded his cyclones to flank the structures, sucking the snarling demons into the swirling masses while Katherine unlatched the vial of holy water at her side. Adding holy water to the cyclones would further weaken the soulless bastards until a Guardian could properly kill them.

She fixated on the first spot she wanted to stream to in order to get the holy water into the the cyclones, but she couldn't move.

"I'm stuck!"

Ari frowned again, barely glancing her way. "What?"

"I can't stream. Here!" She lobed the holy water at him.

Leviathan materialized on the far side of Aqua's roof, just in time to intercept the bottle and knock it over the edge of the building.

"No!" Katherine yelled. The Chains smoked around her neck, impeding her view of the archdemon. Katherine's vision blurred, her legs wobbly from the unrelenting pain of the Chains.

And she'd lost sight of her enemy.

The archdemon's voice rang from all sides. "Aren't you tired of all this yet? If you had only chosen me, you would have none of this pain."

Katherine spun in a circle, enveloped completely now in thick, dark smoke, her superior senses unable to fixate on

Leviathan's position. "It's hard to rise above wretched beginnings, unfortunate circumstances, but I'm trying to do that," Katherine said. "I'd like to think you can do it, too."

"You'll fail, Guardian. Like you always have."

Katherine froze. The demon had said it like she knew something Katherine didn't.

"Don't let her play or distract you. Keep your force woven to the Chains." Ari's voice sounded more strained than she'd ever heard it.

"Are you okay? What's happening?"

She couldn't hear if he answered, but she could feel his force hooking into the smoke molecules, slowly pushing them apart.

"Give it time, and you fail at everything. This nightclub will fail, too. You know that even the sacrifice you made that transformed you into a Guardian turned out to be a failure, right?"

No. All sounds faded—the rush of the wind, the howls of the trapped demons in the cyclone, even Ari's voice reaching for her in her mind. Katherine held her breath, all her senses tuned into Leviathan.

The archdemon smiled as she advanced through the dissipating smoke. "Your sacrifice didn't actually save the woman you gave your life for, because she killed herself two days later."

Katherine shivered as sadness and shame bled through her. Taking the knife stab meant for that deranged man's wife had been the first truly decent thing she'd ever done. She couldn't stand the idea that it hadn't done any good, after all.

Ari landed beside Katherine, his eyes flashing blue fire. "That's a goddamn lie. Don't you dare listen to her, North. The woman you protected from her sadistic husband remained free and unharmed and went on to raise her children successfully. Was it easy for her? No, but she did it. And her children grew up and had babies of their own."

"How do you know?"

"I'll tell you how he knows, it's called 'controlling, misogynistic asshole,' that's what," Leviathan spat.

"I found her and looked after her for years, Kat. I couldn't let the woman you'd died for suffer or struggle too much," Ari said.

Katherine felt dizzy.

Maybe it was the Chains? *"Thank you for that, Grimm. Truly."*

Leviathan made a rude noise. "He wants to do nothing but control you, Katherine. He's doing it telepathically right now. I can feel it. He's coming between us, saying he wants what's best for you. Why are you letting him make that decision? He pillaged villages and captured thralls. He's a human trafficker. That is everything you and Susan B. Anthony worked so tirelessly to overcome."

Katherine clamped her hands over her ears. "Shut up! You know nothing of love or selflessness."

"I really wanted to befriend you, Guardian. But I've come to see you don't know the meaning of the word." Leviathan's eyes glimmered with unspent tears, her cheeks and neck blotchy red.

Katherine shook her head to forestall a wave of compassion. She'd known her own face had worn that stamp of despair many times when she'd shut herself up in her room. But now she understood that she'd been the only one responsible for her loneliness. She had alienated people because it was safer that way.

"You long for connection. I understand that. But your way of going about it is wrong. Leave this island and never come back."

"Believe it or not, I regret to say I can't do that."

Leviathan took a step toward her, her eyes on the Chains of St. Peter.

The hum of power inside Katherine dimmed a notch. Her fingers singed as they wrapped around the iron, her hair lifting from the twin cyclones that Ari moved closer to Leviathan.

Leviathan raised her hands, sucking water from far out in the ocean, then redirected it in one enormous rush at the cyclones, barreling them and the demons within them out to sea. Ari groaned as he tried to build new cyclones, but the air only swirled sluggishly. Kat struggled to pull the archdemon's waves off Ari's slow, twisting air mass, but she wasn't strong enough.

Leviathan strode toward them across the roof. Ari stepped in front of Kat, but she could feel his strength flagging. Her heart knocked against her rib cage. More black-eyed demons had begun to swarm up the sides of the buildings again, clinging to the cracked and pockmarked cement like insects. Screams from people inside Aqua were fewer and far between now. Katherine's gut turned to jelly.

Into the water, Kat. Now or never.

She knew. It was where her power was the strongest, and it was their only chance to defeat Leviathan.

Katherine didn't even take a breath before she attempted to demolecularlize again. This time it worked. She stopped at the bar and stuffed several vials of chrism oil in her pockets before streaming away from Aqua and reforming on top of the waves. She gagged as a rush of nausea ripped through her. "Ari!"

"Here. Above you."

She looked up to find him and Raj levitating. Another new trick. She hoped she lived as long as these two did to see what kinds of badassery her water element would develop.

"You are right where you belong." Ari's deep voice soothed. "You are of the water, North. Remember that."

Leviathan jumped off the building, her mass of brown fuzzy hair quivering, her white shift flapping violently in the wicked winds. She landed on top of a pile of rubble with a loud thud that rocked the buildings and made the water roil and foam. Then she strode down the devastated beach, the water parting in front of her as she moved toward the Guardians.

Katherine breathed slowly—in through her nose, out through her mouth—in an effort to remain calm as she found her balance on the waves. She concentrated on the thread of her power, feeling it warm and wrap more tightly around the power of the Chains. *"I want to heat the water, but I need less air pressure. Can you do that, Grimm?"*

"You got it. I can even do pockets of different pressures, just let me know where you want them."

Leviathan's eyes turned black, her hair lifting, writhing around her head like serpents. As she stalked closer, the water at Katherine's feet bucked harder though she tried to calm it. Clouds built, lightning threading through the darkened skies. Goose bumps broke out along Katherine's arms. *"Ari?"*

"It's me. Lightning will energize the water. Raj and I will protect you from it. Don't lose your focus. You do your part, we'll do ours. I've also sent out a call for Alexios and any available Guardians to help, but so far I haven't had any response."

Katherine sent out an SOS on the main Guardian frequency with the same negative results. No response. The pathway felt completely vacant. Had to be Leviathan.

"She's isolating us, isn't she?"

"I think so. But we have Dorian and Raj, North. We can do this, and we will."

"Would you stop with the positive affirmations? God." She

didn't want a freakin' pep rally. She wanted several other pissed-off, fighting Guardians to help them kick demon ass.

Stupid, damn, telepathy-blocking Leviathan!

Katherine created a small rippling wall of water in front of her to hide her actions from the Devil's daughter. She slipped two vials out of her pocket and pulled out the stoppers. Old words spilled quietly from her lips as she closed her eyes and slid one end of the Chains into the water beneath her feet to build heat.

As the last of the words were spoken, she poured the vials of chrism oil and holy water into the ocean. *"Now."*

Ari and Raj shot lightning into the streams of oil and water. As the blessed liquid hit the water, it sizzled at her feet, the temperature soaring, the voltage raising her hair, but not electrocuting her because of Ari and Raj's insulating powers.

"North, you need to move away from the heat."

"The Chains will protect me." If they didn't melt her alive first. *"Wait for my next signal."*

"I'm always waiting for you." His chuckle warmed her, but she still felt sick. *"She's closer than I want her to be to you,"* he sent.

"Just wait."

The water boiled, steam rising from the top so profusely she was forced to create a dry molecular field in front of her so she could see.

Leviathan paused and narrowed her eyes. "You think you're so smart. Three elementals working against me? You're still no match."

"As much pressure as you can possibly muster! Now, Grimm!"

Katherine bore down on the Chains and her element, bringing the walls of boiling holy water crashing down on Leviathan. The archdemon shot out of the water like a rocket, her screams merging with the booms of thunder from

Ari and Raj's storm, the glow of her melting skin blending with the lightning until, even with her enhanced vision, Katherine couldn't see her. Then the archdemon plunged down out of the sky into the water, blasting a dry crater in the ocean, which quickly filled in with a swirling backwash of red water.

The water under Katherine shook and rippled as though something was rising.

"Kat!"

In a single heartbeat, Ari poured images of himself as a child into her mind. Sitting around a fire, listening to old maritime warriors speak of Jörmungandr, the Midgard Serpent. The most grizzled of the Vikings warned young Ari that when the Serpent released its tail, Gods would die.

No.

Ari grabbed her armpits and streamed toward the low-slung clouds as a giant mouth filled with three layers of razor-sharp teeth breached the surface where Katherine had stood. *Leviathan!*

The monster's brown leathery tongue shot up, wrapping around Katherine's ankle. She screamed, sweat running down her face, her shoulder sockets rending apart between Ari and the monster's tug of war.

Ari shifted his hold, wrapping one arm around her body while both he and Raj hacked at the Leviathan's tongue with their swords. The pain in Katherine's ankle made her vision blur. She gasped and tried to look down. Jesus, the monster dangling above the water, hanging by her tongue. "Let go, Ari! You can't hold us both like this!"

"I'll never let you go!" Ari yelled hoarsely as his sword slammed into Leviathan's tongue. It bounced off as though it were a toy weapon. Lightning forked down, slamming into Leviathan's massive, gray, dragon-like body. The monster shrieked, her clawed, webbed feet pawing the air. Ari hacked, again and again, but his sword didn't so much as nick the beast's tongue.

And his power was draining at a rapid rate.

Raj shot downward, driving his sword hilt-deep into the crease where one of Leviathan's legs met her underbelly. The monster roared, her long, sharp claws swinging wildly, the last swipe impaling Raj through the chest. She flung him across the super-charged air to crash into the water where he sank insensate into the stormy depths.

"Raj!" Kat screamed, uncontrollable tears flooding her eyes.

"You fucking bitch!" Ari yelled, sending an air bubble down into the water after Raj and striking at the archdemon's eyes like an out of control berserker.

A sudden crush of pain made Kat gasp back a flood of bile and look down. Streaks of black climbed up her ankle. She looked ashore to Aqua where demons were beating at the wooden shutters with broken pieces of patio furniture.

God, no. *No!* She was *not* losing to this monster.

"Ari!" She stared into his wild eyes. "Cut me. Cut off my lower leg. You have to do it!"

"Not happening!" He bellowed, veins standing out in his forehead as his sword came down so hard on the tongue that Katherine screamed at the piercing reverb. All three of them began slipping toward the water. Leviathan thrashed harder.

"I'll heal! Do it!" Katherine pleaded.

The clouds swirled and clashed, translating Ari's fury. Rain and hail pelted them. "I can't, North. I *can't* hurt you."

"She's killing me. You have to, it's the only way. Hurry, before your power runs out!"

"Fuck, I'm so sorry, baby. I'm—"

Her body seized.

PAIN.

White-hot and breath-robbing, it seared up her body like

she was dropped feet-first into a fully stoked cremation furnace.

Then...

Blessed cool.

Her eyes closed. Then snapped open. Another shriek from Leviathan, a colossal splash below.

Skin, cold. Head, woozy. Body, lighter. Less pain.

She tried to focus her blurry vison. *Above the clouds?*

They were rising.

Ari groaned low, the sound lighting an urgency inside her.

She twisted in his hold, blinking, squinting. His face was contorted in agony. She put her hands on his cheeks, feeling the echoes of pain he'd taken from her.

"Damn you, Viking!"

His eyes cracked open to reveal crimson irises. She sent her healing element inside him to pull some of the pain back into her body. She gasped, but it was manageable now since he'd mitigated most of it, and she'd already started to heal. He peeled her hands from his face. "Don't."

"Stop the heroics. We'll share it. We both need to be functional to get Raj and finish this." She let Ari into her mind as she probed the water with her element for any sign of the ether Guardian.

Nothing.

Ari sent an emergency call to Alexios, but he didn't answer.

"If she killed him, I swear to God, North—"

"He's ancient and strong and your air will help him breathe as he heals. We have to believe that. But right now, let's fuse our elements."

Ari's thunder rumbled inside her chest. "There's no going back from this," he warned. "Once you share your element with me, I'll always be inside you."

She looked into his haggard face and saw the love and acceptance she'd always craved. "I want that."

Her arms jolted out to the side as the full, euphoric impact of Ari's life force joined with her own. An exploding kaleidoscope of colors that was there, then gone, leaving behind a new level of dynamism in the Chains that still hung around her neck.

Below them, Leviathan's scaly gray body swam in a rapid circle just beneath the surface of the churning water, healing, rejuvenating her power. The current swirled, a huge dimple growing in its center.

A massive whirlpool.

Ari thrust a hand into her hair at the nape of her neck and brushed a rough kiss against her lips before she slipped from his warm embrace and dove. She plunged into the whirlpool's center, the howling of the wind deadening as she sank through the murky water. Instead, she heard the archdemon's piercing underwater vocalizations, driving away all forms of marine life.

Katherine blinked, resisting the urge to wrap her arms around herself and cry. Her remaining foot touched the sandy ocean bottom, and she used her love and trust in Ari to close the door on the fear that beat in the back of her brain.

Her vision shifted, brightening. Objects came into focus. Shadows lightened and swayed from the rush of water pulling at her.

I am of water.

The aqua element surged in her chest, more powerful this time as it was knit with Ari's corresponding air element. Her heart pounded. She opened her mouth.

No water entered.

"North. She senses you. At my signal, clear the water and make haste to safety."

Leviathan was building a watery grave for her. But she

could do this. For Mary. For Ari. For Raj and all the Guardians who worked so hard for their second chance.

For the human lives they all protected.

The boiling holy water hadn't worked. This had to. *I am of water.* Her hands curled into fists, her foot shooting with phantom pains as it regrew. She inhaled and exhaled. Again and again before she allowed herself to believe she could actually breathe underwater.

"Now, North!"

Katherine spun supernaturally fast, forcing the waves to reel back at her command. The water retreated in a booming, frothing roll, leaving a circle of dry sand a quarter-mile diameter wide. Leviathan's monstrous form surged through the edge of the retreating water, landing in a mighty thud against the dry sea floor where crabs scurried and colorful fish flopped amid coral and waterlogged seaweed.

Katherine streamed back to the safety of the water and sent every last thread of her remaining power pouring into the archdemon's form and found...

Sadness. Loneliness.

Despair.

An echoing eternity of it. All of the things the archangel had seen inside her own soul.

Tears swelled in Katherine's eyes, then blended with the ocean. Leviathan rolled and crouched on her hindquarters, her black eyes intent, everything about her seeming to wait for annihilation at Katherine's hand.

Then she shifted back to her human form and hung her head, her long frizzy hair a halo concealing her face.

What the hell?

The archdemon's form flickered in and out.

"Don't let her leave!" Ari's voice barreled through her mind.

"I don't know how to make her stay!"

"Use the Chains!"

Katherine reached up to wrap her hands around the Chains that had bound St. Peter, but before her fingers could grasp the ancient iron, Mary stood beside Leviathan on the dry sand.

"Mary?" Katherine gasped, blinking back more tears.

"Kitty." Mary's sweet voice was as clear as the sunny morning when their world had fallen apart. "People hurt others because their own souls weep."

"I know, sister." For decades Katherine had cultivated an icy front to keep people at a distance. If she had no close attachments, there would be no guilt, no chance of pain.

But oh, the loneliness.

She'd even kept Jade at arm's length as hard as she'd tried to worm her way in. But Katherine had ended up hurting herself most of all because she'd missed out on so much.

"I can't destroy her, Grimm."

Ari's warmth stroked through her mind. *"Mary's not really here. She's beyond the reach of demons. You know that, North. Leviathan's reflecting your feelings to create sympathy. She's using your humanity to try to defeat you because she finally realizes she underestimated you."*

Her heart was beating so fast in her chest. *"What if you're wrong?"*

"Look inside yourself and see if what she's projecting is more about you than it is her."

Katherine stared into Mary's dark eyes, so like their mother's, waiting for a spark of connection.

Waited as the water around her pulsed with Leviathan's dark energy.

Waited for warmth or humanity.

Nothing.

The moment Katherine's hands curled around the Chains, Mary's form winked out. Leviathan shifted into the scaled monster once more. Her long, forked tail twitched, sending a volley of sand hurtling through the wall of water, pelting Katherine like stinging buckshot.

Katherine pulled energy from the Chains, sending out her element to bind with the liquid molecules in Leviathan's form. Katherine's body shook, the rattling of the Chains magnified underwater as her power worked to dehydrate every last ounce of moisture in the archdemon's body.

Leviathan bucked and screamed as Ari drove away the clouds so the sun's potent rays could wreak more devastation. The archdemon's body smoked and her skin began to desiccate. Her claws gouged giant furrows in the sand as she snorted and pawed her way to the boundary between sand and water where Katherine stood.

"I can't hold the water off of her for much longer."

"Okay. Raise your protection shield."

"I don't know if I have enough energy. I can't divert it from Leviathan."

"You have to. Do it now!"

Suddenly, the pressure changed. The water condensed around her, leaden, cold, and unimaginably heavy as though she were two miles below the surface instead of thirty feet. *Hard to breathe.* She dropped to her hands and knees. She ground her teeth together and diverted a portion of her element to insulate herself, and the crushing pressure lifted. She looked over, gaping as russet-colored powder puffed out of Leviathan's scaled nostrils and mouth. She was lying on her side on the sand, jerking unnaturally, the once-shiny scales of her body now shriveled and dull.

But in her defeat...a thread of humanity. The archdemon's eyes, sorrowful.

Katherine raised a hand toward her, but the creature didn't even have the strength to cry out as Ari continued to apply a massive amount of pressure to her form, crushing her withered internal organs into dust.

Soon there was nothing left but a pile of coppery soot. A great rumble shook the earth as a crevasse opened in the ocean floor, swallowing the archdemon dust.

Katherine stood up slowly, shakily, and stepped from the water onto the dry patch she'd created. She looked up to see Ari fall like an angel from the sky.

CHAPTER 29

A ri shot out of bed, his beloved Ulfbehrt sword already in hand by the time the footsteps halted outside Kat's door. He strode naked across Kat's Aqua bedroom as three powerful raps shook the wood doorframe. He glanced back to see Kat scoot up, her blonde hair tousled, her sea-green eyes soft, and those breasts...

He sucked in a rough breath and put a finger to his lips with a look he hoped was one part 'don't worry' and twelve parts 'don't you dare leave that bed.'

"I hear you two breathing in there, mate. The sooner you open the bloody door, the sooner you can resume your celebratory, demon-ass-kicking fuck-fest. Come on now, don't make me pull a Spencer and go the full monty on this door."

Nate Temple, owner of the Minneapolis club, Mirage.

Ari almost laughed out loud when he heard a slap, then a muffled "ow" from the other side of the door.

"There's a female heartbeat out there. Get some clothes on your relentless body, Viking, or somebody's gonna get hurt." Kat slipped into the itty-bitty satin robe he'd relished peeling off her last night. At the moment, however, he wasn't too keen on her wearing it in front of another male, even if said Guardian was already bonded.

"Relentless, huh? I'll show you relentless." He lunged for her. She squealed and snatched a towel from the back of the chair, snapping it across his pecs so hard it left a mark.

"You're going to pay for that."

"Gladly."

Saucy. He growled to hide a smile, cinching the towel around his hips before opening the door.

Nate had an arm around the shoulders of his bonded mate, Jessie Blaze. He moved a half step back, smoothing the feathers of her long white wings so they wouldn't touch the doorjamb as the angel entered the room.

"Thank God the mighty Viking listens to you, Katherine." Nate winked at his Unholy Inc partner. "My eyes couldn't have handled him starkers this early in the morning."

"Get on with it, English. And it better not be bad news."

Jessie's lips curved at Katherine. "I'm sorry to bother you so early and indelicately with my Neanderthal in tow. But as soon as Raj recovered and filled us in on your battle against Leviathan yesterday, we had to come. Well done, you two." She approached Katherine, arms outstretched.

Ari watched the shifting play of emotions on Kat's face as she fought against her inclination to shun physical contact, to ward off intimacy. It all happened in the blink of an eye, but he saw her triumph over the artificial walls she'd kept up for so long. Kat wrapped her arms gently around Jessie's wings and closed her eyes, feeling the embrace so thoroughly that Ari felt its echoes through their soul bond.

"I love you, North."

Katherine opened misty eyes and blew him a kiss before pulling back from Jessie to smile warmly. "Welcome to what's left of Aqua."

"I wish we could stay to help clean up, but unfortunately,

we have to hustle to San Francisco," Nate said. "Spencer's maxed out with Baal still raising hell at Inferno."

"When you get there, let us know if you need some extra hands. My staff is competent enough to handle the cleanup." Katherine crossed her arms under her breasts, drawing Ari's undivided attention until fingers snapped in front of his face.

"Up here, Grimm." Katherine pointed to her amused eyes, then glanced at Jessie. "Looks like you're not the only one cavorting with a caveman today."

Ari advanced on her purposefully, unable to resist touching her for another moment. Countless times yesterday he wondered if he'd ever have the chance to hold her in his arms again. Because of that, last night, not one hour had passed without feeling her skin next to his.

It was healing for both of them.

He pulled her against his side. "You wouldn't want me any other way."

Nate smirked at Jessie. "What he said."

They all laughed.

"We'll let you know if things deteriorate further at Inferno. What we're more concerned about is Alexios," Nate said quietly.

A bad feeling settled in Ari's gut, remembering how Alexios looked on the beach the first day he'd arrived on O'ahu.

Katherine had gone completely still. "What's wrong with him?"

"He's been increasingly absent from Rapture, and when he is at his club, he's...volatile," Jessie responded. The unflappable Guardian leader had always been their rock. If something rattled the Spartan, it was truly cause for concern.

"I don't think he's located Sophia yet," Ari said. "The only other time I've seen him this unstable was when he couldn't find her in the sixteenth century."

"Is he sure she's even reincarnated in current times?" Kat asked.

Nate nodded. "In each of Sophia's reincarnations, Alexios feels when her presence enters the ether. He knows she exists somewhere on the planet, but he can't locate her until she's in danger. Jawahar thinks the difference this time is that Alexios feels her need of him, but can't find her." As Rapture's head of security and Alexios' closest friend, Jawahar Bajwa would be the one to know.

Ari pulled Katherine to his side. "That would drive anyone mad."

"But especially the oldest of the Guardians," Jessie added.

"At various times over the centuries, I've had concerns about how he was able to go on. Having to lose your soul mate over and over like that. To watch her die, not knowing where or when you'd see her again..." Ari trailed off, and the four of them remained silent for a moment.

"What can we do to help?" Kat asked.

"When you have things squared away here, you might want to check in at Rapture. Jaws is completely capable, but your help was invaluable to me at Mirage. There's really nothing we can do to help Alexios find Sophia, but helping out at his club would let him focus on her recovery." Nate smiled and squeezed Jessie. "We should probably leave now to let these two return to their slap and tickle. Unless you want to grab a room of our own—"

Jessie open-mouth kissed him, then shoved him back with a smile. She turned to Kat. "I want to apologize for calling you stuck up and sexually repressed that first day we met."

Kat raised an eyebrow. "Do you now?"

Jessie's smile slipped and a furrow appeared between Nate's brows.

Apparently, Kat's haughty expression was only transparent to Ari. He tried not to laugh. After all their time together at

Mirage, Nate should be able to tell Kat was fronting. *"You're being mean,"* Ari said on their intimate connection.

"Do you really expect me to change overnight? I have decades of bitchiness to beat back, you know."

Her blue eyes blinked up at him as he approached. *"Excuses, excuses. You expect me to believe you aren't strong enough to overcome things you yourself want to change?"*

Too late she realized his intentions. He bent down and pulled her over his shoulder, her mouthwatering ass next to his face. He kept his back to Nate and Jessie so they wouldn't see her nether regions exposed under the flimsy robe. *"In case you'd forgotten, accepting an apology is one of the cornerstones of friendship, North."*

The pads of her fingers played over the muscles of his lower back, dipping beneath the edge of the towel. He closed his eyes to focus on the lesson, but his body had other ideas. Her leg shifted slowly, deliberately, across the bulge in the front of the towel, making him cross-eyed.

"Oops," she whispered throatily, then pushed laughter into his mind.

His fingernails dug into the backs of her thighs to hold her still while he angled his body to the side to address their guests. "My apologies. It seems my mate is more interested in corporal punishment than graciously accepting an olive branch. I will deal with her accor—"

"Oh, stop. Really, Grimm, this responsible, 'teach Katherine how to be nice' side of yours can be so annoying." Katherine paused, then added telepathically, *"Put me down. Now."*

When he did—carefully so as not to expose her bits and his own—she took Jessie's hands in her own with a secret little smile that Ari didn't quite trust. "Look, I'm no an angel. I never will be. I've pretty much deserved everything I've been doled out. So, I'm grateful for your apology. I give you mine as well, even though I'm damned jealous of those gorgeous wings."

Jessie laughed and pulled her into a hug. Ari caught Kat's brief surprise before she hugged her back. "Then all's forgotten."

Kat wasn't the first to pull away. That, more than all her words, made Ari realize she was truly opening her heart. He rubbed at the sudden warmth in his chest as Nate and Jessie bade their goodbyes.

Kat closed the door behind them, then leaned back against it for a moment. His feet felt rooted to the middle of the floor as he looked at her.

She cinched her robe tighter as the tropical sunlight slanted through the windows and struck her golden hair. "What are you staring at?"

"You have no idea how long I've wanted to bond with you."

She moved away from the door. His heart rate accelerated as she moved toward him. "You are a persistent man, I'll give you that." Her lips curved softly.

Her smile made him happy. "I will never give up on you. Don't ever forget that." His skin warmed every place her gaze strayed—his lips, neck, shoulders, chest...

"You're pretty hard to forget." Her lips quirked as her gaze traveled further south. "Perhaps I should say you're a hard man in general."

"Indeed." He closed the last few inches between them, his thumbs hooking under the lapels of her robe to slide it down her sleek shoulders. He bent down to feather his lips against her neck. Her swift intake of breath was all he needed right now.

He kissed his way down her body as he went to his knees

before her. His fingers pulled on the ribbon that circled her waist. As the black satin fell away, he watched his own hands as they skimmed up and down her curves, her skin alive, quivering, reaching for his touch. A poetry all its own.

He built the pressure in the air behind her, then eased her back to float semi-reclined on the dense atomic mass that molded comfortably around her body.

She sighed and closed her eyes. "Ah, fancy tricks. Being so old has a few perks, I guess."

"Old, you say?" He waved his hands at the windows to draw the curtains. No one else was going to partake of the coming view. "That mouth of yours is going to get you in trouble if you don't have a care," he warned, hopeful she would misbehave as he bent to kiss his way up her calves.

"I can handle any trouble as long as I have a fresh coat of lipstick." Her breath hitched as his lips moved to the insides of her thighs.

"Is that so?" he whispered, pressing her legs further apart to nip, lick, and suck on her flesh like it was his last meal. Deliberate. Wanting to savor the moment. The feel of her fingers pulling at his hair. He shifted between her legs, aligning his mouth with her sex. "Then maybe I should concern myself with your lips as well. No?"

He blew softly on the landing strip of caramel-colored hair, then swept his tongue, broad and slow, across her softness. Again and yet again, as her hips rolled. He vocalized along with her.

When she was at the brink, he pulled back on his heels to smile at her.

"O-oh my God, what are you doing? Come back here," she panted, holding out a hand.

"Old men like me, we need our rest, you know."

"Oh f— You. Big. *Baby.* I was only joking. Look at you. My God, you're..." Her body pulsed from her scalp to her toes just looking at him.

His lips tilted in that thoroughly sexy way of his. "I'm what?"

He was going to make her say it. Say it all. Jackass. She came up on her elbows, watching his pupils dilate even more as her breasts jiggled. "Touch me, Grimm. I'm dying for any part of you on me."

When he climbed back onto the air mass to kiss her legs again, her victory felt petty and hollow. She pulled on his shoulders, moving him up her body until he rubbed his stubbled chin against her belly. Then he pressed his lips against her sensitized, reddened skin with velvet kisses. His bold hands kneaded her breasts as he moved up her body, almost making her forget what she needed to say.

"Grimm."

"I'm busy."

Gods, yes, he was, and gloriously so, doing all those lovely things to her neck with his tongue.

But, he deserved more.

"*Grimm.*"

He sucked her earlobe into his hot mouth. "You really want to talk right now?"

No. "Yes. I have to tell you something."

He pulled back, streamed them to her king-sized bed, and lay beside her, head propped on his hand. She ran her thumb across his bottom lip, giving her pulse a moment to settle. He kissed her thumb, then raised an eyebrow at her serious expression. "If you're about to say something nice, I need to get my phone so I can video the moment."

She laughed then, her heart lighter than she could ever remember. "I'm that much of a bitch, huh? Oh wait, I think you called me a harpy."

He cocked his head, running his fingers through her hair. "I know you've got a heart of gold under all that biting wit and emasculating sarcasm. And trust me, someone who has enough compassion to give an archdemon the benefit of the doubt has more love in their heart than most."

Her face and heart warmed all at once. "Don't tell anyone."

The sun slanted through the crack between the linen curtains, highlighting fine lines when his eyes crinkled. "Your secret's safe with me, North."

She knew it was. With her Viking, every piece of her felt safe.

She sat up, sweeping back the errant golden lock that always fell across his forehead. She wanted to see his eyes. "What I was going to tell you before was..." She held her breath, then let it out, feeling almost light-headed. "You're all I've ever wanted. You're my home base. I'm not worried anymore about where life takes us. I will always need to spend time here at the club, but when you need to roam, I have a team who can run this place in my absence. I always want to be by your side."

Butterflies exploded in her belly as his face lit with a glorious smile.

"We'll find our balance," he whispered and pulled her down into the bed's silken sheets and moved his muscled body over her. "My true north."

She opened to him then, opened her whole self—heart, body, and soul—to his deep passion that filled all her empty places. Filled them with his sighs and groans, his sweet, dark whispers, his gritty masculinity.

His big, big love.

She gasped, holding onto his steady shoulders, looking into his intense eyes. His powerful strokes drove her higher. Toward union. In his focused gaze, she saw forever. The unknowns were there in the fathomless blue, yes. The unknowns, like whether she'd be able to give him the family he longed for.

That she longed for.

The unknowns like if they were wise to even try to find a way to bring children into this world with the dangers they still faced. A lifetime of battling demons and archdemons and who knows what else the Guardians would be called on to defeat.

But just now, the unknowns didn't matter. Their fingers entwined on either side of her head, their breath mingling, his body covering hers, giving her promises, ecstasy, hope.

Love.

Her hair tangled on the pillows as the climax ripped through her. Ari's mouth slashed across hers, taking her vocals, giving her back...

More.

He let go, and she felt their power threads meet and knit together.

"As it's meant to be."

"Yes," she breathed back.

He held her as the tremors faded and the hours passed, the sun dipping lower in the horizon amid more love and whispers. Too soon, she could hear the booming of the bass start in the club as the DJ prepared for the show to go on, despite the wreckage across the city. She sighed, not wanting to leave this bed and face the mess downstairs, but really, nothing could get her down tonight.

She smiled and kissed him again. "I guess that's my cue to get to work."

He hooked an arm around her naked waist, not so gently pulling her back into the sheets. "Not so fast, woman. You still have to pay for that towel whipping."

She laughed. "Show me what you've got, Viking."

And so, he did.

Thank you for reading Dark Huntress.

If you loved Dark Huntress then you will love Dark Hunter from the same series.

Read a sneak peek on the next page!

The series continues... Each book is a stand alone with a happily ever after.

Dark Hunter
Guardians of Humanity
Sneak Peek

This isn't your mother's fairy tale. And I'm no prince charming.

I'm the devil next door.

And claiming Jessie is what I desire most.

I was a scumbag before my death and fate gave me two choices.

Fight demons for the sake of humanity, or face hellfire and damnation.

Yeah, not really much of a choice...

Most women who come this close to a demon hunter turn to putty on the spot.

Not Jessie.

This sassy little spitfire is playing hard to get.

Beautiful eyes and heart-shaped a$s that would make any immortal do bad things.

Guarding humanity is tough, but loving Jessie makes me remember what it's like to be human.

Her gentle touch and caring heart make me want to be... more.

So as the battle for good and evil draws near, Jessie's safety is my main concern.

They try to come for her.

Wrong move.

I protect what's mine.

Any time. Any where. No matter the costs.

Nobody messes with my girl.

Sexy meets magical in this steamy full-length, stand alone novel. No cheating, no cliffhangers, and happily ever after guaranteed! This is book 1 of the Guardians of Humanity series.

Chapter One

ONE

Tall, dark, and delicious, he pressed her body against the wall. Full. Frontal. Contact. Mmm.

Lord, he was hot-blooded. His I-got-you-baby shoulders blocked out the world and its problems, his wicked lips descending to that perfect spot on her neck.

She burned for his touch.

Burned and—

Sizzled?

Water hissing as it overflowed the pot of spaghetti.

"Shit!" Jessie snapped out of her fantasy and lunged for the stove, yanking the pot off the burner. Boiling water sloshed across the counter as a new round of moans and headboard slamming began in the apartment next door.

Jessie shivered in response, shooing her ten-year-old Chihuahua away from the hot noodles on the floor. "Whoever he brought home is not gonna be able to walk for a week. Lucky bitch."

And Stupid Nate.

Why'd he have to flaunt his hookup like this?

Every time they talked, he seemed so into her.

She'd never seen him with anyone, so she hoped he might be single and...

You are so lame, Jessie.

And unfair.

She didn't know much about her naughty neighbor other than he had a sexed-up British accent, bedroom eyes, and a smile that made her knees weak.

Just because he knew his way around a woman's body— some *other* woman's body, *gah*—didn't mean she should take her sexual frustrations out on him.

"Looks like we're gonna have to swing by McDonalds before hitting the library, Scourge. You'll have to hide in my purse again." With only two hours before the law library closed, she didn't want to fuss with getting gussied up.

Besides, Mr. Charisma was already occupied next door, and no hunky law students would be prowling the library this late on a Friday night.

She shoved her books into her bag, slipped on her fuzzy boots, grabbed her coat, purse, keys, and Scourge. She hustled out the door and...

Bumped into her fantasy.

"Whoa! Easy there, angel." A deep voice rolled over her skin.

A British voice.

Hell in a handbasket.

Nate.

Jessie ducked her head and pushed out of his grasp because she wasn't wearing a stitch of makeup. Or a bra. *Balls.* Not a good call when you're a double D.

Déjà vu drifted over her from the day he'd moved in and caught her in the same predicament. Except that morning she'd been wearing nothing but a baggy white t-shirt and underwear.

She pulled her book bag and Scourge in front of her like a bullet-proof vest. Then noticed she'd knocked a bunch of grocery bags out of his hands when she'd barreled out of her apartment.

She and Nate bent down to the grocery bags and knocked heads at the precise moment the woman in Nate's apartment reached her throat-ripping climax.

Nate made a low sound like he was in pain, causing all the skin on Jessie's upper body to prickle. Her gaze shot up to find his saturated blue eyes burning with intensity and his lips —*oh wow*—those beautiful lips inches from her own.

"Y-you aren't home?"

His serious expression slid away and a dimple peeked beside his lips. Had she really spoken out loud? *OMG, Jessie.* "What I mean is..."

I'm so happy you're not the one banging that chick into next week.

There was nothing she could say that would make this less awkward, so she handed him a red pepper, wondering what he planned to make with it. "Glad the eggs are okay, and sorry to plow you over," she managed without stuttering again.

He ignored the jug of pomegranate juice, Gruyere cheese, and various types of produce splayed across the floor to pet Scourge, the little traitor, who'd bailed from her bag and now had his front paws on Nate's chest.

"They've been kinda loud, eh? Good for them. I thought they'd be finished by now. How long have they been at it?"

Her mouth gaped for a split second before she recovered. "I am so not having this conversation with you."

The heat in his eyes made her suddenly aware of her pointy, unprotected nipples. She rearranged her scarf over her breasts the best she could. Then she reached for Scourge and stuffed him in back in her bag. "See you around, Nate."

He grabbed her elbow and helped her to feet. "Hey, where are you going so late anyway?"

As casually as possible, she pulled more hair out of her

messy bun to hide behind because these awful fluorescent hallway lights highlighted every imperfection.

"It's not late for night owls like me. I'm heading out for a bite to eat before I hit the library."

Moans started anew next door. Nate stepped closer, raising Jessie's heart rate tenfold.

"I'm a night owl, too, so I'd like to propose a deal for you, Jessica."

Of course he did.

But she'd never tried a foursome, and tonight was damn well not going to be her first.

Her glance raked him over, from his scuffed leather boots, up his jean-clad, muscle-bound thighs, to the snap-front olive shirt rolled to expose his sexy forearms—*doesn't he feel the cold? It's like forty degrees outside*—to those lips, all-seeing eyes, and carelessly artful mahogany hair.

Talk about a total contrast to her oversized University of Minnesota sweatshirt, UGG boots, and spaghetti sauce-splattered yoga pants.

Back away from the bad boy, Jessie. "I...I'm sorry. I really need to get to the library to study. Big constitutional law test tomorrow."

Which she was going to flunk if she didn't get some food and study-time serenity ASAP.

He tilted his head with a lazy smile that made her anything but relaxed. "With your dog?"

"He was at the vet for shots this afternoon. I never leave him alone in case he has a delayed reaction." She glanced down at her baby. "I know it's silly."

"Not at all. It's sweet. So here's what I'm thinking. I'll help you study if you give me a place to hang around for a while. You've got to admit, I can't go in and interrupt *that*." He lifted his grocery bags. "I'll cook us a quiche while you study. I promise not to be a bother."

"What?" He couldn't be serious.

"I'll even quiz you after a while."

"Quiz?" she squeaked.

"Sure. I'll ask questions from the chapter you're studying, and you can answer." How did he get his eyes to twinkle like that? "Then I'll feed you quiche," he said.

"Quiche?"

"You know, eggs, cream—"

She squeezed Scourge so hard he yelped. *Come on, Jess, full sentences.* "I *know* what quiche is."

"If you don't like it, I can make something else. Trust me, I'm an experienced cook."

This was just...bizarre. "I like quiche," she mumbled.

"I remember," he said, his voice deep and thick, trapping her in the memory of the day he'd moved in. How she'd babbled on about *quiche* of all things.

He reached for her doorknob, and she finally shook out of her stupor. "No, wait!" Why would he make her quiche? She pointed to his door. "Go in there and tell them to take their party elsewhere. Good grief, they've been at it for two and half hours already."

"Look, when my mate Dorian got to town and asked to use my place, I didn't realize he was so depleted. I'm sorry."

Depleted? What an odd way to describe horny, but whatever. Scourge squirmed in her bag. "Well, by now I'm sure he's dulled the edge enough to find a hotel for the rest of the night. I'd kick them out if I were you," she said.

Nate shrugged. "I don't want to bother them when they're having so much fun. Come on, Jess. I'd love to feed you." His eyes mapped the contours of her body from top to bottom. He smiled when his gaze made it back to hers. "I promise it'll be good."

Oh, wow. This guy was a walking innuendo.

TWTA: Trouble With a Tight Ass.

Good looks do not preclude homicidal intentions, Jess. Ted Bundy had been a reasonably handsome guy with loads of charm, too.

So they said.

Did serial killers cook quiche, though?

A tiny voice inside her head told her to open her door and hold on for the ride. Jessie peered into Nate's eyes looking for the tell-tale vacancy she'd read about in her undergrad abnormal psych classes.

She shivered. *No vacancy, folks.* In fact, there was so much depth in his blue eyes, she could fall right into them.

Her fingers tightened on her bag strap. "Okay, you can come in, but only for a little while."

Heart thumping overtime, she turned to unlock her door, then cringed when she saw the ungodly mess in her kitchen. "*Crap.* My place is a wreck. Guess this isn't going to work after all."

When she turned around, he was in her space. Like *right there*. She tilted her head back to look at him and swallowed hard. Oh man, he smelled good. Layered notes of leather and vetiver and a vivid memory of the ocean from her childhood when times were actually good with her mother.

"Fuck the mess. Let's get you studying." He tapped her on the nose and walked in.

Twenty minutes later, the stove sparkled, the quiche was baking, and Scourge was fast asleep on Jessie's lap. She shuffled her law notes unproductively. She hadn't been able to concentrate on any of them with Nate's fine ass moving around the kitchen like he owned the place.

At least things had finally quieted down next door, so she'd begun to relax.

Nate sat down across from her at the table and handed

her a glass of Gewürztraminer. "Sorry, it's all I have at the moment." One side of his lips lifted. "Cheers."

Her glass clinked against his before she sipped the wine. "It's nice. I'm a bartender, but I don't drink much, so this is a treat." Between work, school, worrying about her uncle, and taking care of Gramma and Grampa, she didn't have much time for socializing.

She gestured to the oven. "Hey, if you want to go home now, I can bring the quiche over when it's ready."

"Kicking me out already?"

"I thought it'd be more like a *get out of jail free* card for you."

He tugged on a coil of hair by her ear. "Are you kidding me? I've been trying to think of a way to ask you out since way before the mailbox incident last week."

Her pen fumbled to the floor. Thankfully Scourge was on her lap to give her hands something to do. "That was *not* my fault." Her overheating face said otherwise, however. It took a special kind of stupid to get your hair stuck in a metal mailbox. "I'm telling you, poltergeists live in those little black holes. But anyway, thank you again."

She took back-to-back gulps of wine. Seriously, why was he here? She'd bet a whole week's bartending tips that she was frumpville compared to the other girls who crossed his path on a daily basis.

He stood up from the table, and just like that, her fairy tale was about to end. He'd leave now, but that was okay because prince charmings didn't compute in her world. She had bills to pay, grades to maintain, an uncle to avenge, grandparents to care for, and new employers to impress.

Her dreams—and worries—were bigger than a momentary heartbreak by a guy who could charm a chastity belt off a nun.

"Come here, Jess." He held his hand out to her.

"Where are we going?"

His slow smile mocked her. "Do you always need to know all the answers before you leap?"

"Yes. Prosecutors always press for the truth."

He winked, sat down on her couch, and patted the cushion next to him. "So, no defense law in store for you." It wasn't a question. "Gonna save the day as a prosecutor then. That's *brilliant*."

That slight English accent was terribly alluring. As was the invitation to sit next to him.

She chose her favorite threadbare chair instead.

Scourge soon claimed her lap. "I've never asked, but are you from around here?"

He'd moved into the building exactly forty-seven days ago. She remembered it well because it was the same day Uncle Mason had called to tell her he'd been manipulated into selling his nightclub.

"More or less." He swirled the sweet, woodsy liquid in his glass.

It was the first time he'd spoken that he hadn't looked her in the eye. Her curiosity was piqued. "Meaning you're from Minnesota? Or you were born elsewhere, but you've been here a while?"

"I bloom where I'm planted. Now tell me, why law?"

She opened her mouth to call him on his evasive answer, then closed it. This wasn't Moot Court, and acting like a pit bull tended to get exhausting after a spell. Not to mention, it wasn't the best way to get to know a guy.

She drank the rest of her wine and settled back into the chair. A pleasant tingling wound around her legs. "I want to be a voice for vulnerable populations—battered women, children, the elderly, disabled veterans."

"My first impression was correct then. You're an angel in a

world of demons." His eyes seemed to pulse with warmth, sincerity, and ... something else.

Jessie smiled, feeling warm in an entirely nice way. She pushed her sweatshirt sleeves up and petted Scourge slowly, a delicious contentment seeping through her. "I hesitate to correct your assumption, but the only angels in my family are my grandparents, Tilly and Walt. They share a love like you've never seen."

His eyes narrowed slightly. "You must take after them, though. You mentioned they all but raised you."

"Yes, fortunately for me, otherwise my mother—" Her gaze dropped to where Scourge snored on her lap. The wine was making her tongue loose. Most people ended up finding out about her notorious mother eventually, but right now Jessie wasn't ready for over-sharing.

The wall banging re-commenced next door. Nate tilted his head back and belly laughed so deeply she couldn't help but giggle, too.

"No wonder you got so distracted, angel," he said.

No one had ever called her an angel. Not even as a child. It was nice. Especially the way he spoke the endearment, meaningfully, like he was savoring each letter on his tongue.

Moments later, his insinuation dawned on her. She glanced around the kitchen, remembering her 'mess-interrupted' and cringed. "They didn't distract me with their...uh, their..."

"Fucking?"

The illicit word from his lips made her whole body tingle. "No!"

"Oh, but I think they did. And they *are*." His gaze was filled with heat. And he was smirking, the beast.

"That's not what I...*You*...I wasn't leaving because I had to get away from *that*."

He shook his head. "You are a horrible liar. Apropos for an angel."

"Well, give me a break, that sexual *marathon* isn't normal." Scourge yipped and growled on her lap, irritated by her agitation.

"On the contrary. It appears no one has ever showed you how much of a journey lovemaking can be." He paused, his eyes once again tracking slowly from her lips to her breasts, lower, down to her bare toes. Her breath caught and held, frozen while her heart pumped hard in her chest. His eyes smoldered when his gaze returned to hers. "I'd be delighted to initiate you."

Outrageous!

But...she liked it.

Almost as much as she liked the way his lips slid past his teeth on that infernally slow smile. "You are curiously depraved," she whispered.

He stood, lifted Scourge out of her lap, placing him on the couch. "Quite. Put it on a t-shirt for me?"

"No t-shirt big enough to fit your vainglorious ego."

"Be careful, big words turn me on. But tell me, since when does having an ego equate with depravity?" He leaned down to place his hands on the chair arm rests, boxing her in.

She cleared her throat. "Since when does a metrosexual know how to cook?" *Or have a brain?* This guy was more trouble than a wired eighteen-year-old in a strip club.

"I didn't figure you for the judgmental type. Stereotypes can be dangerous."

"More like early warning systems for modern women."

"What are you worried about?"

She blew out a breath, but it didn't help one damn bit. "You."

He raised his eyebrows. "I'm here because I like you."

But why? Why do you like me? "Well, I like you, too. But I don't know much about you other than you drive a beat-to-hell pickup, you're exceedingly permissive with your friends, and by the smell of it, you know how to make a mouthwatering quiche. That's it."

Next door, the man's groans merged with the woman's crescendo of staccato cries. Jessie shifted in her seat, her body achy and warm. The sounds were getting to Nate, too. She could see it in the way his eyes stripped her naked and laid her bare.

He straightened, his hands sliding down his pants like his palms were sweaty.

"What else would you like to know?" His voice was gravelly.

The woman next door *had* to be dying by now from the cadence of those moans. "How can anyone go on for *so long*?"

"Oh, Jessie, that sounds like a challenge I can't refuse." He pulled her up into his arms, and her skin ignited.

Please go to Amazon.com to get your copy of Dark Hunter NOW!!!

ABOUT HARLEY JAMES

Mom by day and freak by night, Harley is a down to earth soccer mom who lets her foxy side fly when writing about witty females, over the top bad boys, and a world of steamy magical romance so hot it'd make a demon sweat.

When Harley's not reading, writing, or dancing in the kitchen, some of her favorite activities happen in the great outdoors with her sexy alpha hubby, their two awesome teenagers, and the world's coolest dog, Finn.

So leave all your worries behind and let Harley make your sultry fantasies come to life!

Want to get up close and personal with Harley? Join her facebook group where we discuss all things sexy and magical. You will be the first to see cover reveals, sneak peeks and exclusive content: Click here to join Harley's Hangout!